The Captivating Flame of Madness

By
Jeff Parsons

A HellBound Books Publishing LLC Book
Houston TX

**A HellBound Books LLC
Publication**

www.hellboundbookspublishing.com

Printed in the United States of America

Dedication –

For Linda,

my wife, my love, and my friend

The Captivating Flame of Madness

Table of Contents

LOST SOULS

May 24, 1944

The damp air smothered Hans with a slow asphyxiation of hot sweat, carbon dioxide, and diesel fuel. Each breath grew more and more tortured, not so much from the pervasive soggy drip of foul moisture clogging his lungs, but from the thought of what caused the U-292 German submarine to shudder, as if in anticipated pleasure.

The U-boat was cruising along the surface in attack mode with other subs in the wolf pack. They preyed upon the merchant cargo ships that crossed the unforgiving sea from Newfoundland to England. Each time the ship shook, a torpedo was sent away through the frigid North Atlantic Ocean towards its hapless convoy target.

Hans sat in the narrow toilet stall behind a flimsy curtain screen, leaning forward with his head cradled by his trembling hands, ashamed of his behavior, but unable to control it any more. He carefully eased a photograph from his uniform's breast pocket. Stroking the portrait of his love, Greta, he wondered yet again how he was going to stay sane – U-boat service extracted a heavy toll upon him.

He winced yet again…

Hans thought he could hear the harsh shriek of the enemy vessels tearing apart after each torpedo hit, but he knew that was unlikely, for the submarine's twin diesel engines were humming along at low throttle in the nearby bulkhead compartment.

He had heard that sound before, the dreadful shearing metal sound of sinking ships, and it haunted him. Like being underneath a waterfall, thunderous bubbling accompanied the dying throes of a merchant ship as it cracked open like a fragile egg shell, the deadly water flooding inside and the sailors within… he swore that he could hear the sounds of their lost souls screaming, just like in his nightmares.

Gott im Himmel… they were dying, he thought. Even if the sailors survived the sudden tumultuous sinking, they'd be cast adrift into the freezing wave-wracked water to die with little hope of rescue.

"Hans! Get your butt outta there now!" Gruber, the head mechanic, bellowed from the engine room.

Hans sighed. He kissed Greta's snapshot and slid it back into his pocket. Standing up, he wiped off the sweat streaking down his face, and left his safe haven. Back to work. The endless war needed him…

Gruber frowned at him, "Did you get lost?"

"No. I just felt sick. Queasy," he lied. "Must be something I ate."

"Uh-huh," Gruber said, tapping on a pressure gauge for the noisy diesel engines.

Hans knew how lame his response sounded. They had just been restocked with fresh food from a submarine supply ship. It was unlikely that the food had been spoiled.

He didn't hear the sound of torpedoes being fired anymore. "Is the attack over?"

Gruber was busy starting the electric engines. They were used for quiet running engines, instead of the diesels, which would be shut off before the submarine slid beneath the waves.

"No more torpedoes left. We'll have to connect with the supply ship again." Gruber looked up at Hans, then smiled slightly, not unkindly. "Hans, this is what we do. Best get used to it. And don't let the Oberleutnant or anyone else know about your… feelings, okay?"

"Ja, thanks Gruber. I'll do my best."

***

The submarine had left the oil-slicked scene of floating carnage and escaped unharmed into the vast rolling sea. Later that evening, Oberleutnant zur See, Herr Werner Schmidt, their commander, gave an announcement over the ship's comm': "We have fought with great valor. Each torpedo struck a mighty blow to the enemy's supply lines. We have saved the lives of many a valiant German soldier. On behalf of the Fatherland, I commend you once again for your selfless acts of bravery."

Hans cringed on the inside. He didn't want to share his emotions with the other crewmates settled around him in the aft sleeping quarters. The crowded room contained bunks stacked three high, filled with crewmen lying on their off-hours, too restless to sleep. The hypnotic tempo of water condensate dripping from the ceiling, piping and curved walls encouraged Hans' mind to wander into places he'd rather not consider, such as the meaning behind Schmidt's words.

Schmidt was right about bravery. Kriegsmarine U-boat service was dangerous. An encounter with an enemy destroyer was lethal in most cases, let alone the technical problems associated with repeatedly diving deep into the briny depths. The experience was unnatural – it took a certain amount of mental fortitude to be a submariner. Even so, everyone was always so solemn after a battle. Perhaps they realized that sooner or later, their luck could run out and death could overtake them.

His friend Fadi broke the silent gloom… He said, "Looks like we've single-handedly saved the Fatherland again."

Several tired smirks were exchanged at Fadi's remark. He smiled ruefully, then said, "I talked with some of the supply ship crew when their officers weren't looking. They said supplies were running short, no one was getting what they needed."

Rudi, one of the pipefitters, said, "Ja, and they also said something else…"

"Rudi, no need to bring that up," Johanne, another pipefitter, grumbled.

"I think it's important. Did you see the expressions on their faces?" Rudi asked.

"They were scared," Rudi said, his voice going low, "…afraid to talk much. One of them said they were being hunted…"

"Ha!" Fadi said. "What do they expect? It's a war! We're all combatants here, even the merchant ships."

"That's true, "Johanne said, sadly. "We must kill our fellow mariners to win this war. Then, if it's our time, we can go home."

Hans thought… *What would we say when we met our maker? That we were following orders?*

***

The boat waited at the predesignated rendezvous

coordinates for the supply ship's restocking of torpedoes and other essentials.

The crew was kept busy with the many routine tasks of maintenance, operations and testing, part of which involved quick certification dives to check for leaks that inevitably sprouted.

During the dives, Hans dreaded hearing the hull's metal shrinking due to the enormous forces crushing against the ship. If the seawater pressure could compress the submarine's high-strength steel, what would it do to him if the ship imploded?

The ship continued to complain like an old woman shuffling across a kitchen floor on a winter morning. In fact, it sounded like his beloved grandmother, Brunhilda, God rest her soul.

Hans had been trained to know the sounds of the ship, so when he heard something new amidst the hull's normal groaning, popping and creaking, he was quick to investigate it. It was a rhythmic tinkling sound that traveled along the piping of the ship's water-cooling system.

He had to fix whatever was making the sound. An unexpected mechanical failure could potentially sink the boat. Also, excessive spurious noise was dangerous on a submarine. The enemy destroyers had hydrophones that could detect underwater sound. If they knew where you were, they could kill you.

Listening carefully, he patiently tracked the sound towards its source, ducking and squeezing through crowded spaces full of machinery, support struts and piping systems. It wasn't much different than working on the plumbing under his grandmother's sink back in Dresden. Except now, he rarely hit his head when he moved without thinking.

The sound originated inside the main ballast area, a large hollow tank situated within the hull underneath the control room. Inside the tank, a careful balance of air and water was maintained to raise and lower the ship's depth, and incidentally, it was used as a backup reserve for breathing air. There were also four other ballast tanks located outside of the hull, fore and aft, and along each side; without sufficient air in the ballast tanks, the ship would sink like a weighted corpse.

What the hell was that? It was almost like a glass bottle bouncing against metal. Perhaps one of the shipyard fitters had left their stash of liquor in there?

He'd have to tell Gruber about it. Gruber wouldn't be happy. The reasons behind mysterious sounds were elusive at times; they might not be able to repair this type of problem at sea.

***

The supply ship never showed up. Schmidt decided to travel back to port. It was a disgraceful waste of diesel, but the ship needed torpedoes.

Hans thought, *Even the angel of death has its limits…*

Still, the crew was in high morale. Back to merry Spain, where shore leave, booze and women awaited them, while the ship underwent an overhaul and torpedo reload.

Then, the unthinkable happened.

A man didn't show up at his workstation. The cook, Alfred, who was also an assistant electrician, hadn't been seen since last night. The crewmen methodically searched the ship, section by section, bulkhead door by bulkhead door. No one could slip past them. When the crew met up in the command center, Schmidt announced that the cook was nowhere to be found. Everyone was to keep a lookout for him.

Where could he have gone while submerged under

the sea?

Gruber whispered something into Schmidt's ear. Schmidt looked at Hans, then said, "Prepare for ascent to surface. We need to recharge the air. While we're doing that, we'll check the internal ballast compartment. We probably have a sound short."

The Captain gave the command. The ship rose to periscope depth. Schmidt scanned the surrounding sea and gave the order to surface.

Hans and another crewman, Dieter, were chosen to enter the main ballast tank.

Hans' slight frame made it easier for him to squeeze through confined spaces, so he was regularly chosen for tasks like these.

The tank's hatchway was unlocked and opened. After ten minutes of letting the tank air out, they entered one at a time through the narrow hatchway. He took a final deep breath before submerging himself into the cloying darkness.

The lights from their electric lanterns did little to dispel his anxiety.

They split up, searching for the cause of the mysterious sound.

Hans left behind the one way in and out of this foul smelling area, cramped with interconnecting metal supporting baffles, struts and piping. Good thing the sea weather was relatively mild; it was difficult enough walking on the slippery surfaces without the boat rocking wildly.

A few minutes later, Dieter yelped. Not a typical sound that one would hear from a seasoned sailor. Hans moved towards his partner, stepping over and bending around obstructions until he got to where Dieter leaned against the wall, breathing deeply.

Dieter's sickened expression said it all – Hans wasn't going to like this.

He saw a head. Just a head. No body.

The head rolled with the shifting of the boat and kept hitting a pipe that passed through the wall structure. *Mein Gott, his teeth...* the teeth hit the pipe, making the tinkling noise.

Hans shuddered – it was Alfred's head. Alfred... who had once told Hans how he missed his wife, his childhood sweetheart, and their two young girls, who would squeal with delight when he pushed them on their tire swing.

Dieter trudged back to the hatchway to ask for direction on what to do next. Hans stood awkwardly in silence, his lantern light playing across what remained of his shipmate, knowing that the only access into this area, the hatchway, had been padlocked closed...

How the hell did Alfred get in here? What the hell happened to him?

***

They never found the rest of the body, so they once again submerged, traveling on a course back to port.

Morale was low. Schmidt authorized a ration of Schnapps for the crewmen, but the drink seemed to make everyone feel melancholy.

Several hours later, loud noises started to bang intermittently against the outside length of the ship.

Fadi joked with Hans, saying that the boat must be looking very sexy to some of the amorous whales in the region.

Hans laughed nervously; knowing that wouldn't be a first in naval history, but it was highly unlikely.

The noises continued to disturb everyone's sanity... Schmidt described the anomaly as a mechanical problem that would need to get fixed at the port shipyard.

Then, another person went missing. It was Gebhard,

the ship's best navigator, last seen going to his bunk for a quick nap.

Again, the crewmen went through the same drill. Gebhard couldn't be found, so after verifying that no other ships were in the area, the submarine was raised to the surface.

When the top hatch was popped opened, a brief waterfall of cold seawater spilled inside.

The banging noise stopped.

A storm was brewing outside. Some crewmen were sent topside, tasked with inspecting the outside of the ship to see what had been causing the raucous banging noises.

Hans was called to duty again, along with Dieter, to search the main ballast tank. He dreaded going in there again. *Will we find what's left of Gebhard?*

Sweating in the dark, even though the air was damp and chilly, Hans groped his way around cold metal and over slippery surfaces. The ship's rocking slowed his progress through the ballast tank.

About halfway through his search, he heard the call to return to the hatchway.

Schmidt wanted them to come see something.

They were directed towards the torpedo room where the nervous crewmen were assembled. What Hans saw shocked him to the core. It was Gebhard, strung up, suspended in midair, electrical wires woven deep into his flesh and connected to the piping overheard, looking like the sacrifice portrayed on the cross he wore around his neck.

Gebhard's skin was a fish-white color, his waxy eyes were bugged out, and seawater still dripped from his body, obviously drowned, yet trussed up here before the group.

They had searched this area not long ago — impossible as it was, it must've happened recently.

Mechanical problem, my ass...

Schmidt took control of the paralyzing situation. "Take him down. Gently. Put him in the machine shop. Men, stay sharp, go back to your stations, make sure that we're running safe and secure, then reassemble in a quarter of an hour at operations. We'll get to the bottom of this. Dismissed." He then motioned for his officers to confer with him, as if seeking counsel on what to do next.

Hans was alarmed that the order wasn't given to submerge the ship – they were extremely vulnerable to the enemy on the surface. Then again, being below the waves had definitely proven to be lethal.

***

Hans went back to the engine room with Gruber and Michael, the machinist mate who assisted with engine repair.

Gruber fussed with the diesels and electric motors. Of course, everything was operating perfectly. They were designed and manufactured by Germans – the best craftsmen in the world.

Hans and Michael talked, faces close to each other, at the aft end of the engine room, near a diesel fuel storage tank, out of sight and earshot from Gruber.

"Are we being hunted as well?" Michael asked softly, reminding Hans of what was said by sailors on the supply ship.

"I don't know. What could do this? And why?"

Michael was about to answer when he was suddenly jerked backward into the inky shadows behind the storage tank. It was so quick that only impressions lingered with Hans: Michael's eyes bulging with surprise, a sudden whoosh of displaced air, and outstretched arms, the last thing Hans saw of him.

No scream. No sound. Just a haloed afterimage of Michael…

Hans hesitated, trembling, then reached forward into the darkness. Nothing there except the sticky bulkhead wall. There was blood coating his fingertips when he pulled his hand back.

"Gruber!" he screamed like a frightened schoolgirl.

***

Hans stared into the darkness, shivering and unmoving, for what seemed like an eternity.

His body jerked at Gruber's touch.

Gruber saw the blood and cursed.

"Michael… he's gone," Hans whispered, "something… he's gone."

"Hans!" Gruber yelled. His grip on Hans shoulder tightened. "We need to leave. Now!"

Hans snapped out of his mental fog.

"Just … just follow me, okay?" Gruber said.

Hans nodded.

They bolted out of the engine room to the all-hands meeting.

Not everyone was there yet. The men kept a wary distance from each other, no longer behaving as comrades, anxious with suspicious looks. Some glared at Hans when they saw the blood dripping from his hands.

At this point, the pounding against the ship's hull had started again. Also, there were scratching noises like nails being drawn across the outer skin of the ship. The sounds unnerved the already tense crew.

When Schmidt arrived, Gruber began, "We lost Michael, Hans said that something-"

Schmidt gruffly said, "That's enough, Gruber."

Hans didn't know what was scarier, Schmidt's

suddenly harsh voice holding fast to his Prussian emotional control or the knowing frightened looks of the other crewmen staring back at him. *Something happened to even more of the others… that's why everyone isn't here.*

There was a sudden flash to Han's left. Others saw it happen too. Officer Waldemar was grabbed by something, a sky-blue misty blur – there he was one moment, and gone the next, pulled through the metal-lattice floor like cheese through a grater, drawn out of sight into the dark decks below. Nothing was left of the man except thin strands of ropy red-brown liquids that spilled into the darkness below.

There was a brief stillness of awful silence, and then all hell broke loose. Screaming crewmen, mindless with terror, pushed and clawed each other in a raging chaos to escape until…

Schmidt's loud commanding voice quickly brought the remainder of the panicked crew under disciplined control. "We're leaving. Launch the lifeboats, prepare to scuttle the boat. On my orders. Move it!"

Shocked as they were by the unusual order, the crew instinctively knew that it was suicidal to remain onboard and, as one, they scrambled to complete their preassigned emergency tasks.

Visibly shaking, Hans put on raingear and helped lift one of the rectangular lifeboat packages up the top hatch ladder. The lifeboat was damned heavy, but he had the strength of adrenaline driving him.

The weather topside rocked the boat from side to side even with its heavy ballast.

Wind whipped the nighttime waves to smash against the lower conning tower. Electric lantern lights lanced wildly into the rain-soaked deluge of Atlantic darkness. Sailors on the outside deck tried to deploy their rafts while holding onto tether ropes. The treacherous wave action almost made some lose their footing, making it more difficult. One raft was almost ready to go.

He heard the sound of an airplane approaching fast from the overcast sky above. He glanced upward. It was probably an enemy dive-bomber.

What! No no no, not now…

Han's teeth chattered. The cold was brutal, especially after being inside the humid ship, but he'd also been traumatized by the insanity of recent events.

With trembling hands, he and his partner gripped their section of the tether rope while they placed their lifeboat on the deck. They held the lifeboat package in place with their knees and, fumbling, started to undo the straps that held it together.

Something heavy splashed nearby into the water, portside of the ship's aft end.

Mein Gott, not a depth charge!

The explosion was deafening, cracking against the ship with a huge wave that swept along the ship's surface.

The wave slapped him hard, forcing salt water into his eyes and mouth. He lost hold of the tether rope as the boat began to list to one side. When he glanced along the ship's waterline rising out of the rough sea, he saw a myriad of long, thick furrows cut into the metal, like claw marks gutting the belly of a dying beast.

Overhead, the plane's engine roared away from the ship into the dark night.

There was no scuttle charge detonation… the ship was sinking of its own accord, with help by a near-hit from the depth charge. The ship rolled suddenly on its port side as it sank into the sea, throwing everyone off balance and flailing into the torrential high-water waves.

The cold gripped him mercilessly, squeezing the breath from him and sapping the heat from his shocked body. His heavy raingear made it impossible to stay surfaced for long as tall waves and fierce undercurrents dashed him about and yanked him under repeatedly, forcing burning saltwater down his nose and throat.

Where's the raft... the raft... the raft...

The raft was lost to his sight long ago in the endless swirling darkness and gurgle of struggled breathing. From a great distance, he heard screams off and on when his head broke above the water for moments at a time.

He knew he wouldn't last long.

The saltwater in his eyes distorted his vision, but he thought he saw a flicker of light. The raft? He was saved!

The light was closer now. But it wasn't above the waves, it traveled below. Moving swiftly, as if unaffected by the weather or waves.

The spectral form of light glowed a pale blue and more followed it, maybe several dozens of them, coming towards him. When he saw what they were, he knew that his time was at an end.

The specters of foreign sailors had come to claim their vengeance.

THE NEW LAW

August 12, 2023
Department of Corrections
Bayonne, New Jersey, USA

Two burly men in solemn black guard uniforms shoved her into the cold medical procedures room.

With a shiver, she self-consciously shifted her thin hospital clothing, trying unsuccessfully to cover more of her skinny, half-naked body.

I'm going to be tortured here, she thought, as she quickly took in the details of the room. It was exactly as she imagined it would be – immaculate and shiny white under the merciless overhead lights. She'd seen these types of rooms before on the Party-sponsored channels. Citizens were mandated to watch the scheduled sentencing of criminals and the accompanying exposé of their heinous crimes against society. The Party brought peace to mankind – breaking the law wasn't tolerated in this perfect world. No exceptions.

Against the smooth concrete walls, glass cabinets

held prepackaged medical instruments and supplies. Her stomach lurched when she saw the tall drug injection machine. It was placed directly behind the plush leather chair that dominated the center of the confined space. The chair could be found in any dentist's office, except this one had confining straps for the legs, arms, body and head. And, instead of an overhead illuminating light and drill setup, a helmet-like medical device was suspended above the chair by a retractable extension that looked like a praying mantis claw.

A technician in a white clinical uniform emerged from behind the drug injection machine. He was a balding middle-aged man with a clipboard that held official-looking paperwork.

"State your name for the record," he said, his reedy voice belying the absolute power he held over her life.

"Meredith White," she said, touching her itchy newly-shaven scalp.

She flinched when the door closed suddenly behind her. She was sealed in this room. *No way out.*

He glanced at his clipboard, then spoke, his eyes locked with hers.

"Meredith White, you have consented to empathetic reparations as part of your sentence. In accordance with Section 8501 of the Party Penal Code, you will be placed in a state of consciousness that is highly susceptible to deep empathetic reactions. The reparations process will then subject you to an experience that will simulate, in your mind, what you have done unto others. Upon completion of this procedure, you will be executed by lethal injection. Do you understand?"

"What? No! I agreed to a reparations procedure because I'd get jail time afterward. Nothing was said about being put to death. Those papers are wrong, I tell you, this wasn't what I agreed to-"

"Here's the final court order." He dangled the legal paperwork before her distraught face. "It's all in here. You signed these papers! Your disagreement is irrelevant."

"But the judge said that… that my family would be safe, but only if I agreed to admit my guilt and signed the papers. How could I refuse that? He said that I'd do some jail time! He didn't tell me that – that I'd be executed. That wasn't in the papers I signed! Why do I have to die?"

"These are the rules of our society. You chose to break them. Now you face the consequences. As written in the court orders, you were given a deal by the judge: your family would be held free of collateral conviction and reparations. If you refuse to accept this court ordered ruling, it'll be duly noted in the case docket, but the outcome won't change one iota. I'll be compelled to call in the peace officers to force you to submit. And, then, the protection given to your family will be rescinded. I'm only going to ask you once – will you comply with the court order?"

My family…

"Yes," she murmured, shoulders drooping with stunned resignation. "What do you want me to do?"

"Sit down on the chair and cooperate. I'll get you prepped for your session."

She shuffled to the chair, feeling lethargic, suddenly realizing this would be the last time she'd walk anywhere. She remembered her lively walks with her two little girls, her husband at her side… the girls were always so excited to see the farm animals romping about in the neighbor's fenced pasture.

Tears welled up in her eyes as she eased into the leather chair. The chair was surprisingly comfortable and relatively warm.

The technician placed a strap over her left ankle,

cinched it tight, and secured it with a lock pin. In moments, her right ankle was also secured. *No more walking. Oh, my darling girls…*

Next, each wrist was strapped and secured into place. *No need for arms anymore.* No longer would she hold her giggling daughters up in the air or hug her husband.

Tears trickled down her cheeks.

She flexed her arms and legs. The straps held her tightly, cutting into her circulation.

Finally, the last strap was wrapped around her waist. She was completely helpless.

The technician lowered the helmet-like device from the ceiling. It looked like a German soldier's helmet from the Second World War, made of thick black steel, but with a mass of tie-clipped, colored wires sprouting from it and snaking up to the ceiling along the extendable support arm.

"Don't move," the technician grumbled as he lowered the helmet onto her clean-shaven head. He clamped the helmet into place with a chinstrap. The helmet was then secured to the chair.

She could open her mouth slightly, enough to talk. Or to scream. Her head movement was restricted: enough to see the door on her left, a medicine cabinet on her right and the blank wall in between, used as a projection area.

Mounted on the ceiling, she saw a recording camera pointed at her. Its solid red LED light indicated that it was sending signals back to the source, which were edited for broadcasting on the Party's television channels.

The technician went behind her field of vision.

She heard the distinctive crinkle of plastic shrink-wrap being carefully torn open.

The technician returned to her left side and tapped

the inside of her elbow. A vein popped up instantly – she'd always had great circulation. Overall, her health was excellent. She lived a life free of fast food, drugs and alcohol (except for that one transgression, the one that landed her in here). *I'm in great health, but I'll be dead soon. How odd...*

The technician rubbed an alcohol-soaked cotton ball over her injection site. He pushed the twin IV needles into her vein. She gave a small yelp – the needles hurt.

"Sorry," the technician mumbled, easing the needles in slower.

She knew he was embarrassed, not from any concern about her pain, but from his momentary lack of medical skill. It made him look incompetent.

Once the needles were in place, like stilettos stabbing deep into her flesh, the technician connected ochre-colored infusion tubes to her IV taps and taped the tubes to her arm. The tubes connected to the drug injection machine behind the chair.

Just a matter of moments. She tried to be brave, to think about her husband and girls, but it was difficult. Her breathing grew ragged and quick.

The technician stepped behind her view and flipped several switches. The helmet hummed with energy. At first, it stung her scalp with sparking pinpricks, then the pain ebbed away, tingling like crawling centipedes. The tubes pulsed. A fiery fluid was forced into her bloodstream. Sweat popped up across her skin as the heat spread throughout her body.

She bit her lip to keep from groaning.

Her thoughts became weird with a raging fever – it was as if they were as pliable as taffy and smooth like silk, flowing free in all directions, unconstrained.

A crisp bright white rectangle appeared on the blank wall before her. It was a projection, about 2' by 3', originating from somewhere behind her. The room's overhead lights dimmed, then switched off, leaving the projection to illuminate the room.

The projection flickered, went black, and then, from the darkness, the screenshot panned in to the glowing Party symbol – a swastika. Essentially, it was the world's united symbol, ever since Germany brought order to everyone from the ashes of the Second World War's conflict. The USA was one of the first to bend knee and obey the superpower. Dropping atomic bombs on at least a dozen major cities had the desired effect upon the country's morale. Other countries followed suit without a fight, including Italy and Japan, the allies of Germany.

The symbol faded away… leaving her in the darkness…

Then, the projection came alive with visceral horror.

Her soul was torn to shreds by what she saw, what she felt, the endless agonizing consequences of what happened, rolling like drowning waves, rippling outward with intense tragedy, the lives of many people destroyed, at least two dozen men, women and children, each life flickering out of existence like a leaf burning up in a bonfire, brutally killed by her terrorist actions, her insurrection upon the Party… their memories inside her… personal… inescapable… unforgettable.

<u>Noooo!</u>

She lurched out of the nightmare and into sweaty reality. Her body was out of control – muscles spasming, heart hammering, ears ringing, teeth clenching… she forced open her mouth and screamed like a tortured soul in hell.

When she could no longer scream, her breaths hitched into desperate harsh gulps of throaty moaning and sobbing.

Her body eventually relaxed, collapsing inward, exhausted by too much empathetic pain; she sagged in the chair, like a discarded limp marionette, no longer capable of movement, held upright and in place by the chair's restraints.

Her brain was overwhelmed by experiencing too much, too fast, too horrible. She squeezed her eyes shut, trying to clear her memory. It didn't work.

The room's light flickered on.

The technician left the room.

Someone else entered and did something to the camera.

"This must be very frustrating for you," a man said, in a tone that was sly, yet dripping with commiseration.

She snapped her eyes open and in the haze of brilliant lighting, saw him smiling at her. He was a tall, immaculately groomed, spry-looking old man wearing a black Party uniform that was perfectly tailored, unlike the mass-produced versions she'd seen on so many Party members.

She thought it was odd that the camera's LED was switched off – it wasn't transmitting.

"I didn't agree –" she squeaked, stopping suddenly, her raw throat becoming uncooperative. She wanted to scream at him. Tell him she'd been tricked. This wasn't what she agreed to. And this reparations process was completely wrong – it wasn't what had happened! On the night of her crime, she heard that Party peace officers had taken her parents away. After a heartfelt hug with her husband and children, she sped off in her car towards the nearest Party facility. They denied having her parents. The weather grew dark and stormy as she desperately raced from facility to facility, each of them turning her aside. Finally, with no place left to go, she sat slumped in her car, head against the steering wheel, tears streaming down her face as the convulsive sobs took over. Looking up, she saw the garish lights of an all-night liquor store through the rain-streaked windshield. The temptation was too much – she had never drunk before, but, this time, she walked away from the store with a fifth of Scotch whisky. The drink smoothed away the raw edge of pain as she drove through the night, going nowhere, a lost soul seeking what she could not find. She ended up in a car accident… she went through a red light and her car collided with another. The other driver was killed instantly. It was all a horrible tragedy, but she wasn't a terrorist!

Memories overwhelming her, she coughed repeatedly until her throat cleared.

While she regained her breath, he waited patiently, then said, "Yes. I know. You didn't kill those people in the reparations scenario."

"What? Why?" she sputtered, aghast.

"As a minimum, jail time, and reparations were required for your felony, but with our new judicial policy, senior Party officials such as myself, are allowed to interpret and enforce the law at our discretion." His eyebrows raised with a question. "Have you ever heard of the ancient expression 'an eye for an eye'?"

"No," she whispered, her mouth going dry.

"You see, your drunken driving killed a prominent Party member: she was my daughter."

"I'm so sorry, I didn't mean to-"

He flashed her a feral predatory grin that stopped her cold. Then, he continued with his calm discussion.

"I never let a crisis go to waste. Did you know that my daughter foiled your terroristic plot at the expense of her own life? Truly heroic. Unfortunately, she wasn't able to stop you before you killed over 30 innocent men, women and children. You see, the more people fear terrorism, the more power they will allow the Party to use to stop it. Not that we need their approval," he chuckled, a chilling sound, "but… winning the hearts and minds of the people does make our job easier."

"That… it's all a lie!"

"Of course! Every aspect of a citizen's life has been carefully conditioned, controlled and manipulated. Everything you've ever known has been a lie. I just thought you should know the truth before your end." He smirked when he observed her surprised expression. "Now, please, try not to get yourself upset. With all those powerful mind-altering drugs coursing through your system, you could subject yourself to a stroke–"

"Why would you care? You're going to kill me anyway!"

"Your body is the property of the Party, or more directly, those who represent the Party, such as myself and others. So, I'd appreciate it if you wouldn't damage… yourself."

He leaned behind her and flicked a switch. A different fluid entered her system.

She started to feel incredibly drowsy. The drug was taking effect – it didn't hurt.

"This will knock you out. It's not the lethal injection drug. But, don't worry, you'll die soon enough, after your vital body parts have been harvested. I, myself am looking forward to a transplant of your liver… for which, I am most grateful." He smiled again. "By the way, I've rescinded the protection for your family… oh, and I've taken a special interest in your parent's case as well. In fact, they'll all soon be joining you in the afterlife."

He flicked the camera toggle to record once again.

She tried to escape the chair, but her limbs were rubbery and nonresponsive. The room went spinning red into unconsciousness.

The last thing she heard was, "In accordance with the laws of the Party, you are hereby executed."

THE RAIN

River Bend Park
Sacramento, California, USA

River bodies were the worst.

Mottled colors, dripping, bloated with decay, shredded by fish, smashed and torn by fierce currents against rocks… altogether unsettling, distinctly horrific, more so because you could still see the remnants of what they once were, human, alive. The touch of humanity, the mementos of a life are what ultimately got to him: their clothes, put on early in the day, with no idea that they'd die in them, and personal items, like a cell phone, a plastic keychain fob saying 'Always look on the bright side of life', a movie theatre ticket stub in a back pocket, a neon-purple plush dinosaur toy, still clutched in a little girl's fingers, as if that would save her…

Damnitall, he thought, scowling.

The memories of the innocent often threatened to overwhelm him. No matter where or how or when they died, they were just people trying to get by day to day, enjoy their lives, think about the future, but… got snuffed out by inhuman monsters.

Detective Francis St. Claire, a.k.a. Frank, certainly wasn't immune to the effect of his feelings, he just had to control them, redirect them, in order to function at his job. He forced himself to concentrate on the here-and-now, what he needed to do: answer the dispatch call, drive to the river, inspect the body of a possible drowning.

The car's heater blasted against the windshield, keeping the wintry morning fog at bay, while the wipers slapped aside the continuous sheets of rain flowing across his view of the road ahead.

Some 'effing drought. California was suffering from a long period of drought, but you couldn't tell that from the recent onslaught of rainstorms thundering across the northern part of the state.

He pulled his unmarked police car into the River Bend Park entrance. Even in this monsoon-like weather, people were outside walking along the paved roadway. They reluctantly moved aside as if offended by his car, the presence of one of man's creations in this pristine natural retreat, or, maybe they were just pretentious, selfish, passive-agressive idiots who believed they had more rights than anyone else. Maybe they knew about the drowning and had come to catch a glimpse of the body.

Despite the people dawdling in the car's path and the fact that the road split several times, he easily found his way to the riverside.

He was surprised to see that the parking lot was almost full to capacity, mostly with news vehicles, all the local television networks and the newspapers too. He was acquainted with many of the news people and their crews, after all, he'd been on the force for twenty-plus years. Most of them were clustered under a canopy of trees at the far end of the parking lot, surrounding…

You've got to be kidding me.

He laughed out loud as he turned off the engine, shoved his wide-brimmed Fedora hat on his head and heaved his chunky body out of the car. The rain spattered off his hat and raincoat, the noise and pattern reminding him of taking a cold shower at home. His joints aching, he walked towards the crowd, no longer the tireless warrior he once was decades ago, for the Army Rangers in Afghanistan.

Attention-grabbing bastard.

It was him! Preston Tucker, his quote-unquote partner, assigned to him to supposedly be mentored, only several years out of the academy, career rocketing upward, promoted to detective already, undoubtedly getting a huge helping hand from his uncle, the mayor. Just the person to be assigned to a major Public Relations case: the recent murder of a prominent businessman who, it turned out, was discovered to have run a god-forsaken sex slave ring right in the heart of sunny California's capitol. Tucker was sure to become famous even if he screwed up.

And now... here he was talking to the press! TV cameras recording, boom microphones extended, questions unleashed and answers given. He certainly did have a flair for the dramatic – they were enraptured by his every word and expression. "We're looking into the matter and will keep you apprised of the situation," he said as a closing statement, then nodded a greeting to Frank and stepped away from the press crowd and its limelight of fickle fame and quotable soundbytes.

What the hell did he tell them?

Frank almost laughed aloud again as he drew closer to Tucker. The Public Relations department were supposed to preapprove any talk to the media. It was doubtful that Tucker had followed protocol.

Let's see your uncle save you this time.

"Hi Frank! Great day to be outside, huh?" Tucker showed his winning smile.

Frank motioned with his head towards the winding path that led to the riverside. The patter of rain grew distant as the rainfall was deflected by the cover of trees overhead. They continued walking down the sloping terrain of the vernal forest, past Bob Carlson, a cop guarding the trail. When they were well beyond the line-of-sight of any of the news crew's parabolic microphones, Frank asked, "Is the coroner here? I didn't see the van."

"Not yet. Must be busy with I-80."

Frank nodded. Not even an hour ago he had heard over the scanner that a pileup of over a dozen cars had blocked off the five-lane highway that led into the heart of the city. There were fatalities, and additional secondary accidents from careless lookie-loo drivers.

He appreciated the additional time to examine the body without the impatient coroner's office people breathing down his neck and asking him when he'd be done. There were always clues to be found on a body, even one that had been in the water. Looking closely was the key – and that took time.

"Who found it?" Frank asked.

"B&W." Boating and Waterways. If they were lucky, they saved people from drowning, but mostly, they pulled bodies from the water. A difficult job to be sure.

Once the bodies were on land, his department had jurisdiction.

"You talk to them?"

"Uh… No. I waited for you." Tucker smiled again but it looked like a smirk. "Based on what I heard so far, I think this drowning may be related to our case. That's why I asked dispatch to contact you."

Frank observed Tucker's face – it was sincere, he

didn't even appear to know how obnoxious he was…

Lying weasel. How could you have heard something?

They could see the pier now. Dock lines secured the B&W boat to cleats on the dock's end point.

A cop was there, Bryan What's-his-name… Bryan Holsted, that was it, some new guy, and he was talking to one of the B&W people. Frank didn't know that department very well. There were two other B&W people on the thirty-foot rescue boat waiting at anchor on the river. He knew one of them, Renee Delacroix, the boat captain, an Armed Forces vet like himself, and also, like himself, of French-Canadian descent.

An oversized tarp on the far end of the pier covered the body which was lying on a transport stretcher. Rain and gusts of wind occasionally shifted the tarp's edges, revealing a partial preview of the form beneath.

As Frank and his partner left the path, the deluge of incessant rainfall resumed falling on them. It sounded like cold chicken being dipped in a deep fryer filled with boiling peanut oil.

Holsted approached them as they stepped onto the pier. After a flash of badges, Holsted stepped aside and let them pass.

Frank hated this part. An awful sight awaited them at the end of the thirty-foot pier. The boat crew watched the two men approach. Renee hopped off onto the pier, causing the boat to rock slightly.

"What d'we have here, Renee?" Frank asked, hiding his revulsive distaste.

"White male, approximately thirty years old, found lodged under a log near the shore about two hundred yards upstream; been in the water for a while, all banged up… the rest… the rest is up to you, Monsieur Inspecteur, sir."

"Okay to look?" Frank gestured to the body.

"Ha ha, very funny, just don't make a mess or I'll call your momma," Renee snorted.

Frank lifted the tarp up to one side.

Tucker inhaled, a sharp inward hiss, despite the ripe stench rolling off the body.

It certainly wasn't a sight anyone would want to see: flesh in advance stages of decay, bones snapped, sharp edges sticking out from the broken skin, jumbled limbs askew, not all turned the right way, chest crumpled inward, and the head… the eyes were long gone, yet a bushy mustache remained beneath a missing nose, but, most graphic, the cranium had been cracked open, leaving a partially hollow shell with a direct view into what little remained of the brain.

Frank felt a freezing chill grip the back of his neck and spread like icy talons down his back. *Something's wrong.* Perhaps being surrounded by death for so long had finally caught up to him, traumatizing him and making his heart thump now with a painful arrhythmic beat, but… damn. Something wasn't right. He began to sweat despite the shivering chills.

Tucker crouched down on one knee near the body. Acrylo-nitrile rubber gloves already snapped on, he searched the corpse's pockets, finding no wallet, no ID, nothing. He eased the shattered head gently to one side. The ragged flaps of scalp and bone shifted with a wet, grisly slap inside the gaping skull cavity.

Frank had the weirdest feeling. It was déjà vu, a sense that he'd already been here, or that he'd seen it before, the moment in time unraveling like some murky nightmare coming true. Something about the body's mustache seemed familiar.

Tucker suddenly became excited. "See, Frank? Look at what I found." He pointed to what remained in the back of the skull. A spider web of bone cracks radiated outward from some central point (fragments long gone, taken by the river). "This is a bullet hole in the Occipital area."

Hmm... Occipital area, huh? Back of the head, you prancing peacock.

"This was an execution," Tucker went on. "Just like the murder of that sex slave pervert. You remember, that creep also took a small caliber bullet to the back of the head. Just like what we have here. A police patrol found the body before the murderer could dispose of it. It didn't have much for clues on it, but that's all changed now. With this body, we have more to go on." He glanced up at Frank. "The M.O. is similar. I bet the same person did these murders."

Tucker continued to babble about his possible new leads while Frank thought's drifted away, searching for the unspeakable truth in a fog of memory.

I remember that mustache. I knew him. Knew him well enough. He came a long way, from a forest hillside, floating down the river, through the lake, even over the dam spillway.

"...and another thing, Frank," Tucker went on, practically hyperventilating with exuberance, "people have been disappearing lately. Way too many people. People of a less-than-reputable moral quality, you might say. I'm beginning to think there's a connection. With the clues from this body, I might be able to tie it all together, or at least, get one step closer to nabbing our perp."

Like hell you will. I'll do everything I can to stop you, you arrogant prima donna. You'll never find a damned thing on me.

While Tucker continued to chatter away, Frank felt his mind escaping to cheerful memories of weekend vacations. He'd have to go again, soon, far upstream into the remote and rugged High Sierra Mountains country, where he'd typically spend carefree days prospecting in dried river beds for placer gold, but this time, there was other work to do.

The flash floods had probably exposed more gold in the ancient riverbeds, as well as the bodies of worthless scum who once preyed upon the helpless.

All scum deserved to die. Time to make sure the other bodies were still buried.

CONTROL

A predator stalked New York City's Central Park.

Her name was Chelsea McCormick. Once as cute and cheerfully wholesome as a teenager as could be, she was now a dirty, vicious street whore, preying upon the helpless… doing anything, anything, anything to get another hit of crystal meth.

She had the haunted look of a new addict: unkempt hair limp as dead grass; dark shadows around cold, calculating, desperate eyes; cracked peeling hungry lips; and pale-white blotchy skin. She could easily be mistaken for a Goth teen in her ragged jeans jacket and pants and black *Plasmoids* heavy metal tee shirt.

Life was hell for her. Not long ago, almost a year past, she'd left home, forcefully kicked out by her disillusioned parents. She still looked her age, young, though the meth habit was extracting its toll.

Just one more hit, she thought.

A sharp spasm of pain twisted in her gut. She bent inward, pulling her jacket tighter as if warding off the cold.

Whenever the flu cramps came, her sweaty skin felt

like it would burst open to release the phantom spiders that burrowed within. Afterward, the ice-cold shivers would linger.

The sensation passed, but the periodic nausea fueled her craving for meth. Her nose was also running non-stop. It was all maddening.

She shivered so deeply she thought she'd never be warm again.

The sun was beginning to set in the clear blue, fall sky. Soon, the long night would come. She'd need a place to crash.

Damn it, I need some ice.

If she had some serious money all would be good, she could get some meth and maybe a room. She absolutely hated having to sleep outside or with some scary creep for a twenty and a bed. If she didn't succeed, it'd be yet another dreadfully risky day in her life. There were more dangerous people on the streets than her – she'd learned that the hard way.

Despite feeling anxious, she sauntered down the spacious smooth concrete walkway, trying her best to be inconspicuous.

No one noticed her. No one cared.

Her potential victims went about their normal lives, enjoying the brisk sunny day, typically unaware and unconcerned, even though they should know better. They were couples, making the circuit around the manmade lake; a cluster of Japanese tourists tossing pieces of bread to paddling ducks; health nuts jogging steadfast, weaving around crowds; rollerbladers and skateboarders showing off their skills; dog walkers holding onto leashes and plastic poop bags; vendors selling everything from hot dogs to Big Apple souvenirs; children squealing with delight, surrounding a performer of some kind, mostly obscured behind a ring of parents.

Chelsea stopped to take in the revelry of the children.

The bubbly sound of young laughter resurrected a latent memory buried deep inside her. She must've been nine years old and the joyous elation she'd felt upon opening a birthday present was nothing less than miraculous. Beneath the bow-spruced silver wrapping was her dream doll. Lifelike, with a variety of outfits, this baby doll would fulfill her instinctive desire to take care of someone, to love. It was a wonderful gift. Her parents had been so thoughtful... but that changed. Her childhood memories darkened after those early years when the veil of cheerful kindness around her was revealed to be a manipulative ruse. Over time, the bliss she'd felt in those treasured princess years soured as her parents imposed more and more draconian demands upon her: demands for her to behave, to study, to do what she was told, to maintain a respectable appearance, to have the right friends and to have no say whatsoever in her life.

Grinding her teeth, she realized that she wasn't angry at the children. They were innocent like she once was. She hated their parents. Adults had created this god-forsaken world, on purpose or not, and their children had to live with the consequences.

Those parents, intent on watching their children so closely, hovered around the nucleus of excited children drawn to the performer.

The children were so happy... she wished she could feel that way again.

Suddenly, unexpectedly, a girl screamed and turned to her parents.

The surrounding crowd went quiet as the mother quickly scooped up her child. The father, fists beginning to clench, took a half step forward before his wife's touch stopped him. As the glaring parents moved away, the girl cried, snuggling close to her mother's neck.

With the moment of drama passed, the children continued with their delighted antics.

Chelsea was astonished when she saw the center of attention. The performer was a woman, ancient, back bowed over, knobby knuckled, light brown skin shrunken like a dried autumn apple and shockingly offset by a trendy cut of stark white hair. Also, incongruously, she wore a loose-fitted, snappy business suit with perfectly matching blouse and pants, and if Chelsea's instincts were correct, the ensemble was composed of outrageously expensive brands.

The old woman's right hand jumped and twitched with a flurry of movement. Connected between her nimble fingers and a marionette figure on the walkway, wispy wires reflected through the fading light like spectral claws phasing in and out of reality.

The puppet figure was about a foot tall, clothed like a cowboy in blue jeans, brown boots, white shirt, red scarf and black wide-brimmed hat. Its hands and feet, and even its head, were comically oversized yet articulated with supple fluid manipulation.

As Chelsea watched, fascinated, the shiny painted doll handed a shelled peanut to a boy, no more than two years old, who hopped up and down, holding the peanut up high like a prize.

The venerable puppet master was undoubtedly an expert in the art form. Intent on her craft, she perfunctorily accepted gratuities with her free hand and stuffed them into a narrow suit pocket.

Crazy ass. Correction, crazy ass with money.

Chelsea's outlook cheered considerably at the thought of taking the old hag's money.

A fleeting pang of remorse disturbed her conscience like the last bubble of air trickling from a drowned person's mouth, rising to the surface and disappearing with a lazy pop as if it had never existed.

I deserve that money, she reasoned. A sense of sanctimonious injustice raged through her, defiant and fierce like a flare sputtering against a dark abyss.

Body aching and nose dripping, she carefully considered her plan of attack. She'd have to grab the money when no one else was around or else there'd be a fight from interfering onlookers. Or, worse yet, the cops would nab her.

Soon enough, the sun crept behind the skyscrapers surrounding the large park. It would soon be dark.

A gentle breeze picked up, tickling the fine hairs on Chelsea's neck with a frosty foreshadowing of the cold night ahead.

It was getting late in the day. Most people had already left the park by now. Only a few scattered souls still strolled by the wind-rippled lake.

Finally, the puppeteer absent-mindedly waved goodbye to her last child spectator. She shuffled away from the main thoroughfare towards a nearby stone bridge. The weathered bridge crossed over a thin channel of lily-choked water and led to a path that meandered through a secluded woody area.

Perfect!

Chelsea caught herself nervously scratching her hands and immediately stopped.

Damn bugs. Real or not, their restless crawling underneath her skin often made her irritable.

Chelsea tapped one foot in tempo with the old woman's impossibly slow pace. Each halting step dragged on.

A wave of nausea suddenly rolled through Chelsea. She almost threw up.

Gasping for air, her craving for a meth hit escalated. She needed to escape the endless insufferable void of pointless existence that had become her life.

Just one more hit… then I'll be brave enough to quit.

Her mantra comforted her. And she meant it. There was a free rehab clinic that was going to open soon on 5th Avenue and 11th Street. She'd check it out.

At that moment, her conscience resurfaced, deciding to bother her like the irritating late-night buzz of an unseen mosquito. She tried quitting before. It didn't work.

The old hag finally passed over the top of the bridge's shallow arch and inched her way out of sight.

Chelsea exhaled a long exasperated sigh. She glanced around to verify that no one was watching, then ambled up to and over the crest of the bridge. The idyllic scene before her was reminiscent of a fairy tale about a nasty bridge troll that stalked hapless travelers, except real life was no fairy tale.

And I'm the troll. She snorted at her lame observation.

What!?!

The old woman was nowhere in sight!

What the hell-

Chelsea raced down to the wooded trail.

Uncertain what to do, she strained her eyes to see further up the curving trail. The old woman could barely walk, so she still had to be close by.

In the woods…

Frowning, Chelsea scanned both sides of the cobblestone trail. She could see maybe ten feet into the wild tangle of trees and bushes. Spruce, pine and scrub brush still held their foliage above a loam carpet of dead brown needles and leaves.

She stilled her ragged breathing and listened.

Despite the background rumble of nearby traffic and cry of city life, she thought she heard something to her left. She waited, cocking her head to one side, straining to hear anything out of place.

There it was again. On her left. In the woods.

It was a… groan.

There she is!

This job would be a piece of cake.

Literally a walk in the park.

Her grin was feral, teeth flashing like a hungry shark, circling closer and closer, about to attack.

As she eased into the undergrowth, her boots cracked dried leaves and softly snapped twigs as low hanging branches closed behind her, leaving no sign of her passage.

The groaning sound repeated, closer, louder, laced with raw pain.

Chelsea's gut gurgled briefly as though in sympathy.

Her stealth brought her to the edge of a small rocky clearing.

Just a running leap away, her victim sat groaning upon a small boulder, facing away from Chelsea. Hunched over, the old woman's head bobbed, and shoulders twitched erratically.

The groaning grew worse as Chelsea closed the distance silent as death.

Without warning, the old woman turned with a scowl. Her wild rheumy eyes locked onto Chelsea's. Bloody droplets sprayed from her distorted mouth as she spat out, "Stay the hell away from me!"

More words would've followed, but were lost as the old woman grimaced, eyes squeezed shut, in the grip of intense agony.

Chelsea's momentum had stuttered to a full stop, unsure what to do, transfixed by the old woman's crazed audacity.

Did she really want to mug a helpless old lady? Her mother's shrill voice chose that moment to haunt her with barbed memories of proper civilized behavior.

"Give me your money, you old witch!" Chelsea

bellowed.

Oblivious, the old woman clutched fitfully at her writhing body with clawed hands, one of which still held the marionette, sending it flying and skipping in a macabre dance across the ground. Leaning forward, her groaning became a convulsive gurgle that ended abruptly. Collapsing with a loose thump onto the stone ridge, she shuddered once, then breathed no more.

Chelsea blinked several times, stunned by the sudden turn of events.

She knew the signs of death; she'd been around it enough lately.

Heart attack? No... Way...

Chelsea's hysterical laughter was cruel and mirthless. She couldn't believe her good luck as she looked around the clearing. Only trees, no people, no witnesses, not even a bird or squirrel.

She knelt on the hard rock beside the still body. The cold ground, as if frozen by the proximity of the Grim Reaper, stung her bony knees.

Close up, the old woman's dress ensemble looked new, albeit rumpled and recently stained with mud spots. It must've come from one of the charity centers that gave out hot meals, clothes and occasionally, a cot for the night.

Chelsea frisked the old woman's suit. The lightweight body moved as easily as a child's plush toy.

The cash she pulled from the suit pockets was astonishing. It looked like at least five hundred dollars, mostly in small bills with coins mixed in.

With this loot, Chelsea could score some meth and stay high for a week straight, maybe get some food and stay at a decent economy hotel. She wondered why the old woman didn't use the money for a hotel. Even a day or two off the streets, here and there, could've meant the difference between life and death.

What an idiot. I wonder…

She hesitated before reaching deep into the old woman's pants pockets. Purple velvet lining slid past her fingers as she pulled forth a slim leather wallet.

It held cash - mostly hundreds, six of them, and some twenties and tens, neatly organized by denomination.

Seven hundred and thirty, if she did the math right. Plus the other five hundred!

There were also credit cards – the high end platinum and gold versions. The driver's license was issued last year… to Pamela Cooper, age 26. The picture showed a perky arrogant executive with a bored smirk on her face. The face looked like the old woman, only much younger!

Chelsea dropped the wallet.

What the fu-

The old woman's body suddenly began to shrivel, rapidly collapsing in on itself with harsh crackling sounds and yellow sizzling sparks of searing combustion. Within seconds, grey motes swirled about in the superheated air, leaving behind the suit outfit, settling to the ground, filled with the fine smoking ash remains of the body.

A wet scream choked in the back of Chelsea's throat as she tried to scrabble away backwards on her knees.

The last thing she saw was the marionette springing up from the ground towards her; its spectral wiry lines whipping towards her face like the tentacles of an enraged octopus, piercing deep into her flesh. The life drained out of her as her consciousness descended into spiraling darkness.

***

The next morning, an odd vacant-eyed old woman,

dressed like a Goth in a jeans jacket and pants and a *Plasmoid's* tee-shirt, entertained the laughing children gathered around her, manipulating a marionette with such skill… that it appeared to be alive.

1642

Salty breeze, the sun slipping beneath the silver horizon, nighttime cooling approaching, the ship Lazarus rolling in the mild sea waves. His wrists gripped tightly by thick rope, exhausted from seasickness, lashed to the ship's mainsail beam, waiting for…

Robarte was agonized by the severity of sudden pain across his young arching back.

When he could breathe, his high-pitched scream was interrupted by the second crack of the whip. Bones tremor, flesh ripped open, muscles spasm, a drawn out wail, blood splashes into the air, running wounds collect into a web of rivulets, dripping to the smooth deck planks, joining his pee as any notion of self-control let go.

He lost count of the whip's lashing. He existed awash in an endless stormy sea of pain.

Eventually, the crack of the whip was no more.

The Captain said, "Let him be for now."

Mercifully, the pain sent his scrawny seven-year-old body into the oblivion of unconsciousness.

***

Robarte awoke in the lowest compartment hold, lying against the cool curving slope of the hull wall, sensing the sea bubbling past on the other side. Earlier, he'd gotten caught stowing away, behind the nearby piles of smooth ballast stones, all because he couldn't stop throwing up from the sudden onslaught of seasickness.

Head swimming with pain, back afire with every movement, he cracked open his green eyes further to see a bull of a man standing over him, chortling mightily, adjusting, tucking, and buttoning his breeches.

"Wake up land lubber! Get yer lazy arse topside!" The man spoke English with a heavy French accent. He had long bright red hair, a beard with braids, a full set of grinning teeth, dressed out in black and wearing a leather jerkin.

I'm not dead! He thought. *But I smell, like... pee, he whizzed on me.*

Unsteady, Robarte wobbled to his feet, assisted by the big galoot, who grabbed Robarte's ear and shoved him up a ladder to mid-decks, a clothesline jungle of gently swinging hammocks, and up another ladder, where he was hoisted aloft by other sailors to the main deck.

The air above was fresh, wind brisk to snap the billowing sails, not at all stifling compared to the various competing stenches of below decks.

Blinking at the sunrise, on a ship of sailors, no... devil-may-care lawless pirates, many staring balefully at him, he wondered if his fate had just gotten worse by stowing away. He'd thought it was a merchant ship. Wrong – there were no trade goods aboard and merchantmen wouldn't torture a hapless young boy.

Shivering, he remembered some words from last

night about how he'd be swimming with the sharks.

Reeling in the grasp of his captor, slouched and unsteady, his stomach rumbled loudly. Gales of laughter erupted around him.

He hadn't eaten for the last three days in Tortuga trying to avoid capture by the governor's men, intent on ultimately killing him. They thought he'd stolen some of their money. It wasn't true, but why believe him? He was a street urchin whelp; father long dead, murdered by constables, and mother, forced into prostitution to stay alive, recently deceased in a brothel brawl that claimed her life. Surely, he was an easy target. He never felt so vulnerable in his short-lived life.

"Maurice, have ye taken account of what this snotgob can do?" the Captain asked, an elegantly enunciated voice despite the crudity of words. He was plainly dressed in loose-fitting seadog clothes, with the exception of tiny gold-looped earrings that sharply contrasted his swarthy cocoa-tanned skin, and a cutlass held in a crimson scabbard on his belt.

Robarte was lifted up, feet now dangling, the mountain-sized man holding him like a kitten, by the scruff of his neck. The giant replied, "He be right clever. Sneaking aboard like a snake, hidden for near a day afore we noticed him, and that only because he blew some chunder."

"Sneaky bastard? Might prove useful. Put him to work."

"Aye, Captain."

***

Time passed like fancy clockwork. Tick tock, tick tock, a relentless schedule, scrub the decks, the gentle lurch and roll of the ship's knifing through the Caribbean waters, his body suddenly awash with sweat, and then, stomach spasming until he was left drained. Repeat again and again, other chores thrown in, clean the bilge, lug coals for the stove, clean the ship's guns, haul tar buckets for patching the hull, pump out seawater, and so on, with insults galore from the crew and the occasional cuff to the head from Maurice, who turned out to be the ship's quartermaster. Then, food, which was often biscuits and gruel, and a shift of sleep, the only thing that was easy to do despite the relentless barrage of vulgarity and cursing above decks and the creaking and groaning of the ship.

More of this pattern, perhaps two weeks, where he eventually adjusted to the sea, felt his back heal, kept his food down, received less abuse, and wondered just what in hell was going on.

Maurice took a liking to him, often showing his affection by calling him a variety of colorful insults, the best one being something in French about a fiddler's fart.

He asked Maurice, "Where are we going?" And knowing the sensitivity of being branded a pirate, "Are we searching for Spanish ships?" Something a privateer would do...

"The Captain has Letters of Marque for certain, but we're looking for something else. He has a Spanish map that'll lead us... to something that'll protect us... and then, we go for the prize."

"Why would we need protection?" he asked, realizing that he used the word 'we', which would include himself as part of this unruly bunch.

"Where we're headed, 'tis the greatest hoard of treasure ever. And the greatest danger ever... we'll need all the help we can get... 'tis bloody cursed deviltry to be dealt with. Best not talk of such things. Get back to your work, lad."

***

Shortly thereafter, land was sighted. The wind was full in their ship's sails, sending them swiftly to a large verdant coast that spanned the western horizon. Perhaps it was the vast unexplored continent he'd once heard about…

The Captain told the sailing master to take a northerly course along the jungle coast.

As the sun crept towards the jungle canopy, they eased into a small cove of clear, light-blue water. He could see the sea floor, deep below, and colorful fish, some larger than him, swimming blissfully unconcerned through a scattering of shipwrecks.

Excited, several pirates pointed to the shoreline. Looking up, he saw a tall column of weathered rock embedded in the sand, above the high water mark, and, even from the distance; he could see that it was carved with many symbols, all of which looked like a flying snake.

The buccaneers went ashore via three longboat skiffs. No one stayed on board.

No guard for the ship? Guess we need everyone… but why? We're looking for something that'll protect us… what's there to be afraid of?

Chilled, and not from the caress of a gentle shore breeze, he disembarked onto the land, feet momentarily uncertain on stable, unmoving ground.

Robarte was loaded up with several bags of supplies hung over his back: lantern, rum, tinder, rope, and other unseen items.

Maurice called him "donkey-boy". Several other sailors took to joking with him as well. Some pirates were friendly enough in their own crude way, like Maurice, but from the stories he'd overheard some of his shipmates brag about, they were, often enough, truly despicable people, completely barbaric.

With this motley group of scallywags, he went inland, deep into the tropical forest. Onward, onward, onward, he trudged into the vast unknown of thick undergrowth and sultry mangrove and palm trees. The winding line the trailblazer cut through the greenery almost seemed to be arbitrary, except that the rocks on the path's ground were worn smoother than elsewhere.

Once, a black cat the size of a large guard dog bared its teeth at him from deep within the foliage. It looked far more dangerous than the wild boars he'd seen in Tortuga.

"Jaguar," Maurice whispered.

The jungle was damp and steamy with rotting plants and no airflow. It got far worse when the flies found the pirates and harassed them nonstop. Tempers became short.

Robarte's burden made it difficult to shush the pests away. Thus, their tiny stilettoes sunk into him with little to no interruption from his occasional swats.

The line's movement stopped abruptly when someone ahead had a veritable conniption fit. A beautiful red, blue, and green feathered parrot had taken a dump on some pirates, and flew off squawking, which was due cause for a round of raucous laughter.

Since it was late in the evening, the Captain decided it was time to stop and setup camp. A frying pan was yanked out of a bag loaded on Robarte's back. The cook, Alfred, who was Maurice's friend, began the process of making a meal for everyone. Alfred wasn't really a good cook. Primarily, he was the ship's carpenter and by default, the surgeon.

Robarte dropped his burden of bags several paces away from the chosen campfire site. He lay down against a remarkably smooth-barked tree that reached up high into the star-freckled early night sky.

When the campfire was fully ablaze, it put his mind at ease, keeping thoughts of the odd nighttime jungle at bay.

Soon, thick slabs of salt pork were roasting on the cooking pan, making him drool unconsciously. It was a rare occasion to get real meat, aside from fish, which filled the belly but was lacking in taste – even that was far better than dry, hardtack biscuits and mystery gruel, their mainstay. Alfred tossed him a rasher strip, landing still sizzling on his exposed legs, causing him to yelp and toss it onto a large leaf nearby. Alfred laughed and called him "ma petite chien", something French about a dog.

The tough pork went down just fine, bite after persistent bite, with a lot of chewing involved, along with short gasping slugs from one of the many rum flagons he'd once carried, most of which had been taken away by the crew. Staring at the fire, he dozed away into sleep to the off-tune medleys of drunken singing, laughing, and farting.

***

He woke up, head throbbing.

Too much rum.

The blue sky was barely visible through the overhead canopy. Thankfully, the jungle air was still mildly cool.

His back ached when he sat up. He was accustomed to sleeping outside, but not atop a thick tree root. *Ouch!*

Maurice gave him a smack across the head. Incidentally, Smackhead was also one of the names Maurice had bestowed upon him.

"Grab your gear," Maurice rumbled, undoubtedly feeling the rum's aftereffects. "We're moving out."

Robarte grabbed what he could see and went

looking for the rest. He found six empty rum flagons scattered on the ground. That left four full rum flagons for the crew, as far as he knew. Maybe someone else also carried rum.

Rum's almost gone, uh-oh...

They walked and walked. It was a slow, staggered march with many stops considering that it was difficult to cut a trail through the densely packed vegetation.

Midday at least, head bowed down like a donkey, he heard the gasps of his fellow mariners. He looked up to find himself before a strange vine-covered, carved stone mountain, bigger and taller than any building he'd ever seen, even the governor's palace in Tortuga.

Maurice spoke in a flat voice, saying, "That's a pyramid. Built by the savages."

"People made this?"

The structure led up into the sky via a steep rise of wide stairs placed atop gigantic stone blocks. The Captain led the way up the steps, the crew following, careful to avoid the crisscross tangle of thick, leafy vine stalks.

Robarte set his burden of bags down on the loamy forest floor. "What is this place?" he whispered to Maurice, hesitant to break the unusual silence of the surrounding forest.

"A temple, I think. The Captain said it's cursed. He's looking for something here. Something dangerous. The Spanish map called it God's Fury. We'll need it for later on."

"What is it? What happens later on?"

"I've told you enough already. Unless you want to be shark bait, keep yer teeth together."

Some of the pirates had already reached the top. Their arguing, a mix of French and English, echoed loudly across the jungle top.

Robarte went up the stairway. Occasionally, he felt

Maurice's hand on his shoulder to steady him. The steps were wide but vine cluttered, and they barely had enough depth for him to set his feet on. He nearly slipped and fell when he saw a human skull, mouth gaping wide open, poking out from the leaves to one side of the stairway.

When he reached the top, he saw that it was a flat square, clear of any vines, but loaded with the skeletal remains of those who'd been here before and never left, including Spanish conquistadors and a priest. And, exactly in the center, there was a carved stone altar, like he'd seen in a church, except this one was of a reclining lizard-like creature, maybe a dragon, and on its upraised belly, it held a wide flat bowl. He'd seen that kind of bowl before – it was used in slave quarters to catch the blood of sacrificed chickens.

Something sparkled in the bowl.

Something which drove the pirates mad.

God's Fury...

Pirates around the altar began attacking each other, wicked weapons drew blood, and the fighting raged out of control. The Captain roared commands for them to stop, but they were driven by a madness frothing from within, cursing epithets to imagined insults, swords and knives slashing through the air, and now, pistols drawn.

"They're going to kill you," a silky voice said inside his head.

Startled, but being no stranger to the idea of people hearing voices, he said, "Maybe I can become more useful?"

"Aren't you afraid of dying?"

"No. Afraid of living..."

"Come to me."

Six pirates had fallen around the altar. More would also die here – the fighters went berserk, more pirates joining in. Alfred the surgeon couldn't save them now, for he had fallen to an errant sword stroke when he tried to help a wounded comrade. Maurice backed away from the melee fighting, shaking his head, seemingly lost in self-inflicted despair rather than molten hot anger.

Robarte moved in a trance-like state through the fighting pirates, barely aware of the battle surging around him. A pistol shot nearby, dropping a pirate, the screaming and yelling loud and irrational.

He stood on his tiptoes and pulled a large diamond-like orb from the bottom of the bowl.

At that moment, the chaos around him dissolved like a sand castle hit by a rogue wave.

Confused, pirates slowly lowered their weapons. They stared wide-eyed at Robarte, seemingly convinced that he'd caused their momentary insanity. Some murderous glares also locked onto him, finally looking elsewhere as the Captain approached Robarte.

The Captain said, "I knew you'd be useful."

"Hide that," Maurice said. "In your tunic."

When the sparkling object was hidden away, the men calmed down visibly.

A third of the crew lay dead and dying...

***

Back onboard, Robarte was locked inside an officer's quarters. The cozy forecastle room was isolated far away from the main crew quarters, but he could still hear the murmur of their nervous conversations – many had died, and the boy was somehow involved. Much of the mutinous talking ended after the Captain made a bloody example of someone far too outspoken. Maurice came by to give him his meals, passing them under the door, and shying away from any conversation.

He didn't know why he was being treated this way, but he suspected that he was the only one aboard who could hold the orb without going stark raving mad. He didn't mind at all. The cabin had a comfortable hammock, it was relatively quiet, he didn't have to work, and he got fed. And it wasn't as if he was alone, the voice inside his head kept him company, telling him about the pirate's plans to use the orb to acquire treasure, a terribly dangerous adventure. And he and the orb talked about other things, like his tragic life back at Tortuga.

No doubt the crew thought he was daft, having conversations with no one at all.

****

This time, the sea voyage was short, lasting two days.

When the cabin door opened again, it was Maurice looking apologetic, saying, "Come along, we're at the island."

"What's on the island?"

"The biggest treasure ever. You'll see. And, Robarte, I'm sorry."

"For what?"

Maurice just shook his head.

The trip inland only took half a day through a forest of lush trees and tangled undergrowth. He didn't have to carry anything except for the orb in his tunic. Except for Maurice, the pirates kept a distance from him, separated by fear.

They reached a cluster of squat stone buildings hidden within the jungle growth. The buildings were ancient – crumbling on the edges, splotched with lichen and mold, and cracked in places by squeezing vines. Long abandoned by the people who'd once lived there.

Squinting, his eyes adjusted to the piercing clear blue sky breaking through the thinning forest canopy.

Just ahead, there was an enormous open space, easily wide enough to swallow three large ships, keel to masts and all, essentially a steep hole in the earth that plunged downward to a light-green, algae-choked pool. Many shallow cave entrances lay exposed along the waterline.

There was a thin wail coming from the hole despite the absence of a breeze.

The Captain swaggered over to him, bent low next to one ear and said, "If anything happens, anything untoward mind you, pull out that bauble. Understood?"

"Y-yes, Captain," he stammered, remembering how important it was to stay useful.

The Captain nodded, then stood up and addressed his crew. "Alrighty, lads, there be treasure here aplenty in this pool and its grottos. Tossed in by the savages, gold, silver, and jewels, sacrificed to their heathen gods… all that waiting below for us. Let's get to it!"

A ragged wave of thirsty cheers went 'round the group. They approached the cliff edges, setting up belaying ropes, tying them to trees and throwing the free ends over the edge.

Robarte gagged. The pool's smell was worse than a cesspit.

They're actually going down there?

The noise from the cenote hole was becoming louder, at first like dry leaves scraping across a cobblestone street in the wind, then becoming like the screeching of wooden reed flutes, similar to the dreadful chorus he'd often hear from outside the church.

When the wisps of vapor trails began rising from the waters, Robarte knew that something supernatural was happening. He was too terrified to run. The pirates didn't run either, though their steadfast behavior was likely due to gold lust.

The wisps grew in number and size, becoming full scale apparitions of human beings, dressed as they died, looking the part of the newly dead, angry at this intrusion, the foresaid violation of their resting place. Judging from their nature, it was doubtful they ever rested – souls somehow condemned to dwell in this forsaken ritual site by unknown gods or witchery. And it wasn't just natives, it was other people as well, such as pirates.

That scared the buccaneers greatly. A cry went up and the men backed away, stumbling from the edge of the hellhole. The ghosts whipped through the air, unstoppable by mortal weapons, wrapping themselves around and through their pirate victims, who felt the slow, agonizing death of being torn asunder from inside out.

"Take out God's Fury and go forth to confront the ghosts!" The captain yelled.

"Nuu- no, no, no!" He cried.

A pistol cocked behind him. "I shan't tell you again, boy."

Shuddering, Robarte drew the orb from his tunic. He stepped forward, shaking all over, blinking back tears. He held the orb aloft in his right hand. The orb's sparkling became brighter as he reached the cenote's edge. The ghosts were clearly agitated by the orb's light. A ghost came at him before he could react. The orb blazed with brilliant white light, difficult to look at, as the ghost attacked it. The ghost was shredded in fiery discharges, but still it didn't stop, furiously assaulting the orb before disintegrating. As more and more ghosts closed on him, angrily seeking to destroy the orb, he got knocked about. By this point, the orb scorched his blistered skin as all the ghosts hammered away at it. The orb took hellacious damage.

"You should let go now or else you'll die," the voice said inside his head.

Robarte's burnt flesh stuck to the orb, making it

impossible to let go until a massive jolt from the ghosts broke his grip. The orb went over the cliff edge, and pursued by ghosts, it bounced several times against the jagged rocky wall, finally shattering but ten feet above the murky pool.

God's Fury flared like the sun then disappeared. Suddenly, the wailing of ghosts stopped. The jungle was quiet. No birds. Nothing.

The ghosts were gone.

The Captain was dead. The cackling roar of the surviving pirates roused him from his shock. "The treasure's all ours!" he heard them yell.

The pain hit him. He looked at his right hand. The skin was peeled back, exposing blackened bones, muscle and cartilage beneath. His mouth bobbed open and closed. *I'm going to die!*

He was even more horrified when a tall godlike humanoid figure levitated up from the pool and glided to the cliff edge before him. The creature was a nightmarish corpse – virtually clear – he could see a distorted view of the jungle through it. When the death's head skull looked at him, he heard a familiar chuckle inside his head.

You were in the orb? He thought. *What have I done?*

"You saved yourself," the voice replied. Amazed, he felt his hand heal instantly.

Terrified pirates decided to open fire with their pistols.

As if exasperated by their annoying behavior, the godling looked quickly from one pirate to the next and to the next and so on. Immediately after, their screams gurgled wetly as their bodies melted like candles in a fire. Soon, just gooey blobs remained steaming amongst clothes and personal items.

Three pirates remained, empty hands held up in a supplicating gesture: Maurice and two others.

"Thank you for freeing me," the voice said to Robarte.

The ghosts did that.

"Yes, but only someone as innocent as you could've brought me here. And this is one of the few places where I could've been set free. I owe you a debt of gratitude."

You can't help me, he said, looking away to the ground.

The godling transformed as it approached him. It kneeled before him, fully human in appearance, and lifted his chin gently.

"Mother!" he blurted.

She was exactly as he wanted to remember her, shiny raven black hair, mischievous green eyes, warm smile, curvy soft figure that he hugged and cried into. It was her before the world went to hell…

"No..." the godling said in her soothing tone, gently stroking Robarte's soft hair, "I'm not your mother, but I thought this shape would please you."

"I miss her so much."

"I know. Robarte, what can I do for you?"

"Tell me. Are you good or evil?"

"I am whatever I need to be. What do you want to be?"

He thought for a moment. "I want to be a pirate. A pirate captain. With many ships. And a crew for each of them."

The godling, now his mother, waved one delicate hand casually, and the ghosts reformed and clustered about, all showing fealty to him. In the distance, across the world, he imagined that he heard the sound of wooden ships and their undead crew being raised from various briny depths.

"And, I want to go to Tortuga. To right some wrongs."

His mother smiled...

OVER AND OUT

She was on the last leg of her 260-mile triangular flight plan, almost home, when trouble appeared on the near-horizon in the form of dangerous thunderclouds.

"Brookhaven Flight Control, this is Pilot Renee Thibeault, November-5-7-9-0-Alpha, requesting course change to 1-6-0, over."

The response: "November-5-7-9-0-Alpha. This is Brookhaven Flight Control. Course change approved, maintain altitude 5,000-"

And it stopped in mid-sentence. Suddenly Renee heard nothing but static.

Huh? she thought. She tweaked the radio's microphone again and said, "Brookhaven Flight Control, this is November-5-7-9-0-Alpha, over."

Again, static.

She repeated her dialogue three times on the same frequency with the same results.

Out of the corner of her eye she saw a bright red streak, zipping down through a break in the clouds. In her vision, its afterimage reminded her of a meteor. It startled her, but she remained focused on flying.

She checked her instruments. *160 degrees, 90 knots,*

5000 feet, level flight...

Every minute or so, she did this, taking in the data with a sweeping glance. Not that it was necessary to do it that often. She could feel any major flight changes through her left hand on the steering yoke, her right hand on the throttle, her feet on the rudder panels, and her butt on the uncomfortable seat. *Flying by the seat of my pants...*

Just ahead, as she watched in disbelief, a wall of dark, angry-purple clouds billowed upward from the Connecticut landscape. The upper level was already becoming a dark grey, overcast mass pressing downwards upon her; the thunderclouds ahead made her flight all the more oppressive.

Well... that FAA forecast sucks... this isn't clear and sunny like they promised.

A slight tremor began to affect her every movement. She was terrified and rightfully so. Her Cessna wasn't built for flying through thunderstorms. If she flew through the heart of those clouds, her plane could be tossed to the ground, twisted and crushed, discarded like an empty beer can on a Friday night drinking binge.

Where was flight control? She was frightened to be alone.

She knew there wasn't enough fuel to fly back to her last airport. If she chose to possibly survive the experience by flying through the thunderclouds, the FAA might revoke her student's license. They had their insane rules; she was only VFR rated, not IFR rated; she was supposed to fly in clear skies only.

Why hadn't the FAA known about this weather?

And why aren't they answering? Even the stationary radar beacons weren't working. Thunderstorms messing with radio signals – that didn't sound right.

She called in again, this time directly to the FAA, hoping to reach Poughkeepsie, Westchester or

MacArthur Towers… or anyone at this point.

Static. Not even scratchy static with the hope of a snippet of conversation. Just the universe's eternal hissing white noise.

Was her radio broken? Not possible. It had been thoroughly checked before takeoff.

Ugh! The plane unexpectedly dropped about thirty feet. She fought with the controls to level the plane out.

The thundercloud ahead was exerting its disruptive influence on the surrounding atmosphere. The effects would get worse. No wonder, because the cloud's shape swelled like bubbles frothing from an overheated pot of boiling blood, reacting almost irritably, as if sensing her presence and being most displeased.

The rain began in earnest, changing from a spray of mist to staccato bursts of big drops cracking upon the Plexiglas windshield. She hoped that wouldn't keep up – the noise was shredding her already frazzled nerves.

Right now, she experienced the epitome of being alone: isolated in a small confined cabin, a mile above the ground, surrounded by approaching clouds, the smell of nervous fear wafting in the musty air, and an ever-present damp coldness that the heater couldn't dispel.

She was running out of time and getting closer to the thunderclouds.

Where the hell are those airport towers? She spotted an area near the bottom of the thunderclouds that appeared to be clear of turbulence. Maybe that would work, if she lost some altitude.

That's when she saw it. It looked like… a kid's Mylar balloon?

How did it get up here? Maybe a thermal updraft from the storm?

She peered through the rain-streaked window on her left, and suddenly she could see hundreds of silver balloons rising from the foggy ground, some already near her altitude.

The balloons rose from a huge building, directly below. She could barely see through the fog, but she could tell that the building was on fire, surrounded by pinpoints of lights from emergency vehicles. Must've been a balloon factory?

Oh no! If she could see the building fire, then she was way too close to the ground.

She pulled up on the yoke to rise in altitude, realizing that if one of the balloons got caught in the plane's air intake, the engine could shut down, and she might go into a stall, or worse, a spin. Once, during a flight lesson, she had accidentally sent the plane into a nosedive, spinning, spinning, spinning, before her instructor pushed on the right rudder to stop the spin and pulled them out of the heart-wrenching acceleration, a certain preview of death.

Since then, she'd had more training, but, if the engine fully shut down, she'd still have to land somewhere: in a parking lot, highway, or open field.

Looking back up, she noticed that there were several balloons in her flight path, and more were rising to her altitude. She almost felt as if they'd hurried to get here and go no further. Well, thunderstorm updrafts were fickle. *Time for evasive maneuvers.*

With gradual sweeping arcs, she flew around the balloons. She took care to make no more than forty-five degree angle turns. Any more than that could cause a stall.

While performing this aerial ballet, she called on the radio, trying to keep her voice calm and not yell with frustrated fear, "Anyone out there? This is November-5-7-9-0-Alpha, pilot Renee Thibeault, third leg solo, Poughkeepsie to Brookhaven, requesting altitude change from 5000 to 1000, over."

More static.

While on the radio, she hadn't seen a balloon near her left side, then...the impossible happened. It exploded like flak in a World War II movie. Her aircraft lurched sickeningly in the air. Her fast reflexes countered the violent clockwise spiral and brought the plane back into level and steady flight.

She fought the sudden urge to throw up.

She hadn't hit the balloon, yet it had exploded near the left wing. The wings were situated above the cockpit, so she looked up at the wing's lower surface to check for damage. It wasn't broken or warped, but structural damage was often hidden – the wing could snap off at any moment or it could be just fine.

And then she saw that on the wing's under-surface, there were several dozen gobs of a mostly translucent, goo-like substance, the size of chicken eggs, each containing a glowing silver dot inside. They reminded her of a predator's eyes shining with malicious intent on a cold, wintry night around a camper's nighttime fire. *They're alive!*

They had come from the balloon. She remembered how it had looked close up, just before it exploded. Those weren't balloons... they were living creatures... eyes.

The balloon-creature on her plane was arranged like a large shiny cluster of bulbous grapes, consisting of so many eyes, along with several ribbon-strands dangling below, whipping in the wind.

Mother of Mercy! The eyes were oozing along the wing towards the cockpit. They were moving, even against a vicious cross wind!

She couldn't just get out of the plane and slap them off the wing. She felt frozen with terror. She had to get a grip; she had to fly the plane. Maybe she could outrun the creatures in the sky.

Yet more of the eye-monsters appeared ahead. They

were closing in on her plane's trajectory. She banked the plane, left or right, as needed, swerving to avoid the floating eyes.

Another explosion on the starboard side! *Are they full of hydrogen like an old Zeppelin?*

The thundercloud was fast approaching. To get to the clearer area beneath the thundercloud, she had to lower altitude now, FAA be damned. She couldn't do a descending corkscrew pattern to lose altitude. Not with those monsters chasing her. They'd be on her plane in an instant.

She pushed forward hard on the yoke and accelerated downward in a ramping slope, being mindful of the increased speed. The left wing was in questionable shape – hopefully, it'd be okay with this steep dive.

About a half-dozen of the eyes were still clinging to the wing, the closest being an arm's reach away from the cockpit. That one seemed to stare at her. *What if it gets to the cockpit?*

Her plane skidded sideways and her air speed was dropping… dropping… dropping. *The plane could stall!*

If it stalled and went into a spin, the excessive wind speed could snap the left wing off. She upped the throttle – she had no choice. The engine protested mightily, but the airspeed picked up.

The wings were intact, the eyes were gone, the rudder was… not just sluggish, it refused to move. She looked towards the rear… and screamed.

Something huge engulfed the entire rear of the plane. Writhing against the Plexiglas exterior, it was fleshy, wriggling, feathery and colorful. It looked like a winged starfish.

A rasping grind defined its viscous movements over the rear cabin and tailpiece, accompanied by a sharp acidic smell that soured the air. She desperately tried to budge the ailerons and rudder, but the controls were locked in place.

She was momentarily thrown off guard as the plane was jerked sideways. She quickly countered the violent movement and held the yoke steady in a controlled dive. She must have hit one of the floating eyes dead on.

The windshield was covered with a clear, runny goo. The propeller's outline appeared to be uneven, ragged and fuzzy. The plane started to vibrate terribly. Prop strike!

She looked desperately into the overcast dark sky. There were more balloons floating towards her plane. Their spectral light was highlighted against the dark skies above. She'd might have been enraptured by their beauty, if she wasn't so terrified.

Maybe the approaching storm would prove a blessing after all. Maybe she could hide inside the clouds. She was enormously relieved to be approaching the lowest part of the thunderclouds where the air was still shrouded with delicate vapors, but hopefully, less dangerous.

Wisps of fluffy white whipped by the windows and surprisingly there was little rain. So far, there was only mild turbulence, so she pulled back on the yoke and leveled the plane out at a two thousand feet elevation. No sign of the eyes! They must have followed her last trajectory or simply refused to enter the thundercloud.

I lost them! Feeling very lucky, she quickly checked her map and did a quick course guesstimate. She figured out that soon, she'd be over the Long Island Sound, that short stretch of the Atlantic Ocean that separated Connecticut and Long Island.

The plane bucked upward once, then fell a few hundred feet. This happened several times again, but to a much lesser extent. The thundercloud was like a rollercoaster, but not as scary as she thought it would be.

The storm was only just starting to form, so perhaps she'd be safe for a while.

She tried to relax but couldn't. Sweat trickled down her itchy body, adding to the chilling effect of the cabin. On the verge of panicked tears, she felt like she was missing something important, something terrible. The creatures could be sneaking up on her and she'd never know until it was too late. In her imagination, she could almost see shapes moving within the mist...

She fumbled with the radio, hands shaking, and called in to Brookhaven Airport again.

Static. Before. During. After.

I just want to go home.

She thought she might be over land by now, so she gently pushed forward on the yoke and lowered her altitude. The plane was holding together, despite the teeth-rattling shaking. If the cloud mist cleared away, she'd need to keep an eye out for roads and fields in case she needed to make an emergency landing.

At a thousand feet, she leveled out the plane. Everything below was shrouded by patches of shifting fog, making it difficult to see any details, but she could see the welcoming lights of her airport tower ahead – Brookhaven!

Her flight plan was nearly completed. She was going to make it! She was going to be safe!

As she approached her airport, the fog below began to clear, allowing occasional glimpses of pandemonium: fire trucks were parked on the smoky streets, nearby fires were blazing out of control; cars were being driven recklessly, accidents were everywhere; scattered police and National Guard were trying to herd terrified people, who were running away from... what?

The world below seemed filled with horrible monsters: swarming clouds of ravenous lights roiling through the fog, tentacled mushrooms sprouting from the earth, blood-hued spider webs blossoming like frost patterns across a windowpane, all of these nightmares and more, stalking, trapping, attacking and devouring people. Chaos, fear and death.

"Brookhaven, Brookhaven, I don't know if you can hear me. I'm a pilot, November-5-7-9-0-Alpha, making an emergency landing on runway 33. Over and out."

She engaged the wing flaps and decreased the engine speed as she brought the rattling plane in for a landing. The plane's flight leveled out close to the tarmac and landed with a single mild thump.

Her trembling body slumped into the seat. She eased up on the throttle and the zipping by of runway lights slowed to a crawl as she taxied to the central hanger. She pulled up to a parking zone and shutdown the plane. The engine coughed loudly and shook the plane's frame as it abruptly shut off.

She was shocked by the sudden appearance of two creatures emerging from the wind-swept fog.

Almost humanoid in shape, but only in a crude, vague sense - they were bereft of unique patterns like unfinished clay figurines. As they approached, their appearance transformed, randomly emerging on their anatomy. Their skin surface sprouted armored bone and barbed quills, a myriad of fierce eyes glared, large teeth gnashed from orifices diverse and deadly, and slim appendages, four in all, crackled with ozone as they whipped through air.

They stared at her, at her doorside only several feet away. As she stared back, her overwhelmed mind threatened to slip away into a fugue of numbed confusion and disbelief.

Seeming to shrug, simultaneously, their appearance shifted into a human form, albeit with large-framed bodies and features, similar to an artist's depiction of Neanderthals.

They talked in a guttural language with each other, and one of them yanked her cockpit door open. Dank, earthy air rushed into the cockpit. He extended his hand to her.

She hesitated, then took his hand. For a monster, he had a surprisingly gentle touch as he helped her exit the aircraft.

NOTHING PERSONAL

Gerard lived for online hacking; it gave meaning to his life. The glittering paradise of wealth was the long-awaited result of his tenacity, but the best reward of all was the absolute power that allowed him to destroy people, their reputation, their finances, their freedom, their lives… it was a *rush*…

And with power came privilege. The pinnacle of privileged success that now excited him, even with his refined sensibilities.

Very soon, he would exit his Lamborghini and take the next steps towards the ultimate power trip: The power to defeat death.

And his timing was perfect. At only twenty-five years of age, Gerard was in excellent physical health, blessed with a well-toned muscular body, and was a handsome Native American with the promise of the world's opportunities at his feet. Magnificence surrounded him – his life choices were positively charged with potential.

And yet, there was a calm restraint, a worldly wariness, a preternatural caution that regulated the incredible life he led. His scars, physical, mental and spiritual, had never left him. Fear, anger and pain were the identifying brands of crushing poverty, seared into his soul during childhood, still smoldering, even now as he waited in his custom-built car, sipping a fine, belly-warming aged scotch, staring out into the chilly Maine night at his destination: the corporate headquarters of Atahensic Pharmaceuticals.

Looming before him stood the modern three-story building with its smoke-tinted glass façade. It seemed out of place in the surrounding wilderness of snow-tufted evergreen and oak. A green banker's lamp, glowing in the lobby, was an unnatural source of light holding back the primal darkness of the forest. The moon above was but a waning sliver of silver light upon the starry cloudless sky.

It was almost midnight – the specified meeting hour.

The president of the company, Jacques Fournier, awaited him inside, long after normal work hours. The meeting time was odd to say the least.

Gerard had acquired critical details of Fournier's background identity. He often sold such commodities to other entrepreneurs. He was considering moving on to another mark, someone he could victimize, when he stumbled upon a cryptic exchange of deleted messages in Fournier's personal email account. The exchange began with a low-level company executive.

'I need direction on how to handle an outside inquiry about the immortality treatment.' Fournier's tersely replied with: 'Never use personal emails for company business.'

From that moment, Gerard's time was spent on infiltrating the company's computer defenses to learn more about the treatment. Hacking into the system took almost a week of intuitive research, crafty programming, and careful online probing. He downloaded every file describing scientific data, statistics, studies and deployment strategies.

He found repeated references to immortality. Speed-reading through some of the data firmly reinforced his hunch that they had actually discovered the secret power of eternal life. It gave a tantalizing glimpse into this company's ability to confer eternal life upon favored clients.

This discovery was by far the ultimate jackpot!

He had to attain that power for himself. But how? What could he do? Then, he figured out their weakness…

Immortality was a secret Gerard was sure they didn't want spread – angry violent mobs of desperate people would storm their facilities, but that would be the least of their worries. Governments would go to war to acquire this power. He had leverage for blackmail… they'd have to give him the 'treatment' or suffer the worldwide consequences.

Gerard emailed the mark, Jacques Fournier at his company address, saying 'I have some extensive information regarding your company's immortality treatments. I will refrain from releasing this information to the press and the authorities upon one condition: you provide me with the treatment. I hope that we can reach an agreement, for your sake.'

As usual, Gerard worked via an untraceable network of false identities, disposable equipment and satellite bounces.

Fournier responded within minutes, his email message saying, 'That is beyond my authority. I've forwarded your communication to my superiors. You may expect a reply within the hour.'

Gerard was confused. Fournier was the president of the company. He didn't need permission from anyone, unless there was some kind of decision-making process with a governing board of chairmen.

Fournier was stalling for time – he was scared.

Within five minutes, an email message popped up from Fournier. 'You will provide your information to us exclusively and also sign a non-disclosure agreement. We will then provide you with the treatment.'

Gerard laughed when he read 'non-disclosure agreement'. Businessmen had no appreciation for the conniving treachery of cyber-thieves – he'd do whatever he damn well pleased.

He replied, 'I suggest an exchange at Faneuil Hall in Boston.'

It was the best public place that he could think of – they wouldn't dare try to hurt him there. Also, it was near his penthouse, so he knew the area well. He could watch them beforehand, to see if they looked like they'd double-cross him – he doubted they would, surely they'd know the consequences of trying to outwit him…

Fournier replied, 'The treatment can only be administered at our corporate location. Be there at midnight tonight.'

What! Their office was in the middle of nowhere in upstate Maine! 'No deal. I need a neutral site.'

'The treatment must be applied onsite. This is not negotiable. Be there, on time, tonight. If you do not comply, you will discover that you no longer have a future.'

If I don't comply… who the hell did Fournier think he was? Gerard was furious with Fournier but cheered up considerably when he realized that he'd still be getting what he wanted. Nothing to worry about. He was safe – he had his backup plan. 'I will be there,' he typed back.

He shook his head in amazement. They thought that their precious secret would be protected by paperwork. Fournier's email compromise of their secret meant nothing to them; giving Gerard the treatment was written off as the cost-of-doing-business.

These people were clueless.

"Just business – nothing personal," Gerard uttered sarcastically as he left his penthouse.

On the long drive from Boston to the backwoods of Maine, he thought about other things he could do to Fournier. Tormenting Fournier would be a great way to celebrate the beginning of Gerard's immortality.

Thereafter, he would have time to develop brilliant schemes over the years, decades, centuries… it was exciting! He craved the rush of hurting people – payback for years and years of the world abusing him.

Personally, he'd never let go of a grudge; it would be a personal vendetta for him. Actually, he decided that he'd start with stripping Jacques Fournier of his assets… after the transaction was complete.

It was time for the meeting.

Gerard finished off the fiery scotch in his glass, checked his perfect hair in the rear-view mirror, and adjusted his suit tie – he was ready to take this business arrangement to the next level. He would take what he wanted and then destroy them.

He grabbed his small backpack. It contained marked-up hard copies and a zip drive of the blackmail documents. Of course, he kept everything backed up in his network system and online storage areas – they'd never find his penthouse, let alone his hidden data depots. Let them think he was a fool – he'd been underestimated all of his life, and ignorant people always paid the price for their arrogance.

Opening the car door was a shock. The cold air gripped his entire body like a bracing jolt of electricity. Good thing he had a serious belt of scotch rumbling through his system. Gerard breathed deeply to help clear his head – in childlike fascination, he was amused by the cloudy frost he exhaled.

Looking up, he beheld the Milky Way in its glorious splendor, making him wonder why he hadn't taken the time to admire it. The awe-inspiring swath of sparkling stars and nebulous gases reminded him that he was part of an infinitely larger mystery. For a moment, he felt a pang of sorrow for having lost touch with the wellspring of his Native American heritage. *How did I ever forget my love for nature?*

No time for melancholy... Jacques Fournier awaited him.

The path from the parking lot to the lobby was swept meticulously clear of ice and snow. The lobby's double doors slid open with a muted squeak, practically the only sound present, apart from his breathing.

The banker's lamp on the receptionist's desk cast a verdant-green glimmer upon the lobby. The building's interior was designed to create a warm old-fashioned ambience. It was almost like walking into an epic movie set that glamorized the 1920's with modern technological highlights like computers, telephones and copiers managing to blend in unobtrusively.

Decadent rich snobs – totally old school.

From the looks of the place, Atahensic Pharmaceuticals did well in their business by providing valuable research and development services for other pharmaceutical companies – never appearing to be dabbling in anything themselves, yet making scandalous amounts of money and always hiding behind the scenes.

It appeared that Jacques Fournier was hiding as well – Gerard was alone in the lobby.

Where the hell is he?

Empty corridors led off into the darkness on either side. Straight ahead, behind the receptionist's desk, there was another set of sliding double doors, which led to a spacious outdoor atrium.

In the center of the atrium, there was a snow-covered meadow surrounded by artfully arranged trees and shrubs, all completely enclosed within the building's pentagonal perimeter. A dull glow of light flickered from atop a flat outcrop of stone. And exposed by the light, the outline of a man facing him: Fournier.

The sliding doors opened and closed quietly as he entered the large frozen paradise. Shivering, Gerard walked toward the light, noticing it was cast by a kerosene lantern – a quaint touch to a midnight meeting.

Fournier stood in front of a massive grey stone table. Cleared of the snow, its unnatural lichen-covered surface was highlighted by a film of clear ice. Rising from the granite bedrock, it had been shaped into an altar by an incredibly old, probably long-forgotten prehistoric culture. Undoubtedly, the building had been constructed around this ancient artifact.

Fournier was as his hacked records had depicted: a tall, thin, well-groomed, middle-aged, precise man of apparent Gallic descent, attired in a rather expensive business suit, hands clasped behind his back, calmly watching Gerard approach.

"You have brought the documents?" Fournier's voice was a gruff whisper.

To Gerard, a whispery voice was an unimaginable weakness for a company president to have and he felt a surge of contempt.

"Yes. They're here," Gerard said, pointing to his backpack. "The treatment – I get it, before you get the documents."

Fournier's delicate, refined features were briefly disturbed by a slight smirk that flashed across his placid face.

"As you wish. Lie down on the table."

Gerard laughed on the inside – he didn't see a non-disclosure agreement on the table; perhaps they'd take his word on him keeping quiet. When he got closer to the pale light, he noticed worn petroglyphs on the table's side, and on the top, was that dried blood as well?

Fournier sensed Gerard's hesitation.

"You'll need to recline for a while. The initial effect is… disorientating."

"You've taken the treatment?"

"Yes. I've earned that privilege."

"What's involved in the treatment?"

"I'll give you an injection. Then, you'll be on your way to immortality."

An injection. That was mentioned in several of the process files he had discovered. Fournier was being truthful; however, Gerard had his doubts… Surely, Fournier couldn't possibly believe that Gerard would just show up with all of his blackmail leverage stowed in his backpack.

"How do I know that you won't give me a lethal injection?"

Fournier's words cut through the tense moment with a hard edge. "I always prefer to behave in an honorable manner, as any good businessman should." From a hidden suit holster, he pulled out a small pistol and pressed it to Gerard's forehead. "If you're really afraid of death, let's put you out of your misery right now…" Fournier's sneer faded like the afterimage of a flashbulb. He shook his head ruefully and tossed the weapon away – it disappeared beneath the fluffy snow.

"That doesn't prove anything. You could still kill me with the injection."

Fournier sighed. "Yes. That's true. But I always like to keep my options open. After all, who knows what arrangements you may have made to protect yourself? Things that I wouldn't even know about…"

He suspects that I've taken precautions. Smart man, after all.

"You got that right." Gerard was careful to not reveal any details.

"It makes good business sense to keep you alive, but what I'd really like to know is how you gained access to my computer files… and the companies."

"It's very complicated... Basically," Gerard drew out the word in disgust, "your personal accounts are ridiculously easy to infiltrate and your company," he laughed. "Let's just say that they need to monitor third-party access from 'trusted' sources."

"I'll pass that information along to my IT department. And, after our transaction tonight, may I rest assured that you won't provide any difficulty for me and my company?"

Not a chance.

"Of course," Gerard smiled as he lied, "I get what I want, and you get what you want."

Fournier's eyes narrowed, and then he nodded.

"So… what's it like, being immortal?" Gerard asked.

"I feel fulfilled… I finally know my place in the universe."

Fulfilled? By what? You look like you've never enjoyed a day in your life.

Gerard lay down upon the uncomfortable stone table. The table's sheen of cold ice stuck to his suit clothes, and the hair on the back of his head. *Damn it! I just got this outfit!* He hated ruining expensive clothes.

"What's next?" Gerard asked, hiding his exasperation.

Fournier pulled a thin syringe from his jacket pocket and examined it against the nearby light. An amber liquid squirted from the needle as he pushed the plunger, tapping the syringe. He pressed Gerard's arm, expertly finding a vein and injecting the syringe's fluid into Gerard.

Gerard felt warmth creep up his arm to his chest,

spreading into his body. It felt… soothing… euphoric… tranquil. Eternal life was going to be wonderful!

"This feels great. Is this how you feel all the time?"

"No. You just need to be relaxed. We wouldn't want you to die of a heart attack before you became immortal." Fournier gave a sepulchral chuckle.

"Wait… this isn't the treatment?"

"No. It was just a preliminary sedative. You'll be getting the treatment when the Goddess arrives." Fournier looked up to the sky, seemingly enraptured. "Ah, excellent timing… the Goddess is here."

A ripple of darkness sped across the stars above, descending, coming closer to where he lay helpless.

This is really happening!

Gerard was ecstatic – his grandmother had told him of the Star People, mysterious tales about the Gods of the Sky… it was all true! *Wait! Atahensic Pharmaceuticals!* He remembered that Atahensic was the name of one of the Gods!

The legend of his tribal heritage landed nearby, quiet as a falling snowflake and gliding closer to Gerard.

The soft ambient glow of the lamp revealed more details: it was humanoid, definitely female with a voluptuous body, but with enormous birdlike wings and a beautiful face. She was a goddess; a goddess of love…

Hypnotized by her presence, Gerard gazed into her eyes and welcomed her sensuous embrace as she easily lifted him from the slab. She held him close to her surprisingly warm body, exciting him even in his drugged stupor.

In an unexpected surge of whirlwind movement, the Goddess leapt into the sky, taking him with her. Her wings flapped hard, a lurching acceleration that left him shaken and dizzy. He looked down, seeing the ground move quickly away until the lantern below shrank to become a star itself upon the surrounding dark forest.

His breaths began to hitch in frantic gulps as the frosty air thinned, but his frightened distress was comforted when he looked back into her beautiful eyes. In the starry darkness, they shone with the fervor of reflective light. She leaned forward slowly, kissing him on the lips, repeatedly, feverishly, passion culminating, kisses moving down his neck. He became deliriously light-headed.

She was draining the life force from him at an alarming rate, yet, in juxtaposition, he also felt her incredible power being given to him in return.

Gerard felt a burning sensation spread throughout his body, regenerating and energizing him with strength and vigor even as he was near to swooning from excitement.

Suddenly… he was falling.

She had let go of him! He felt an empty soulless heartache at the thought of losing her…

Gerard plummeted to the ground, wind buffeting and tumbling him wildly about.

He glanced through squinted eyes at the fastly approaching ground, then… impossible pain and nothing…

…nothing…

…nothing.

Nothing until distant sounds lured him from a dreamy unconsciousness: some mechanical equipment, maybe HVAC, and an occasional squeak that sounded like sneakers on a linoleum floor. For an unknown amount of time, he continued to doze intermittently, lying on a cold hard surface. Eventually, he finally awoke, easing open his eyes, when he sensed that someone was near him. Over him. Looking down upon him.

Fournier's face came into focus.

He had that slight smirk again – this time it didn't

leave his face.

"Time to wake up."

"What happened?" Gerard blinked several times, wincing at the sharp smell of urine and feces.

"You're immortal, as agreed upon in our deal."

Gerard remembered everything now – he should've been dead! And, apart from being uncomfortable, his body felt great. He tried to shift his position but was unable to move. He was restrained! And naked!

His arms, legs and chest were firmly secured by thick leather straps holding him onto a stainless-steel table. Glaring at Fournier, Gerard lifted his head to find out where he was. His table was one of many, all holding people, completely filling an enormous dimly-lit room, similar to the bleak layout of an underground parking garage.

He noticed that there was a thin tube of blood leaving his right arm, and entering his left arm, another tube of ochre fluid. The tubes disappeared below the edge of the table. He never felt so helpless in his life.

"What the hell is this?" Gerard sputtered with rage.

"Call me old-fashioned, but I like to conclude my business arrangements with a personal touch."

"You're making a big mistake!" Gerard warned as he struggled helplessly against the table's restraints. "If you don't let me go right now your precious company's secrets will be uploaded to all of the major news networks and government!"

"Did you know that we actually considered recruiting you?" A distant sadness crossed Fournier's face. "But in the end, you've proven yourself to be untrustworthy, just a common thief... We've been monitoring you since your first intrusion into our privacy." He smirked at Gerard's reaction. "Why so surprised?"

"Holding me here will only make it worse. When the

authorities find out…"

"No one… is going to find out anything. We've scoured your penthouse for documents and then burned it down. All traces of your network activities have been located and purged. In fact, you no longer exist… we wiped your records clean."

"You fool! I also sent hard copies in the mail! By now, my personal courier will have delivered the trade secrets of your operation."

"No. She won't. She's right next to you. Over here…" he pointed to Gerard's left side.

He'd never seen his courier before – it was safer for both of them to operate that way. Hell, he didn't even know that she was a woman. She was naked, like him, securely strapped in place upon a table, with tubes coming and going from her body.

Fournier gestured towards the courier. "She's permanently sedated, like everyone else here. We decided not to kill her – that would be a terrible waste. She's being harvested for blood-"

"What! You're vampires?"

"Oh, nothing so vulgar. Or fictional… Actually, we've learned how to tap into the blood's cellular mitochondria, extract some of the energy therein and then return the blood, along with nutrients, back into the harvested body. It's the perfect renewable resource to satisfy the thirst of our Goddess and her companions, and the faithful, such as myself. Welcome to the company, Gerard… I just wanted to let you know that we do appreciate your personal contribution to our success. As you say it's just business, nothing personal."

"Wu-wait…" Gerard cried out. "We can… make a deal, I know a lot of things, I can…"

Fournier winked as he lifted up a section of the brown tube for Gerard to see. At one point in the tube, another thinner tube of clear liquid was joined into it with a connecting plastic valve.

"This drug, in the thin tube, will put you out for good. Actually… to be more accurate, you'll still have some awareness of what's going on around you, but… you'll be unable to do anything about it. Imagine… being like that… forever…"

Gerard's eyes went wide with fear.

Fournier turned the valve.

The clear liquid began to flow into the brown fluid.

"Welcome to immortality, your eternal life awaits you."

Gerard screamed for the last time before slipping into an endless waking nightmare…

THE EYE OF THE STORM

"Spare a smoke?" John Doe asked. John was a rugged, handsome man, dark skinned, straight black hair, grey eyes, dressed in stained blue sweats, sitting in a plastic chair before the impatient Doctor Schuster.

"Patients are not allowed to smoke," the Doctor replied, taking a deep pull off his cigarette with one stained hand, and rifling through John's case file with the other. Ashes rained like volcanic pumice onto the paperwork.

John's file described his problem: he had no idea who he was.

But, he instinctively knew that he liked smoking and he knew that the Doctor was a self-absorbed, indifferent, arrogant loser stuck in a dead-end job.

With the curiosity of the passively observant, John looked around the Doctor's cramped office. The wan light from the iron-barred cloudy window touched upon a faded diploma in a cracked frame, dusty medical reference books, stacks of patient files piled atop a scarred metal desk and most importantly, no sharp, breakable or throw-able items; overall, a safe room for mental patients to listen to the Doctor pontificate about their stay at the New York City Behavioral Assessment Center.

The Doctor inhaled wetly, much like an overweight toad would, and said, "Your record states that you fell off a building. A skyscraper no less." He exhaled with disgust. "And your fall was broken by a tree. You survived with critical injuries and… this cannot be right. Your injuries were healed by the time you arrived at the hospital. Hmmm, more likely you just fell out of the tree and the EMTs completely misdiagnosed you. Incompetent fools. One thing they got right – you have amnesia. You can't remember anything before the accident."

The Doctor flipped through the hefty file again, blowing a jet stream of smoke towards John.

"We do not know anything about you. You had no ID on you and no one has come forward to claim you. You have been here three weeks… much longer than our regulations typically allow for isolated observation, but due to the nature of your case and the mishap we had with your preliminary therapy, the administration extended your stay." He scowled. "It was speculated that you were suicidal, hence the intensive sedation regimen, however, I needed to assess your base state of mind, so I took you off the meds two days ago when I took over the case. I have a week to make a decision about your future."

No happy drugs? He thought. *No wonder I've been edgy lately.*

This mystery about his past was truly annoying. Doctor Neumann, his previous intake assessor, had told John exactly what the EMTs encountered on the night of his accident: a suicide with rag-doll twisted limbs, pulverized bones, blood everywhere, and miraculously, John was clinging tenaciously to life, just barely. But, by the time they pulled into the ER, he had fully recovered, except for his memory loss.

John hesitated, then asked, "What happened to Doctor Neumann?"

Doctor Schuster's caustic expression made him look like an angry gorilla. "While you were hypnotized, he left the session, and… promptly quit this hospital. Any ideas on why that would happen?"

"No idea. I only remember him starting the session, and then, someone shaking me out of it. But, I've been having visions ever since."

"These visions are known as impressions. Basically, they occur because your mind was tampered with, due to Doctor Neumann's complete ineptitude, no doubt, and these impressions give you false memories and notions about reality." He shook his head with sour exasperation. "Hypnosis therapy was a bad choice of treatment in My Professional Opinion. It has left you confused."

"I'm not sure how I feel, confused or not, but I see things in my visions and I'd like to know why. I hope it's not from my past… it's all indescribably… horrific. Is it normal to see such dreadful things?"

"You have been experiencing episodic hallucinations related to your memory loss, but it is normal to feel anxious, and-"

John tuned out the Doctor's rambling while he thought. *Anxious? Yeah, I'm going crazy thinking about it… oh wait, I'm already crazy. Supposedly.* He stifled a smirk while the Doctor kept droning on and on – something about all this, something unknown, gently tickled John's mind with its curious distraction.

"-this immersion therapy, to face your fear, may help dispel the hallucinations. Your record states that you experience them when you are relaxed, typically before sleeping. I can simulate that state of mind in a series of tests. I will first observe your reactions, and from there, I can recommend a treatment program to help recover your memories. If you concur, we can start tomorrow morning."

Sounds like pop psychology to me. Oh, what the hell can it hurt?

"Yes, please," John replied.

"Good. I would rather not send you away without a proper diagnosis. It does not look good on the paperwork."

John wondered how many people the Doctor had sent away to a drug-induced hell, condemned by a maliciously incompetent and indifferent diagnosis; innocent people trapped, crushed and forgotten within the system, doomed to die an early pointless death because it looked good on the paperwork.

"Of course, I understand," John agreed, silently fuming. *Paperwork? Is that all people are to you?* "But what if the therapy doesn't succeed?"

The Doctor frowned, radiating a scathing message of contempt. "I am just a humble civil servant doing my job, Mr. Doe. The system will take care of you, one way or the other. Someone will come by with paperwork for you to sign within the hour. In the meantime, enjoy your lunch."

The Doctor waved his hand imperiously at the door behind John.

Two burly orderlies came in, lifted him up from the chair and took him away. They frog-marched him down an ancient, antiseptic-doused hallway to the cafeteria entrance, where they shoved him forward into the crowded dining area. His innate sense of balance prevented him from stumbling, but many of the patients, all of them men in this ward, snickered at him anyway.

John entered the food service's assembly line. He grabbed a molded tray, a glass of water and a spork, all crafted in faded once-cheerful plastic colors. Tonight's dinner was slopped into the tray's partitioned areas: an open-faced turkey-remnant sandwich, unnaturally spotty mashed potatoes, coagulated gravy and a dried cherry tart.

Still fuming at the Doctor's behavior, he sat down at an empty table and stabbed hungrily into his meal. *I guess I'm not fussy when it comes to food.* Many times, he had overheard other patients gripe about the food. It seemed like that was all they ever talked about.

The tables around him had become quiet.

Suddenly, he was pelted by food from all sides. The deluge stopped after several volleys. Mocking laughter cackled around him.

He wiped away mashed potatoes that clung to his eyelids. He blinked several times to clear his vision.

Some of his attackers thought this harassment was hilarious. He listened to their cruel jibes as he continued to clean the food off himself. He was incensed; with the drugs having worn off, it was a new depth of feeling for him to experience. Still, despite the deep, dark mood of livid anger boiling within, he didn't react with an outburst of retaliation. Strangely, his anger was distracted by a powerful curiosity, his mind observing the situation as if it was on the verge of remembering something incredible. In a way, it was like trying to define something elusive by the effect of its absence.

The scornful derogatories directed at him took on a sinister vulgar tone.

Then, chaos erupted – a full-scale food fight broke out. It was a bizarre attack targeted against a select few: those who were naturally docile and those who were drifting in and out of a fog of drugged lethargy. They were assaulted en masse by food, gooey handfuls grabbed and hurled forcefully from close range, followed by plates and utensils. The innocent patients covered their heads, cowering in a vain effort to protect themselves from the barrage. Their cries of fear and pain were soon drowned out by the feral howls of the attackers, who seemingly became frenzied into more hostile behavior by the innervating presence of weakness, like the smell of blood drawing a hungry predator.

John slid off his chair and hid underneath his table, astonished at how quickly the situation had become volatile.

Aggressive patients began beating their trays against the hapless victims. The trays cracked and split and fragmented; sharp edges drew rivers of blood that spilled and spattered, screams became shrieks of terror. Some of the innocents lay on the floor. No longer moving.

A large group of doctors, orderlies and support staff had assembled at the cafeteria's open entrance doors. At the vanguard, a line of orderlies waited with riot batons ready, like pit bulls straining on their leashes.

Why aren't they doing SOMETHING!

Suddenly, with an enraged roar, the orderlies swarmed into the cafeteria. They grabbed hold of patients and repeatedly beat them senseless. Even the previously afflicted innocents, lying unconscious or worse yet, were subjected to brutal attack, as if years of repressed rage demanded cathartic reparations. Likewise, the aggressive patients fought back, some picking up chairs and wielding them.

Time to go.

John crawled under the table to the nearby wall. A patient moved to attack him but was felled by a passing orderly. The crack of a baton upon the patient's head resounded like a thick watermelon rind being snapped apart. The patient collapsed to the floor. The orderly charged towards the main battle that had developed in the center of the dining area.

Other support staff flooded into the cafeteria, but, overall, there were more patients than facility workers…the brawl was totally out of control.

The doctors had also entered the cafeteria behind the support staff, seemingly drawn by an impulsive momentum, but had stopped short just a few running steps inside the double doors. And by now, they were looking quite agitated, fingers flexing into knotty fists, bodies trembling anxiously, hungry eyes reveling in the carnage like a bloodthirsty audience at an ancient Roman coliseum game.

They were so fixated on watching the cafeteria's manic spectacle that John snuck past them into the hallway. He was actually crawling away when one of them, a particularly waspish woman psychologist, happened to glance backward. With a growl, she made a running leap and speared him in the lower back with a spiked heel.

He yelped from the piercing flare of pain. She kept on kicking him even as he tried to stand up. He stumbled and fell to the floor, and was attacked again and again by more forceful kicks, this time with another doctor joining in. John took a shoe tip to his left eye – his vision in that eye went dark. Something was torn loose. His eye hung limp in its shattered socket.

He felt betrayed. These people, these doctors, with their lofty impassive demeanor, were supposed to protect him! Anger exploded from within.

No!

Sometime thereafter, as unknown seconds of insanity roiled around him, the assault against him stopped.

The sounds of raucous battle grew at the doorway: desperate scuffles, guttural grunts of crazed exertion, shrill screams of pain and fury, squeaks of shoes sliding and slipping, bodies landing on the wet floor.

He attempted to stand and was surprised that he was able to do so, albeit with a lingering twinge of muscle stiffness.

Looking back, his troubled vision gave a disoriented view of a nightmarish scene. Several lifeless bodies lay sprawled on the blood-slick floor. The doctors fought each other, swinging clipboards and stabbing with pens. One doctor still raged on with a pen stuck in his eye – the pen moved whenever his eyes darted about. Other doctors resorted to tooth and nail attacks, animal-like in their screeching ferocity, all pretenses of personal integrity and self-defense ignored.

In the long hallway ahead, it was no different. Patients and staff wrestled with each other.

It occurred to him that he could now clearly see this tragedy unfolding before him. His eyesight was restored.

Shocked as he was by this epiphany, he knew he needed to get away from the fighting. Immediately.

Many doors lined the long hallway before him. Four additional corridors branched off the hallway and, at the far end, there were security doors that eventually led towards the way outside. There was only a slight chance that the security doors would be open, but perhaps he could hide in one of the rooms along the way.

He bolted down the hallway.

That was a mistake. His movement attracted attention. He almost made it to the security doors when a bloodied hand groped at his sweatshirt. He was confronted by an angry patient who held on with an unshakable grip.

John hands sprung up in a reflex reaction. "Wait!" he pleaded.

A wet fist smacked against his chin, sending him reeling backward. His back hit an office door – it popped open behind him as he fell to the floor. His head bounced against the cold tiles.

The patient landed hard on John's chest, knocking the wind out of him. Stunned, he felt hands close around his throat, throttling his breath and lifting his head up and down, banging it with devastating effect against the floor.

He couldn't breathe.

He fought back, clawing weakly at the patient's wiry arms.

Spinning red and black dots squeezed in from the edges of his vision. The patient straddling him was fading away.

No!

His survival instinct kicked in. Furious adrenaline fueled his muscles, but the energy wasn't needed anymore.

The patient atop him squealed like a stuck pig, released the death grip on John's throat and lurched upward, staggering out the door, tearing at his own face. John saw blood and viscous goo streaming down the patient's face… he had gouged out his own eyes.

Lying on the floor, through a haze of blood pounding back into his head, he saw the people in the hallway attack each other with wild abandon, far worse than anything he'd seen earlier.

What the hell's going on?

More people had arrived in the hallway, pulled inexorably towards the epicenter of pandemonium – he now understood, it had to be him. Intentionally or not, his presence was a catalyst that seemed to summon forth the primal instincts lurking inside the raw subconscious, with anger and fear being easiest to access. He was something more than human, something far more powerful, as dangerous and unpredictable as a rabid timber wolf tearing through a herd of penned sheep.

Guilt overwhelmed him. Maybe this devastating

pathos had always swirled unseen around him like a hurricane's treacherous winds, taking lives whenever he got angry and leaving behind a twisted swath of utter grief and tragedy. It was almost too much to bear – perhaps that was why he had tried to kill himself before.

I can stop this.

Focusing on peaceful thoughts, he stood up and walked out into the hallway.

The ongoing struggle bruised, bit, scraped and tore flesh around him, driven by an all-consuming fierce furor.

He watched helplessly as one of the patients, a gentle, mildly retarded man, was pummeled by two patients and an orderly.

John bent his will towards the assailants. His body shook from the enormous amount of effort.

Stop it!

The attackers stopped and looked at each other with confused expressions.

Yes!

Feeling light-headed, he stepped forward to help the afflicted patient, but was suddenly pulled into a side office by strong calloused hands.

The door slammed closed and he was spun around. He was in an observation room that was brightly lit, with lime-green paint peeling off the walls and stuffy uncirculated air that tasted of ammonia. Doctor Schuster stood before him. An orderly held John's arms firmly from behind, fingers crushing into John's triceps.

The Doctor beamed with an expression that was oddly euphoric, confident and conciliatory. He waved the orderly away. The grip released from John's aching arms.

"I just realized what has been going on, John." The Doctor's tone was hushed like a preacher sharing a profound revelation with his congregation. "I had listened to Dr. Neumann's recorded sessions with you and read his notes. I had refused to believe it. Up until now. Turns out the fool was afraid of you. He left because he knew what you are. John, you are the source of what is happening here. You are evil."

The Doctor's right hand moved in a deft streak, plunging a hidden scalpel deep into the side of John's throat, leaving it to quiver there as John staggered backward.

Thick arterial blood welled around the contours of the embedded scalpel blade.

NO! I don't deserve this…

He yanked the scalpel out. His trembling fingers couldn't plug up the thin deep gash; blood sprayed out quickly, pulsing with each heartbeat's struggle.

Breathing hitched, vision swam and dizziness spun; his overwhelmed body began to shut down from severe blood loss.

The doctor smiled with maniacal glee: eyebrows raised high above wild eyes and lips pulled thin over bared teeth that hissed out a low throaty chuckle.

John understood everything with perfect clarity in that instant.

With infinite sadness, he realized that there was nothing he could do to change the inherently cruel nature of mankind. This problem couldn't be solved by persistent acts of kindness. The aggressive people of the world would always terrorize the meek. It was time to correct that, not by encouraging them to behave decently, like he had probably tried before, but by encouraging them to destroy themselves. The pure of heart would also suffer as a result, but some would survive, and in the end, true evil would be exterminated from the world.

When he willed his body to heal, in a searing flash of white light, his senses fully returned to him and he knew what he had to do. He gave into his anger. Fully. Embracing it – *that feels good.*

The Doctor and orderly immediately attacked one another: struggling, grasping, clawing, biting, and falling to the bloodied floor. Other calamities erupted into savage violence throughout the hospital and spread outward into the world with a dark madness; the last days of evil mankind would be snuffed out by an unstoppable apocalypse.

I have become Death. Woe be it to the wicked.

BRUJA

John was alone in the dark.

The relentless downpour of cold rain kept his skinny body soaked and shivering as he stumbled through the nighttime woods of pine, fir and cedar.

He was a scruffy 12-year-old lost in the remote mountains of California's Klamath National Forest. It had been almost two days since he'd run away from his "blended family" at the park campground. At the time, he'd been terribly angry, resentful that his dad had remarried after the divorce. All of those problems seemed to be insignificant now. He was afraid.

He fell again to the unseen forest floor. His shorts snagged on something thorny as he staggered back up. New blood dripped down his scraped knees.

Thunder boomed and lightning flashed, several times in succession, sputtering illuminations upon the nearby gloomy area. Large raindrops began falling.

He saw that he had tripped on a jagged piece of cut lumber rising from a moss-covered stone foundation.

The derelict ruin was probably once a small cottage. He was lucky that he hadn't impaled himself on an exposed timber shaft.

In the lightning flashes, he had seen the remains of other houses as well. Most of them had collapsed into jumbles of shattered wood and glass edges, but there was one house still standing. About a hundred yards away, in the dark, on his left.

He could barely see his hands outstretched before him as he groped his way through the tangled, wet undergrowth and around an occasional tree branch.

Why are there houses way out here? He wondered, deep in thought. *Maybe they're from the Gold Rush Era?*

He'd visited ghost towns before – like the term implied. He thought he felt the presence of ghosts around him, like the half-heard whispers of long-dead secrets, waiting to come to life again.

Lightning continued to explode with rolling thunder.

Just ahead, he saw the mansion intact, two stories tall, but modest by today's standards. Undoubtedly, it was an opulent extravagance in its time.

As the flickering light subsided, the house appeared to wobble before his eyes.

That's weird. Sheesh, I'm so darn tired.

He rubbed his eyelids – red afterimages of the house flared in his eyesight. When his vision adjusted to the darkness, he thought he saw a faint glimmer of light coming from ahead. He blinked several times. It was still there. It was from inside the house.

What is that?

He felt his way through the scratching brambles towards the fuzzy mote of light.

Another lightning flash – a quick one that resulted in a long, resounding crash in the woods far behind him. It sounded like a tree had gotten hit.

Now that he was close to the house, he could see that it was dotted with freckles of remaining white paint, standing out like pus on dead grey skin. Boldly climbing a few steps to look inside through the lighted window, he saw a small room with some furniture shapes in it, but that was it. The light source came from an adjacent room, behind a closed door.

Wading through waist-high weeds, his wrinkled fingertips trailed along the rough, weathered wallboards until his sneaker bumped against an elevated flat rock. He stood before the front door. Faint light trickled onto the doorstep from a crack along the door's bottom.

The door creaked when he pushed on it, opening onto a warm, cluttered living room that had three other doors and a stairwell going up.

The light source was a fireplace hearth.

In the hearth, a greasy, black kettle pot was suspended above a smoldering bed of orange coals.

Someone lives here.

A pair of worn plush chairs faced towards the dwindling fire…one of them had a blanket draped over its wide back.

On an end table between the chairs, a stoneware mug of dark fluid sat alongside a huge leather-bound book. Judging from the condition of the once-fancy furniture, decorations and wall sconces, the house had fallen long ago into a prolonged descent of water-rotted decay.

Hmm. Something's cooking…

The aroma was heavenly. But there were other scents present in the house as well. Aside from the pervasive, earthy smell of mold, his stuffed nose could sense something else… distant, subtle and elusive, making him feel uneasy.

Hunger overwhelmed the vague warning from his instincts. He was starving – bubbly saliva collected at the corners of his mouth.

Moving forward, he grabbed the thick pot handle.

He yelped and pulled his hands away. The metal was

hot! He waved his hands in the air to cool them. The pain eclipsed his hunger for several stinging moments.

"Are you hungry?" a gruff voice asked from behind.

Startled, he whirled around, drops of water flying off his dirty sweatshirt.

At the open door, an old woman stood tall, dressed in faded archaic clothes, carrying an armload of firewood. She was rail-thin, yet from the way her knobby fingers gripped the wood; she also appeared to be quite strong, in a wiry, resolute way.

"Suh-sorry," John stuttered, forcing the words out, "I'm lost. I'm cold and hungry and it looked good. I'm-I'm hungry."

Water streamed down his body onto the warped wooden floor while he waited for a response.

A smile slowly crept across her craggy face, revealing teeth arranged like a shattered picket fence, stained black and reddish-brown.

"Of course. Have a seat," she motioned gracefully to a chair. "I'll get the fire going and you can dry off and have some stew. You like stew?"

"Yes!" John replied eagerly, a little more excited than he intended to be, suddenly ravenous.

After closing the door, she placed some split logs onto the ashy coals and dropped the rest of the logs into a wood storage box. Using an iron poker, she dug into the coals and stirred them into a crackling flurry of activity.

He watched the colorful flames as they whipped about in a lively fury that was mesmerizing, hypnotic. Over the last two dreadful days, he'd forgotten the blessed feeling of warmth. Without thinking, he moved closer to the growing fire. Water dripped off him and spattered into steam on the hot hearth.

The old woman chuckled while he blissfully soaked up the heat.

"So, you've been outside for a while," she said casually, with a touch of a Spanish accent.

"I got lost in the woods. I saw your house when the lightning flashed."

He glanced out the window. Outside, rain streaked down, silent as silver meteorites. His ears were still ringing, but despite the raging storm, he was amazed at how peacefully quiet it was inside the house.

"You're a very observant lad – maybe that's why you found my house – lucky you," she said, watching him discreetly.

"My parents will be looking for me. Do you have a phone?" he asked, hopeful.

"No," she smiled again. "Nothing like that here."

Her eyes sparkled like emeralds near the fire. She stirred the pot with a wooden spoon and ladled some stew out into a bowl.

"Here. Sit down, already." She remarked, handing the bowl and spoon to him.

He sat down cautiously – the chair groaned but didn't break. Its comforting warmth helped to drain away the cold dampness afflicting him.

"Go ahead and eat," she motioned and smiled again. "It's not often that I get visitors. I value my privacy, as you might guess."

He sampled the chunky stew. Turnips, potatoes, carrots and peas gave it a familiar flavor and texture, but the tasty meat within it was unfamiliar to him, and the gravy had a rich, juicy blood aftertaste like drippings from a fresh-cut steak.

He began to wolf it down in earnest.

"Not so fast," she chuckled. "You can eat as much as you'd like. Plenty of time for that." She paused, gazing into the fire. "The storm won't clear 'til tomorrow. No sense going out 'til then. I'll take you to a logging road. You can follow it back to the main road and find your family."

Chewing away with his mouth full, he bobbed his head enthusiastically.

Thunder rattled the windows, but the sound didn't penetrate much farther into the house.

An anguished howl, coming from the second floor, accompanied the thunder.

He stopped eating, or even moving, rounded eyes riveted toward the stairs. After moments of ensuing silence, he looked back at the old woman with a questioning look.

"My dogs don't like the weather much," she grinned, lopsided and uneven.

He went back to finishing off his stew.

She continued to stare at him with her thin, narrow face scrunched up in a shrewd, thoughtful expression.

"Would you like more?" she asked.

"Yes, Ma'am," he said, giving her the bowl.

"So polite. By the by, what is your name?" She handed him another steaming bowl of stew.

"John Ramos. What's yours?" He dug into the delicious stew.

"My my. It's been sometime since I've been asked that. Leticia is my name. Leticia Vasquez."

A jolt of electric sweat prickled like sparks igniting across the surface of his skin.

Around the family campfire, one of the scary stories he had heard was about a witch, a *bruja* in the Spanish language, who had lived in this area many, many hundreds of years ago when the Spanish ruled California. Her name was Lettie...

It's not her. Stop being silly.

She leaned closer to him, looking concerned.

He noticed that she had a multitude of miniscule warts sprouting like mushrooms across her leathery skin. Also, his nose wrinkled at her sour smell; it was as if she never washed herself.

"You're looking a little pale. Are you feeling well, John?"

"Um… not really. I think I have a cold or something."

"Oh dear," she fussed in empathy.

She vigorously stoked the fire again with the poker. The light caught her dirty, dishwater-colored hair, seemingly transforming it into molten silver. He thought that, once upon a time, she must've been exceptionally beautiful.

"I have just the thing for you!" she smiled widely and clapped her hands together softly. "Do you like cider? Just made it no more than a week ago. I could heat some up for you, if you'd like?"

"Yes, please," he said.

She nodded and went to the door beside the stairs. It was a kitchen door; he saw as she entered, door slapping closed behind her. Tromping about within, she hummed to herself and moved things about, apparently looking for something, with a clatter and bang of pots and pans.

He heard another noise, coming from the top of the stairs.

It wasn't a howl. It was a whimper. And it wasn't from a dog.

Someone's up there!

Curiosity aroused, he left the stew bowl on the end table and approached the steep stairs. The second story landing didn't appear to be as dark as it should be.

The old woman was still humming away in the kitchen.

He crept up the stairs. A few of the steps squeaked as they sagged, adding nervous tension to the anxiety he felt.

Upstairs, there was a short, low-ceilinged hallway that contained a door on both sides and also at the end.

The end door was especially interesting to him – lines of soft light outlined the door's edges.

There it was again. A sobbing. From straight ahead.

The sobbing stopped when he pushed open the end door.

The musty room was illuminated by the pale electric-blue glow of weird symbols covering the floor and five large cages.

The metal-barred cages were enclosed within a runed pentagram of grey-white salt, each cage arranged near the tips of the star, closed doors facing inward.

Dark shadows crouched within two of the caged confines – the shadows moved closer to him. They were children, his age: a boy and a girl, watching him wide-eyed, mouths agape, their disheveled, filthy bodies pressed hard against the interwoven cage bars.

"Help" and "Let us go." They simultaneously cried, pitiful and desperate in their pleas.

He rushed towards them, feet scuffing the pentagram, spreading salt across the blood-sticky floor. A sharp, acrid stench of defecation, urine and sweat surrounded the cages – his nose twitched and his eyes watered. He felt like he could sneeze at any moment.

There were no locks on the cage doors.

"What… how do I open them?" he asked, boggled.

"We don't know! Hurry or she'll get you too!" the boy screeched, frantically shaking the bars on his cage.

Then, the girl said something truly awful: "She's going to eat us!"

John felt his body go slack with chilled shock and fear.

In his dazed stupor, he noticed that the children suddenly went still and expressionless, quietly eyeing the door.

John's heartbeat raced as he turned.

The old woman was there, blocking the exit, with a

porcelain pitcher hanging loosely in one hand.

"Well now, this does complicate matters," the old woman said. "Most unfortunate..." She gestured with her claw-like free hand.

The room spun and he lost his balance; he heard his body hit the floor just before he lost consciousness.

***

He was slowly roused into awareness by the muffled cries of people calling out his name. Many people.

"Mom! Dad! I'm here!"

He bolted awake, realizing that it wasn't a dream.

The room was well lit by narrow windows. The storm had broken, and tree-filtered daylight clearly showed the decrepit state of his nauseating confines.

He was lying inside one of the cages! With a low groan, he shuffled his body to relieve the pain on his backside. The hard metal cage lattice had left aching marks from where he had lain. He sat up and cradled his throbbing head in his hands.

The people calling out his name were nearby!

"John. That's your name?" the boy asked. "Those people are looking for you!"

John let go of his head and shook his cage door. It wouldn't budge. There was a crude lock holding it shut. His rescuers were so close and he was trapped in here!

"Help!" he yelled in frustration. His voice didn't carry very far.

"Stop that!" the girl hissed. "She'll hear you! There's a better way…" She pointed to a sliver of bone next to his cage. "Use it to open the lock."

Squeezing his arm through the cage's bars, he stretched real hard and finally grabbed the bone from beneath a knobby tuft of green mold.

He inserted the bone into the lock's crude keyhole.

He had no idea what to do, fumbling around, his hands shaking.

"Move the tip of the bone. Find the lever inside and gently turn it." The girl suggested.

"Okay. Hey, why does my cage have a lock and yours don't?"

The boy spoke, "Don't know. She's crazy. She locked us up in here using witchcraft. Maybe she didn't have a lock at the time?"

The bone kept on slipping whenever John applied pressure to the lock's internal mechanism. He sighed, then slowed his breathing to help calm his trembling hands. It worked – he went back to picking the lock.

"Hurry. Our rescuers are getting farther away," the boy said, eyes darting around desperately. "She's probably outside, casting her illusions to hide the house again. The lightning storm must've…"

The lock clicked, opened and fell to the grimy floor with a dull thump.

John scrambled out of the cage in an instant, crawling to the nearest captive, the girl, when she shrieked, "Look out!"

He turned and saw the old woman striding down the hallway, hands gesturing, arcane energies gathering like dried leaves caught a whirling vortex of fire.

What! Not again!

He dove toward the room's door and slammed it shut.

A feathery gust of wind brushed against the outer surface of the door.

Something heavy hit the hallway floor, hard.

Listening intently, he heard slow, wheezing breaths on the other side of the door.

"You did it!" the girl cheered.

Hesitant, he yanked open the door.

The old woman lay sprawled on the floor,

unmoving, except for her wild rolling eyes, which looked dazed until they focused on him.

The old woman's lips oozed spittle as she babbled, "Ooooohhh."

She must've gotten paralyzed by her own spell – it had rebounded off the door!

He was stunned by the sudden, fortuitous turn of events.

"Let us out, quick, while you still can! We'll go find the search party," the girl said. "John! You can be with your family again!"

"Nnn-ooooohhh!" the old woman gasped.

Evil crone.

The hope of seeing his family again spurred him into action.

He pulled open the cage doors – it was ridiculously easy.

The boy and girl eased out of their cages slowly, stretching and grinning widely.

"I told you he could do it," the girl marveled.

"It was wise of you to summon him," the boy admitted.

Summon? What?

"Hmm…first things first," the girl said, directing her brilliant smile towards the paralyzed old woman.

Invisible forces dragged the old woman across the uneven floor into a cage. The cage door slammed shut and flared an incandescent bright white as it welded to the cage.

"Nasty witch. Let her starve," the boy grumbled.

"Now… John." The girl stared at him, coquettishly. "Thank you for setting us free. We've been locked up for ever so long…"

"Centuries," the boy clarified.

"What are you? What are you doing?" John asked, in shuddering breathes, afraid of hearing the answers.

"Oh dear…still confused?" the girl smirked with malevolent compassion. "Poor thing. Who are we? Let's just say that we're your worst nightmares come to life. We love chaos – encouraging it, causing it, savoring the flavor of fear. The witch had imprisoned us. You set us free. How sad. Now your world is going to suffer again…"

The boy and girl laughed as they transformed into… something else.

The air surrounding them began to infuse with writhing wisps of vapor, struggling to push into the boy and girl from all sides, as if insanely enormous entities, monstrous and terrible, had forced their way into this dimension and protruded the images of a boy and girl, images no more real than a child's finger puppet.

"Before we set out, how about a snack?" the girl said, looking at John, hungrily.

John screamed, one last time…

THE DAISY

Wynnclyff Mental Health Facility
Northern Maine
Winter 1923

The screams of the damned reverberated off the cold, damp, brick walls. The relentless sounds created an overlapping chorus of anguish conducted by the pathos of insanity, revealing a glimpse into a hell of physical, mental, and spiritual torment. The souls locked up in Wynnclyff were the afflicted, the lost, the forgotten. It was the end of days for them. There was nowhere else to go.

Ralph Dobson knew all about that. Intimately. Five years of day-to-day nursing work at Wynnclyff provided him with a comforting, predictable solace that would be too painful to leave. He tried not to dwell on the past; there were too many patients here who needed him now.

He thought the new doctor, Stefan Fellman, had personally reached rock bottom when he'd agreed to work at this decrepit facility. Northern Maine wasn't exactly the place to be for ambitious psychiatrists. The truth was despite the exemplary patient accommodations; the facility was still a horrible place. For Ralph, it was about serving others.

Young Dr. Fellman was following Ralph on his rounds through the separated men's and women's wards. Ralph dispensed medications prescribed by the head doctor and administrator, August Heinrich. Soon, Fellman would take on more duties, such as prescriptions and treatments, to relieve the excessive burden on Heinrich.

Ralph had his doubts about the bespectacled Fellman, who seemed to keep the patients at a distance both physically and emotionally. He often kept a monogrammed handkerchief pressed to his face, presumably to attend to his perpetually runny nose. Ralph thought that Fellman might not be used to the musty stench of long-unwashed patients.

That prissy weakness brought Fellman down a notch in Ralph's assessment because, although he didn't expect everyone to have the same zeal he had for his job, he at least expected everyone to do their job. Fellman seemed perfectly content to let Ralph do all the work: pushing the medicine cart, reviewing the medications list, dispensing the medicine and, most importantly, making the patient feel like they were still human, simply by talking with them.

To Ralph, the medications maintained the patient, but the personal attention he gave them provided some meaning to their lives – casual conversation held at bay a total surrender to insanity. To this, Fellman seemed indifferent at best. Indifferent, at least until he inquired the overall status about their next patient, Alice Boudin. "She sees and hears things," Ralph said quietly, as he checked his medication list. "She hallucinates about characters from books she once read, mostly Alice's Adventures in Wonderland. She believes she's Alice.

We've used our basic antipsychotic treatment, but-"

"She hallucinates often?" Fellman asked, rubbing a hand over his baby smooth chin. "She's predisposed to experiencing and dealing with potentially frightening episodes then?"

Surprised, Ralph paused to reflect upon an answer. Fellman sounded extremely intelligent, probably used to getting his way. Frankly, he just veered so off-topic that Ralph wondered what the man was thinking. "Uh, yes, I would think so," Ralph ventured. "She's had her hallucinations since childhood, some forty years now, but they became worse after she lost her husband in the Great War."

"What exactly has been her treatment plan?"

Ralph's starched white uniform crackled as he straightened his back; the hallway wasn't the proper place for such discussions.

"We're not a well-funded place as you may have noticed, so our treatments are simple, mainly a regimen of structured activities, anti-psychotics and sleep aids. We rarely cure anyone here. We just try to help our patients through their remaining years on earth."

"Yes, I understand. I've come here to help. I've made special arrangements with Heinrich to allow me to do research..." Fellman's voice trailed off as Ralph opened Alice's four-by-ten cell. It housed a lice-ridden cot and rudimentary toilet and sink. As usual, a waft of urine, feces and sweat escaped the cell. Despite being curious, Fellman took a step back, handkerchief held firmly to his nose.

Arrogant miscreant, Ralph thought. *This is all beneath him.*

Alice shuffled forward in her stained smock and ragged slippers. She stared at Fellman, as if trying to figure out if he was real or not. She then frowned at him.

Ralph stifled a dangerous chuckle – it wasn't good

for a staff nurse's career to laugh at a doctor.

Alice shook her head then turned to look at Ralph. She beamed, smiling beautifully, even with unkempt hair, runny eyes, and a scattering of missing teeth. "Hello Ralphie. How's my favorite lad doing?" Alice had a British accent, an especially rare commodity in rural Maine.

"Right as rain, Miss Alice," he responded, trying to imitate her accent. "How's the leg been treating you?"

She touched her right thigh. "The cold makes it ache ever so much. Did the chemist give me an elixir for it?"

"Of course, these here pills will do you right." He handed her three pills of different size, shape and color. He then poured her a small cup of water. "Here you go, love."

With a well-practiced tilt of the head, she took the pills and swallowed them with a gulp of water. She drank the rest of the water and gave him back the cup.

"Thank you, Ralphie. See you this afternoon?"

"That you will. Good day, Alice. I hope you enjoy your lunch."

As Ralph pushed the medicine cart to the next patient cell, he noticed that Fellman was watching him closely, and probably had been the entire time with Alice. Without a word, gesture, or expression. Just staring. In Ralph's opinion, the man was daft when it came to care and concern for the patients, and was downright creepy. According to rumors, Fellman hailed from Switzerland. Ralph wondered if all Europeans behaved so dreadfully.

He's up to something.

For the rest of the shift, Fellman remained silent, even when prompted for his medical opinion, which resulted in non-committal grunts for replies.

They parted ways after finishing the woman's ward.

Ralph shuffled toward the cafeteria. He'd grab a

sandwich and as usual, talk for a while with some of his coworkers before calling it a night.

The next morning, while he was attending to his ritual of loading up the medicine cart, one of the orderlies, Jenkins, came up to him and said the big boss Heinrich wanted to see him... *now*.

"What's he want?" Ralph asked, wondering why Heinrich, an impossibly busy man, would want to see him.

Jenkins shrugged. "Don't know, pal."

Heinrich's office was an unorganized clutter of stacked boxes and patient file folders. He glanced up from a spread of papers strewn across his desk.

"Dobson! Is Alice Boudin on the standard regimen?" Heinrich barked.

"Yes sir," Ralph sputtered out.

"Her health and psychological state are stable?"

"Yes, she's doing well enough. She still has the hallucinations, but she has adjusted well to them."

"Thank you, Dobson. That will be all." Heinrich dismissed Ralph with a casual hand wave.

Ralph left, confused and silently fuming. His shift work helped to distract him from his growing frustration. He even felt grateful that Fellman didn't accompany him on his rounds. Apparently, the arrogant prima donna couldn't be bothered doing real work. Ralph wondered how long Heinrich would tolerate this unprofessional behavior. The man wasn't going to be much help with patient care.

Unfortunately, Fellman showed up moments before Ralph started to attend to Alice.

That's no coincidence.

Alice noticed Fellman as soon as Ralph opened up her cell door. Her face screwed up in disgust at Fellman, once again with the handkerchief over his nose.

Ralph dispensed her medication and assessed her

general physical and mental health. While he attended to Alice, Fellman observed her behavior with a calm, cool, clinical detachment. Finally, after the exam was complete, Ralph closed the door to her cell and turned to Fellman. "Why are you here? And why didn't you show up at the beginning of the shift?" Normally he'd be more deferential, but Fellman's arrogant demeanor irritated him to no end.

"Just dropped by to see our fair patient," Fellman grinned crookedly with a mysterious flicker of emotion.

"When are you going to actually do some work around here?" Ralph shot back, his anger etching acid into his confrontational tone.

"You're doing fine by yourself. I've things to do on the schedule, my fellow. Must go," Fellman muttered as he walked away.

Later on that evening, Ralph enjoyed dinner with his friends in the cafeteria once again. They sat around a table, drinking tea and nibbling their food, discussing the latest news about Germany's economy, Mount Etna's eruption in Italy and the deluge of tropical storms in the South.

Their friendly chat was interrupted by one of the new orderlies approaching the table. The man pointed at Ralph and said, "Heinrich wants you to report to the boiler room."

Odd looks were exchanged around the table.

"The boiler room? Why? What's there?" Ralph asked, completely mystified.

"He didn't say," the orderly said as he walked away.

"Ya don't know anything about furnaces, do you?" one of his friends asked.

"Nope. Not a thing." Ralph stood up, said his goodnights and left for the boiler room.

The boiler room was in the basement. It was just as he expected it to be: warm, humid and shadowy. It actually didn't smell as bad as he thought it would, but then again, he was used to far worse smells. A loose string of temporary light bulbs led a clear path through the cluttered jungle of groaning, creaking and sweating pipes. At the boiler, Chuck, one of the maintenance men, grinned through his bushy beard and jabbed a gloved hand toward a corridor on the left-hand side that held three doors, probably storage rooms. Brushing aside a stray cobweb, Ralph walked to the last door, which was slightly ajar with a strong light shining from it.

He heard Alice's voice coming from within. "What's that contraption for?" she asked.

Ralph opened the door and was momentarily stunned by the dismaying sight revealed before him. In the center of the room, Alice sat on a wooden chair, strapped to its armrests, underneath a bright ceiling lamp. She stared wide-eyed at Fellman, who was adjusting the height of a nearby elevated tray holding a syringe and three small drug bottles.

An orderly, McCormick— a decent fellow— stood at the back of the room, looking bored, leaning against one of the shelves lining the walls. The shelves were filled with various electrical spare parts, some of them possibly older than the ancient building.

Ralph's temper got the best of him – he hated seeing his patients abused. With a raised voice, he thundered, "What in hell are-"

Fellman spoke over Ralph's words. "Mr. Dobson, good, you're here." He gestured toward four metal poles, situated six feet equidistant from Alice and connected to a modified transformer and some other unidentifiable electrical equipment. "You… have been given the rare opportunity to assist me with my research."

"What research? And what the devil are you doing to Alice?" At the sound of her name, Alice struggled against the straps binding her to the table. Ralph ground his teeth and scowled at Fellman. "Does Heinrich know about this?"

"Of course Heinrich knows. He approved this research. That's why I'm here!" Fellman's voice was calmer when he resumed speaking. "Actually, it's all basic research at this point. I stumbled onto a concept after I read about spirit mediums, you know, the people who hold séances?" Fellman smiled, not unpleasantly. "I want to find the source of fear, so that I can eradicate it. I want to free mankind from war, oppression and misery."

"So you want to scare Alice?"

"I do. Just a little. But, to be honest… I won't be scaring her." Fellman paused, melodramatically. "Her own imagination may do that, through an interaction with an ectoplasmic energy, for lack of better words, that enables her thoughts to manifest. At least, that's my educated guess. I don't really know exactly how it works, but… it does."

"You've done this before?" In a disgusted revelation, Ralph understood the probabilities of why Fellman had to come work out here in the middle of nowhere. He was forced to leave his last place of employment, or worse yet, he left before the authorities had caught up with him in due time.

"Yes. I've facilitated this experiment elsewhere with *some* success. I've discovered the best test subjects are those who suffer from acute psychosis, in the form of visual and auditory hallucinations, but also, along the way," Fellman paused, checking the connections on his machinery, "I believe I discovered a connection, a gateway to another realm, a spiritual realm, if you will…"

"That's insane. Fellman, you're a dangerous man. This is going to stop – now!"

"Ralph! Please. Think clearly," Fellman said calmly, as the orderly inched closer to Ralph with an obviously reluctant look on his face. "My experiments were approved by Heinrich."

Ralph looked at the orderly, who nodded. Ralph glared at Fellman, hating the man intensely.

"Okay. I'll help," Ralph conceded. "But Alice better not get hurt…"

The orderly relaxed his composure and returned to lean against the shelves again.

"Excellent!" Fellman said, a slow grin forming on his face. "I would wish for nothing else, believe me. Now. The procedure. First, I inject the subject with a neuron-stimulating drug that encourages hallucinations. The effect takes place fairly quick, so don't be alarmed. She'll be fine. I'll adjust the control knobs on this device, which essentially transmits electromagnetic waves and… oh, most importantly… don't move or interact with whatever you may see."

"What will I see?"

"Wondrous things. Frightening things I hope – remember, I'm looking for the source of fear within everyone, what you will see will be a manifestation of her-"

"Hmph," Ralph grumbled, patting Alice's hand. "I'll be here the entire time, my dear."

"Miss Boudin, this won't hurt much, I promise," Fellman said. He gently slid the needle point into an inner elbow vein with smooth practiced ease and slowly injected the clear fluid.

"The experiment has begun. Five cc's of Lot Ten-C have been injected at-" Fellman checked his watch, "at 6:42 p.m. and ten seconds."

The orderly wrote down the information on a chart.

"6:43:00. Turning the EM machine to a setting of three out of ten." Heinrich nodded to the orderly, who moved the machine's dial.

The machine made no noise. Ralph expected at least a crackle of warming vacuum tubes.

Alice started chuckling.

Ralph's vision blurred. He blinked several times to clear his vision. Then a headache emerged in the center of his head.

The orderly seemed to be experiencing similar symptoms. If Fellman felt it, he hid it well – he must have been used to it by now.

"The effect will level out soon. It's perfectly normal," Fellman murmured as he watched Alice.

Alice was in her own fantasy world. She giggled and babbled nonsense. Then, near one of the vertical metal poles in front of Alice, a blur of cloudy blue movement repeatedly appeared, and then just as quickly disappeared. Alice laughed loudly.

Ralph's heartbeat started to hammer.

The orderly had seen something, too, judging by the astonished look on his face.

Fellman just smiled. "First indication at 6:43:32. Write that down."

The orderly tore his eyes away from the scene and jotted down a few quick notes.

"6:43:50, turn the knob to four," Fellman ordered.

Ralph's headache pain increased: his head began to throb, his eyes ached and his ears rang. He pressed his palms to his head, closed his eyes and breathed his way through the pain.

He opened his eyes to Alice's bubbling laughter. She was so ecstatic that she practically rocked the chair up and down.

Ralph's breath caught in his throat, strangled with fear at what he saw.

The recurring apparition soon became very clear. It stood over six feet tall, wearing a formal Victorian blue waistcoat, checking the time on a fobbed pocket watch and saying "Oh dear! Oh dear! I shall be too late!" It was the White Rabbit from Alice's Adventures in Wonderland.

Ralph was terrified by the figure before him.

"6:44:20, turn the knob to five," Fellman said, rapt with awed curiosity.

The orderly yelled, "Oh hell no!" and switched the machine off. The apparition dissipated into wisps of ether.

Fellman stepped up to the burly orderly, face to face, hands clenched into claws, looking as if he wanted to strangle the man. Fellman's aberrant behavior was every bit as startling as the apparition had been.

Alice groaned, "ohhh" in a disappointed voice.

"Fellman! What the hell was that?" Ralph demanded.

Fellman snagged out of his angry fugue and said, "I'm not entirely certain, but that wasn't the reaction I was looking for. The machine… projects her hallucinations. Apparently, Miss Boudin has adapted to her psychosis quite well. I need another test subject. Maybe someone who has been directly exposed to raw fear. You have witnessed firsthand what it's like to *look* into a patient's mind! Isn't that exciting, Ralph?"

Ralph was surprised that Fellman even knew his first name. "It sure was something, alright." Ralph glanced at Alice, who appeared sad as she was released from the chair and led away by the orderly.

***

Just before his daily shift, Ralph approached Heinrich in his office.

"Do you know what it takes to run this facility?" he asked Ralph.

Ralph was caught off-guard by the question. "Uh, planning?"

"Yes, but mostly *money*," Heinrich stared at Ralph for several heartbeats, as if trying to burn the concept into Ralph's soul. "Everything costs money! Money we don't have, even with Thomaston Prison sending us their low-risk psychotics. We're operating in the red, do you understand?"

"Yes, sir. Uh, I came here to talk to you about Doctor Fellman."

Strangely, Heinrich didn't get upset. "Well, I *am* talking about him. We're receiving a healthy compensation for allowing him to do his research here. Without that, it would only be a matter of time— months, maybe a year at best— before we'd have to shut down the facility. Everyone would be let go, including our patients."

"I didn't know that." Ralph was surprised, but he pressed on and spoke his mind. "His work, even he doesn't know what he's stumbled onto and the dangers are-"

"A calculated risk, like all experimentation," Heinrich finished Ralph's sentence. "You don't think he's discovered something incredible?"

"It certainly is incredible, quite beyond my understanding," Ralph admitted. "But why use Alice? He said she's not even a good test subject."

"That's exactly what he reported to me."

Ralph was stunned. "Oh, well, then… that's good."

"I've authorized him to select from the prison people."

"Is that safe?"

"He'll be setting up shop in the secured wing. Two guards should suffice. I'm expecting you to continue assisting him."

Heinrich's statement wasn't exactly a request, more

an expectation.

***

Ralph worked through an entire day without seeing Doctor Fellman. On the end of the second day, he was summoned to appear after supper in the secured west wing area. He had never worked there. It was upgraded several months ago to help take on the temporary overflow of Thomaston prisoners. The prisoners were relatively low-risk offenders experiencing psychological difficulties, but still warranted extra precautions with a new unit of guards and orderlies.

The main access doors to the west wing were reinforced metal, and lock-up protocol maintained by a rotating shift of guards. There were only a dozen or so prisoners, but the rumors going around said that once the facility was past a probationary evaluation period, a flood of state business would be sent their way.

A stern, dark-blue uniformed guard escorted Ralph to an open door of a first-floor storage area and entered with him. The room was much larger than the last one, and it was stripped bare. Even the shelves had been removed. Fellman's equipment was there, essentially the same set-up as before, ready to go.

Another guard and an orderly were in the room. They eyed Ralph's entrance, virtually indifferent. The guard sported a shiny black eye and stared balefully at the prisoner, who was tightly strapped into the chair.

"So good of you to show up, Ralph," Fellman said. "Would you be so kind as to take notes?"

Fellman handed Ralph a clipboard, with loose sheets of paper and pen. "Let's begin, shall we? As you know, the purpose of this experiment is to evoke fear and find its root cause, so we may discover how to eliminate violence, the end result of much of the fear in this world."

Ralph thought it interesting that Fellman never introduced his prisoner. It was as if Fellman considered him to be a mere test animal. Fellman's type of indifferent amorality bothered Ralph considerably.

Fellman poked the needle into the prisoner's arm vein and injected the drug. The man appeared unconcerned.

"Five cc's of Lot Ten-C have been injected at 6:51 p.m. and zero seconds," Fellman announced as he glanced at Ralph.

Ralph transcribed the information. He watched the prisoner, who was just a normal-looking man, middle-aged, easy to miss in a crowd, yet confident and extremely calm, even under the influence of the drug.

Fellman held up three fingers to the orderly, who cranked the transformer dial. "6:51:30, EM setting at three, Ralph."

Ralph wrote that down. He then felt the beginning of a familiar headache.

Nothing happened.

No apparitions.

"Should've seen something by now," Fellman's voice trailed off. He motioned to the orderly. "6:52:00. Turn the dial up to four."

The orderly did as he was instructed.

Ralph's headache began to throb in earnest, each pulse seemingly cracking apart the jagged plates of his skull.

Everyone else seemed to feel it, too.

The prisoner sat with a slight smirk, looking casually around the room. He seemed to take pleasure in Fellman's apparent failure. He turned to the guard with the shiner. "Aw shucks, is that hurting you, big fella? Would a lollipop make you feel better?"

The guard growled back in reply.

"No results at four. 6:52:25, switching to five." Fellman motioned to the orderly.

"Yes, be a good ol' boy and do what you're…" the prisoner started but never finished.

The air rippled before Ralph's eyes, dust motes sifted downward from the ceiling, and there was a God-awful vibration that tore into everything. His skull seemed to be just barely holding his brains from exploding outwards. The pain was mind bending.

Ralph experienced a bewildering sensation. It was if his awareness spread outward from his body and encountered the various emotions of everyone in the vicinity, especially the prisoner, who was remembering something horrible that he had once encountered and tried many years ago to suppress. That otherworldly memory was fast approaching the room from some distant place; Ralph knew, because he felt its overpowering presence.

Suddenly it was there. No gradual transition. Its mystical presence continued to be overwhelming – so much intelligence, wisdom and power, gathered from eons of existence.

The presence evoked different reactions from everyone within the vicinity. Resurrected from an inconsolable grief, Ralph's innermost fear, one of facing his unquenchable guilt, manifested before them.

It was her.

His wife, Lydia.

In a beautiful summer dress, just like she'd wear on their picnics in the park, on those magical, happy days, before she died of the Spanish Flu. He had been unable to stop her from dying and never forgave himself for that. The world without her was a lonely empty illusion – he had tried to fill the void by helping others. It never worked. It never did. He had failed her…

"Lydia?"

Tears started rolling down his cheeks. She was twenty-three again, alive, pretty and her smile lit up the world for him.

"How?" He started sobbing aloud. "I'm so sorry. I miss you so much. I …"

She slowly extended her arms to him, her blissful smile blending with a compassionate expression of love and concern. His vision blurred into a radiant vision of her, only her. Blinking away tears, he walked toward her open arms.

Then, from somewhere else, someone slammed into her. That person fell to the floor as if they'd smashed against a brick wall.

Suddenly, the room's atmosphere surged with an impossible power that flashed with blinding spark lightning, grasping gusts of wind, and shifting displacements of space that shook the building to its foundation.

Ralph, maintaining coherence, stopped in mid-stride. He barely noticed the atmospheric violence – he wasn't affected by it, but rather confused – why would someone attack her? And then it came to him. He knew what the other people felt… he knew! The vision they saw was of a malevolent super-being. Like a movie, Ralph instinctively knew that this perception was what you made of it, what you brought with you… it was neither good nor evil, it was simply a mirror reflection of who you were on the inside.

His wife, once a hundred pounds, was a blur of decisive movements within the room, acting with preternatural speed against the room's other occupants, the last move clasping Fellman's head in her hands. She gazed deeply into his bulging eyes, then let him slide limp to the floor, his body trembling and mouth gasping like a fish out of water. At that moment, the room's energetic cacophony began to dissipate, and the lights ebbed back on.

Lydia walked several steps toward Ralph, holding out a daisy, her favorite... As the room's crackling discharges, rolling thunder and numbing vibration dwindled away to nothing, her presence lingered on long enough to throw the daisy to Ralph with a heartfelt kiss, just before she faded away into the ether of surrealism. He held onto the flower as he slumped to the floor.

The orderly was leaning over the transformer, which had been switched off, and he was... vomiting. Both guards lay on the floor, still breathing, but apparently unconscious. Fellman was both screaming and laughing. The prisoner wasn't there anymore – all that remained of him was a wet, oily puddle on the chair, dripping to the floor, along with some shredded tufts of clothing scattered about the chair. Many footsteps approached the room.

Ralph's world receded to the daisy he held cupped within his hands. It was her favorite flower.

***

"Shock," Heinrich said to Ralph, leaning over him.

Ralph blinked several times, waking up in a clean white-sheeted bed. The room was one of the several spares located in the employee dormitory.

Heinrich smiled reassuringly, "You had a bit of excitement during the last experiment. You were in shock. After you stabilized, I gave you a sedative to help you sleep. It's been two days."

It all came back to Ralph and he started to tear up over Lydia. He had lost her all over again.

Heinrich interpreted Ralph's initial reaction differently. "Everything's going to be okay. The prisoner died of natural causes, Ralph."

"Wait... no, something happened to –"

"Natural causes. Natural causes, Ralph. Happens all the time. And it sounds much better in a report than what the orderly and guards were saying before I had a talk with them. They're fine now. Fellman, however…" Heinrich frowned, "he's lost control of his sanity. We're his caretakers now, Ralph, a service provided by his employment contract, at least until he gets better or back to himself again. Ralph, I need your help." Heinrich moved closer and sat on the edge of Ralph's bed, leaning in to whisper.

"Ralph, the investor behind Fellman's work wants this research to continue. So do I. You've got the moxie for it. You've seen what Fellman did. You can look through his journal notes, and I'll give you all the help you need, orderlies, guards, equipment."

"I can't leave my patients, they need me," Ralph struggled for the words.

"Well… you can still work during the day if you'd like, but I'd prefer to arrange for someone to take over your patients. Free up your time and energy. Ralph, without this research grant, our place goes under and all our hard work… it will be all for nothing. You know what to do. You're an educated man, Ralph. You can control the science, make it safe. I'll get good people to work with you, I promise. Whoever you want. And don't worry about the deceased prisoner, the paperwork is already taken care of."

Ralph knew that it was risky, but… his mind replayed the euphoric vision of his Lydia, once again vibrant with life. He saw the fresh daisy in a glass of water on the nightstand. It was a reminder of his youthful springtime, a sweet season when life bloomed with endless joyful possibilities; not at all like the years of darkness since then, wasting away, lost in anguish and longing.

The daisy gave him hope. He felt… forgiven…

loved…

"I'll do it," he said.

***

When the procedure and equipment setup were perfected, Ralph proceeded with the experiment in the secured area.

"Five cc's of Lot Ten-C have been injected at –" he checked his watch, "7:12 p.m. and 40 seconds." The orderly wrote down the information on a chart. Ralph watched the patient struggling in the chair and smiled to provide whatever reassurance he could. It didn't help…

Undoubtedly, Fellman knew what awaited him…

THE VARIANT

He awoke.

His face was mashed up against a cold slab of dirty, gritty, concrete pavement. A mottled brick wall was close to his head. He was lying in a puddle of sour smelling urine, and something darker – blood.

That's when the pain hit him. All at once, all over, there was no escaping it. His head radiated the most pain. A pounding behind the eyes, like hot lava seeking a way out, shifting between his temples with each movement of his head.

Where am I?

Dazed and confused, blinking, lost between the city's glaring lights and dark shadows, he found himself inside an alleyway, about a body's length away from a busy street's sidewalk.

The relentless chatter of night people and honking taxicabs echoed in the steamy air.

He was disoriented, not knowing the time. His watch was gone. And the familiar bulge of his wallet was also absent. He couldn't feel the shoes on his feet. Maybe they were gone, too.

He turned his head slowly to look behind him, wanting to know where he was.

Further down the alleyway there were other people, slumped against the walls or sprawled beneath the garbage. Derelict drunkards by the look of them.

His body ached, stiff and raw, wracked with pain. He coughed and spit up a massive wad of blood; sticky and gooey, it dribbled in rivulets down his chin. He tried to roll over, but there was no way in hell – it hurt too much. Maybe some ribs were broken.

The flash of streetlights strobed intermittently through the parade of people walking past the alley's entrance. Glancing directly at the lights elevated his headache to a new level. His gut clenched and up came a black-speckled spray of bloodied vomit. Weak and dizzy, he consequently passed out again.

He woke up to the dry heaves. More blood coated the pavement. Throwing up blood was bad. He knew that – somehow.

Why do I know that?

To distract himself against the rolling waves of nausea, he struggled to remember who he was.

How did he know about the dangers of blood in his vomit?

Yes, he knew about medicine. That was it.

He began to cough up more blood. He tried to clear away the frothy phlegm from his lips, but, when he reached for his mouth, his arm muscles cramped up. He groaned through cracked lips as he let his arm droop back to his side.

And still, the people walked by, ignoring him and his occasional moans for help – so typical of city people.

Typical of New Yorkers.

That was it. He was in New York City. The revelation brought him no joy.

His throat had become so swollen and sore and his

lungs were clogged. He couldn't take in enough air. He needed to sit up. A burst of feverish throbbing made his head swoon with dizziness and his movements sent scorching bolts of agony throughout his sweaty body. But, with persistence, he was able to push himself up into a sitting position against the wall. He coughed violently, and out came a thick blob of coagulated black blood.

Able to breathe again, he gazed at his dark reflection in a puddle. Underneath the purple bruises, his swollen face had an odd expression, almost as if a porcelain doll's face had been cast in a rictus of intense suffering. And, most startling, bulging from his crusted eyelids, were his fiery red eyes. His eyes! They looked like they were about to fall out.

He'd been hurt badly. By a group of punks, at least a dozen of them. Now he remembered. They had surprised him at the nearby subway entrance. They had quickly beaten him, robbed him and left him for dead, tossed into the alley.

If only he could get some assistance from a passersby but he was in a dangerous-looking alleyway, and to them, he probably looked like a wino.

Moving slowly, he reached up and touched his tender head. Underneath his matted hair, there was a large, angry bump. A concussion in the very least. Hopefully, there would be no permanent brain damage.

He knew about brain damage. He definitely had some medical knowledge.

Who am I?

His name, his name was...

William Chung!

William's foggy thoughts were violently interrupted as his body shuddered with another onset of wet coughing. As the coughing fit subsided, he reached out to the crowd of people passing by. They continued to ignore his feeble attempts at getting attention, walking past him briskly.

His memories were coming back to him. It occurred to him that he was suffering from short-term amnesia. He knew that because he was a lab specialist and an M.D.

But what had happened?

Why am I here?

William closed his tired eyes and struggled to remember.

After a few moments, it all came back in a startling flash of recollection.

***

William was a technical specialist in a small private R&D lab undertaking classified viral DNA work for the U.S. government. When government cutbacks left the lab without work, his boss, the owner and also an M.D., was forced to lay off everyone except William, who was needed to close down the project.

On the last business day, his boss was contacted by a business interest. The potential client had some Pentagon R&D work that needed to be completed despite the widespread government cutbacks. They offered just enough money to keep the lab going and the two of them employed. His boss took the contract, even though the lab work involved mutating the Zaire Ebola virus. The virus was classified as a Biosafety Hazard IV pathogen – it was extremely contagious and had up to a 90 percent lethality rate.

His boss was confident their lab containment setup could be quickly upgraded with some procedural modifications. They would simply have to be extremely precise, careful and conscientious.

After signing a surprisingly short stack of

paperwork, they received a secure travel case of Zaire Ebola virus samples and a standard document of generic lab safety procedures.

To William, the entire situation seemed far too lax in its security protocols. This was a deadly virus, after all. But then again, it was work, so it was best not to ask too many questions.

After two months of creative frustration, they got lucky. Extremely lucky. They created an unexpected mutation, a variant of the Ebola. They tested the killer virus. All the lab rats died within the same day of exposure. The contact and airborne transmission vector had an estimated 100% lethality rate. Quick and deadly.

William and his boss were ecstatic – they had created nature's ultimate form of death. Better yet, they controlled it. The knowledge gained from future experiments would also provide a wonderful opportunity to advance the field of virology.

With unrestrained enthusiasm, his boss contacted their employer and explained the successful outcome. The response was rather unexpected. Representatives of the business interest would be coming by within the hour to collect all of the samples, including the new strain, along with any related documentation. His boss objected strenuously, saying that variant Ebola needed to be further studied. They hung up on him in mid-sentence.

With sad resignation, his boss told him to prepare the virus samples for shipment and meandered away to collect the documentation.

Something was wrong with these people. They just didn't understand how important it was to learn from this work. William decided not to let them have the virus. The future of viral R&D was at stake.

He quickly did what he had to. And without the boss being able to see him, William slipped into a bioenvironmental suit and entered the isolation room's airlock. After a disinfecting cycle, he left the airlock and walked to the storage refrigerator. He removed the stubby glass vials of variant Ebola, placed them inside a Ziploc sandwich bag and made sure the seal was perfect. He then created new vials that looked like the variant Ebola vials. These he left inside the refrigerator.

After leaving the isolation area and removing his suit, he placed the Ziploc baggie in his shirt pocket and exited the building through the back door. As the door eased closed behind him, he heard yelling and some of it was his boss' voice, shrill with fear. And, gunshots. William bolted.

Those people, who are they? Terrorists. What am I going to do?

He couldn't go to the police. One way or another, the vials would eventually end up in the hands of the supposed terrorists, the rightful owners by contract. The terrorists would probably just tell the cops that the vials were common medical samples, maybe even for something as innocuous as a new common cold medicine. If the legal process was drawn out, they could just steal the vials from the evidence lock-up, or bribe someone else to do it. Either way, William would be treated as a petty thief, desperate to say anything to avoid jail time.

Maybe the feds could protect me?

He then realized the government would more than likely charge him with something dreadful – maybe even some kind of conspiracy to kill all of mankind, posing him as a terrorist! They also wouldn't use the variant Ebola for medical R&D. They'd use it in their weapons arsenal. That was unacceptable.

Maybe he could force the government to be sensible? They'd have to listen to him if he threatened to release the virus. With this kind of absolute power, maybe he could demand an end to all worldwide violence? Then people would finally be able to care about each other. He could do it. Because he'd be the one in charge!

He was about to enter a subway entrance when something hit the back of his head…

***

The tragic memory haunted him. He noticed that his thoughts were rapidly becoming scattered, fuzzy and tenuous.

As he opened his eyes to watch his fellow New Yorkers go about their lives, he wondered about his earlier plan. He wasn't so sure about what to do now. He was confused.

This virus is too dangerous. In the wrong hands, he thought, just before he hacked up a chunky stream of blood, and then continued to cough again many times, gagging with a shaky rattle, trying to clear his lungs.

In the midst of his convulsive outburst, he witnessed a young woman approaching the dark alleyway entrance with alarmed trepidation, saying something comforting, reaching a hand out to him, but being pulled back at the last moment by her group of friends, one of whom said William was drunk and to leave him be.

The spastic cough stopped.

Damn, those muggers beat the crap out of me. Wait, something else is going on here…

The rats. The lab rats had the same initial symptoms he had right now…

The rats had bled out everywhere, from every orifice, including the dark unseen spaces within the body, shutting down vital organs, filling the lungs; a certain death by hemorrhagic nightmare.

Oh no…

He slowly reached for the vials in his shirt pocket. His shirt pocket was damp and no longer bulging – jagged glass shards poked through the shredded fabric into his hand.

The vials were broken! The virus had been released. Airborne, for hours and hours, before a constant stream of people passing by! And it was near a subway access stairwell.

Oh my God – the subway!

In Zaire, the virus' origin, the contagion wouldn't have spread beyond any of the small isolated villages because anyone infected would be dead before they reached another village. Here, in the Big Apple, it would spread like a raging firestorm.

William had been a fool with naive dreams of creating his own benevolent dictatorship. He had caused this tragedy. He simply hadn't counted on getting mugged – how appropriate that the senseless arrogance and cruelty of mankind has caused its own downfall. There would be no hope for a vaccine to be developed in time.

William's vision became sporadically blurry as he slumped onto the cold concrete.

Sometime later, through a bewildering mental haze, he realized that someone was kicking him in the leg, trying to rouse him, apparently. It was a cop. One who gasped and quickly withdrew several steps after rolling William over.

William went unconscious then awoke again.

He saw a flicker of hazy images. EMTs hovered over him; an oxygen mask approached his face and cops held back a curious crowd.

He finally succumbed to eternal sleep.

The world began the process of dying along with him.

AT ANY COST

The process of dying wasn't what Ellen thought it would be. After 62 years of feisty survival, there was no enlightened wisdom to be gained in her last days of agony.

Aside from painful, dying was rather boring. She sat alone in a dimly lit exam room of a free clinic, waiting for the doctor to come through that door and tell her the news.

More dreadful news. Well, she would make the best of it.

She had lost everyone and everything a long time ago. And now, in her cancer-wizened decrepitude, her social interactions were distant at best, made so by others with their shallow, inane expressions of concern and sympathy. She preferred the people who showed they didn't care. At least they were honest in their own brutal way.

To be fair, how could anyone understand? How could they know everything she ever was would be forgotten as if her life had never existed? What a cruel joke. Feeling insignificant, she wished there was something to help her with this – spirituality, religion, anything… she had nothing.

She wanted to live, yet she wasn't sure why. Maybe she was stubborn. Most likely, however, the alternative was terrifying.

There was a knock on the door. Doctor Hopewell entered the tiny room. As usual, like the waft of antiseptic stench that followed him, the shabby middle-age man didn't make a big impression on her. His lab coat was not white and clean. Instead it was mottled with brown splotches.

Normally, she would have stood to greet him, but she felt too damned tired, and remained slouched in the hard plastic chair.

He smiled. Not a real smile, it was the same condescending smirk of someone who lived for power and was barely struggling to be polite.

"How are you today, Ellen?"

"Not good. Spent the night throwing up. And the morning, too."

"I'm sorry," he said, in a tone that was more exasperated than sorry. "The results show that the standard treatment process isn't having the results we need."

'We?' What's this 'we' crap? And then, it hit her. She always knew the cancer would kill her, but the cold, hard facts still stunned her.

"How much time?"

"You should put your affairs in order," he mumbled without emotion. "One to three months, best guess."

Is that all there is to it? She felt like it was just another thing to do, checking out sof life, not much different than checking out of a hotel and moving on.

"It's inevitable. Even if you had insurance…" Like her, everyone who came to his small clinic was desperate – without options. The framed M.D. degree on the wall blurred into oblivion as her eyes unfocused.

"There is an alternative," he ventured.

Her foggy attention tried to grasp what this seed of hope could be…

"I feel… *bad* about what has happened to you. Life's not fair," he said. "I know of a treatment plan that may help you. But it's risky. No guarantees."

"Go on," she coaxed.

He sighed. And looked at her. Like he was sizing her up – she'd seen the expression before from used car salesmen.

"I've been doing some research," his voice whispered. "On my own, no FDA bureaucracy experimenting with cures for cancer. My treatments have had mixed results so far, but I'm getting closer. I'm sure of it."

She stared at him, unblinking.

"I use an ancient Chinese herbal solution. Among other things, the extract contains a natural solution of Betulin, mostly from the Chaga mushroom, which has also been speculated by Western medicine to combat cancer cells. With your help, maybe I can get closer to the cure, and you…" He grinned awkwardly and shrugged.

"What would I need to do?" Her entire personal universe awaited his answer.

"Nothing drastically different in your lifestyle," he chuckled, once. "Good food, exercise and the rest. I don't anticipate any side effects – you're one tough cookie."

"Side effects? What does being tough have to do with that?"

"Irrational fears," he said as he glanced into the fractured wall mirror and frowned. "Or so I was told."

"Hmmm, I don't have time for those," she said. She had always been pragmatic – she didn't shy away from making difficult decisions.

"Good for you," he quipped with precise inflection. "And, since this research is too important to be stopped by governmental interference, I'd need your solemn promise that you won't tell anyone, or… you're out of the program."

"Of course, I swear."

"Excellent. We'll talk more on your next visit."

***

Ellen still felt awful when she arrived home. *Oh well*, she brooded, *nothing ever happens immediately*. Doctor Hopewell was good at taking blood from her arm, but she'd avoid sitting down for a while, the two treatment shots in her butt were still tingly. It was the only part of her body that didn't have some vestige of skin sores.

Later that night, aside from some mild nausea, she felt a little better. While waiting for some green tea to finish steeping in the kitchen, she lounged in her comfy chair, watching one of those ghost investigation shows on television. She liked them immensely even though she knew they were faked. If a ghost ever appeared in her life, it'd probably be annoying. Maybe it'd make rude bodily noises just to get her upset…

There was a flash of light, behind her, in the kitchen, accompanied by the sound like a short burst of rainfall.

What the…

She muted the television. The apartment was silent.

She walked into the kitchen and flipped on the light. The teakettle was fine. It was where she had left it on the stove, taken off the gas burner that she had used to heat it…

Whoa!

On the floor, she immediately saw about half a

dozen insects. Mostly cockroaches. These monsters scurried about when the lights were off. Typical for any big city. Except in this case they weren't moving. Some were upside down, lying on their backs. They appeared to be dead. She prodded one with her foot, grateful that she had her slippers on at this point.

Yep. D-E-D spells dead.

Maybe the landlord had sprayed the tenement today? That would be a first. She shook her head warily and grabbed the broom and dustpan.

***

When Ellen came in for her weekly routine visit, she was escorted to an open exam room. Within ten minutes, Doctor Hopewell entered. He took some blood tests while they talked.

"Why do you do the bloodwork and not a nurse or technician?"

"Better quality control," he grumbled, impatiently.

She had the distinct impression he didn't want her lingering around the clinic.

Perhaps she wasn't good for business. She wasn't a pretty sight. The ancient scars of radiation therapy still lingered across the ravaged battlefield of her skin. She'd lost the war for her life when the skin cancer had metastasized as a brain tumor. Time was not on her side.

"Any relief from your symptoms?" he asked as he prepared a syringe.

"I think some of the lesions on my skin are getting better." She gently stroked the rough skin on her fingers. She used to have fine, delicate hands – long ago, when she had a life.

"I see," he murmured, injecting the treatment shot into her upper arm. *Ouch.* "Anything else?"

"I'm throwing up less, but I'm enjoying it more."

There was an uncomfortable silence after her joke.

He looked at her sternly. "Excuse me?"

No sense of humor.

"I don't throw up as much and it hurts less now."

He seemed surprised.

"Ahh, then, that's great." He stood up. "Okay. I'll see you next week," he mumbled as he left the room.

***

Miraculously, even with the occasional flutter of ethereal dizziness, Ellen had more energy and felt more alert. Maybe because of this hyperawareness, she started to experience things differently.

At night, she was lying in bed, rereading her favorite romance novel. She lay the book on the bedcovers, rubbed her eyes, and yawned.

That's when she saw it. The air itself, just beyond the foot of her bed, was rippling, like the billowing of a wispy curtain in a gentle summer breeze. She was fascinated, but equally terrified, as she watched the vision. It was as if the universe's structure had suddenly unraveled, then re-adjusted to a new pattern before smoothing to normalcy.

What the heck did he give me? Magic mushrooms? What's wrong with me?

She must be more tired than she thought. She placed her book on the nightstand and switched the lamp off.

Damn!

The spot where she had seen the illusion had a faint luminous glow throughout it. It faded after several minutes, leaving her trembling beneath sweat-soaked sheets.

Frikkin' 'shrooms.

She fell into a fitful sleep, dreaming of demons tempting her and had more macabre spectacles in her sleep…

***

In the morning, Ellen discovered a dead rat under her bed. She screamed like a schoolgirl. Eventually, cringing at the thought, she got up enough courage to sweep the shriveled body into the trash and toss it into the alley's dumpster.

She cleaned the area thoroughly and sprayed it with disinfectant. She called Doctor Hopewell. His receptionist put her through to him immediately.

"Yes, Ellen. How may I help you?"

"I want to tell you about something that happened last night."

"I'm listening." The sound of paper being shuffled in the background made it seem as though the doctor was distracted, only half-listening.

"I saw a pale light hovering in the air. And the air… it shimmered. Like heat waves above a desert road. It didn't move when I moved my eyes, so there was nothing wrong with my eyes."

He was silent.

She wondered if he was surprised by her lucid observations. She was amused. What did he think? She was always a human train wreck? She was once an Air Traffic Controller, but… a decade of tragedies left her all alone, living in the slums on a meager pension, waiting to die. Having no health care really sucked…

"How did you feel at the time?" he finally asked, robotically.

"Well," she replied, assertively, "before I was terrorized, I was actually quite relaxed. My thought processes were somewhat fuzzy, but far less cluttered. I was very aware of my surroundings. And, when I woke up this morning, I felt great! It's amazing. Should I be concerned?"

"Hmm… I think you had a hallucination. It happens. It's similar to having a dream when you're half-asleep." He paused in thought. "My guess is that you were tired. I don't think there's anything to worry about, but I'll see if the County can comp you a CAT scan. Besides, it isn't a constant problem, right? And, you said that your skin lesions have been healing?"

She nodded to herself and said, "That's right."

"Okay, try to get some sleep. Let me know if anything else happens."

The phone clicked off.

Oh well, it's all good. She remembered their talk about 'irrational fears.' He seemed to say that any cure was worth some side effects.

She agreed – until something terrifying happened several nights later while she slept.

Ellen awoke with a yelp of surprise, leaping off the bed, bouncing off the dresser, head spinning, hands flailing… PAIN!

She ran from the bedroom into the kitchen and still, the slicing blows followed her, seeming to pass through her body like scythes, leaving an awful itching and burning sensation. The dark kitchen was slightly brighter than the bedroom, but she saw nothing that could possibly be attacking her.

She fled from her apartment to escape the unknown menace.

She was in her pajamas when she called the clinic's toll-free number from the pay phone in the nearby all-night convenience store. The clinic's message service took down her phone number and hysterical information. She wasn't in immediate danger, so she was told to wait for a return phone call.

Ten minutes later, Doctor Hopewell called, tired, but attentive. She told him about the attack with the resulting welts swelling on her.

He told her to meet him at the clinic ASAP, before it was officially open, and hung up.

She was furious with him. *What the heck did he do to me? Open my mind to alternate realities, or, is my subconscious now bringing my nightmares to life?*

DAMN – she felt AWFUL, like she was near-death again.

She shuffled over to the clinic. She was probably a sight to see in her frumpy pajamas, bare feet, and wild hair, looking quite crazy.

No one messed with her.

By the time she arrived at the clinic's front door, she was much calmer. In a detached way, she had faced the inevitability of what was happening to her. The doctor opened the door for her and led her into an exam room.

She showed him the white razor-thin scratches on her arms. They were the source of her welt-lines.

There was no blood on her.

He examined her arms, tracing one of the welts with a fingertip, then, with her permission, he examined the rest of her body, discovering more welt-lines underneath her pajama top. Still, there were no other marks anywhere else on her body.

"Well? Do you believe me?" she asked. *Damn, am I losing it?*

"Let me see if I understand you," he droned in a supercilious manner. "You said that you were seeing things, and now, you're not seeing them, but they're attacking you?"

"Something attacked me in bed." She started to wheeze and felt light-headed. The blotchy, floral patterns on the wall faded in and out, appearing to be slowly breathing, writhing, soon, aware enough to reach out and strangle her.

"Let's look at the facts. You have deep scratches on

your body. You said that something invisible attacked you, but no one can validate that. The simplest explanation is that you had a psychotic episode triggered by…"

His voice had a metronomic cadence that was irritating to her.

"The simplest explanation? More like the simple-minded explanation! You're saying I imagined this?" She held up her forearm and pointed to the scratches. "These are real."

He sighed. "You caused them yourself, during the episode. It's just a side effect magnified by your overactive imagination."

"I was attacked!" she affirmed. (Although, by now, she was starting to wonder.) "Why would I make this up and come disturb you in the middle of the night when normally I would be sound asleep? Does that make any sense, doctor?"

"I don't believe in the supernatural… or whatever it is you call it!" He stopped bellowing at her and resumed talking in his quiet, practiced voice. "Look, no one will take me seriously if a case study patient of mine has a severe psychotic reaction to the treatment. I'm sorry. I won't be able to work with you anymore."

"But, your treatment works! My health has been improving!" Sweat appeared on the inside of her shaking hands. "My skin is clearing up and I'm almost never sick anymore!"

"I can't compromise the study."

"Please! I want-" she lowered her tone, "-I want to live."

"No. I can't afford to continue treatment on unqualified test subjects."

"Afford? Wait! I can help!" She restrained herself from grabbing onto him. "What would it take? How much money?"

He looked pensive. Thinking it through. "What I have to do – it's not cheap. I still have to pay off my investment loan. And, the herbs and manufacturing process are terribly expensive." He glanced into her desperate eyes, then looked away, "Probably $500 will do. $500 a treatment, that is."

Her chest muscles tensed over her heart, painfully constricting her adrenaline-rushed breathing.

What was she going to do?

If she used her life savings, she could only afford one more treatment. Maybe she could work out an advance on her disability payments… but she needed that for rent and food. If the treatments stopped, she'd probably regress and die. Money would have no value then. On the crux of her momentous crisis the street-wise part of her wondered if these injections were just a scam to squeeze money out of her. But, no. Overall, she *was* getting better, her recent weird events aside. Inside, she knew it was working.

"I can do it. It'll take a while to arrange." From his silence, she could tell that he was waiting to hear more of a commitment. "I'll have it for you on my next visit. And thereafter, as well."

"Let's keep this arrangement between us, shall we?" Baring his teeth, he smiled like a predator. One with bad breath. "I'll come by your apartment when you get the money. Will that be okay?"

"Uh, sure." *I can't do this.* Her life expectancy drained away from her with each heartbeat, like blood seeping past a desperate hand held up against a mortal wound.

"Tell you what. Since you're here anyway, I'll give you a treatment shot right now, for free."

She smiled convincingly, but, actually, she felt seriously depressed, her eyes focusing on nothing at all.

***

Ellen was tormented by a chilling anxiety. How could she pay for any more treatments? Maybe a loan company could buy her disability payments and give her a lump sum payout after scalping their own percentage?

When she got back to her place, she saw one of her neighbors must have closed the door. Nice people, but still strangers nonetheless. She entered the apartment. The morning sunlight's rays filtered through the kitchen curtains.

She flipped on the lights. Her 'hallucinations' had happened at nighttime, several days apart. She should be safe for the near future, but she'd still need to be careful afterwards. Not like she had any other choices, except maybe living out on the street. She shuddered at the thought of it returning.

She spent the day calling loan companies. They were always cordial at first, but after an exchange of a few terse questions and answers, they refused to do business with her. One agent actually said that disability payments went away when a person died, and, as such, she didn't have much to bargain with. They must have had access to her medical records… or some abbreviated version of them. Or maybe a payout wasn't allowed for some reason.

Maybe she could ask one of the pawnbrokers for an advance? That thought gave her a sad idea, similar to committing emotional suicide, an agonizing violation of her soul as she reflected upon the reminders of a kinder, gentler past.

Later in the evening, she brought her jewelry to a nearby pawnshop. It hurt to part with her cherished memories: an anniversary necklace of pearls, once clasped around her neck with a passionate kiss from her sweet husband; her sister's favorite earrings they always shared, like all of their jewelry, along with their deepest secrets; her mom's ring, slid onto Ellen's finger, given with a deep heartfelt love of hope and joy, a last act, from a deathbed.

All of these people were long dead.

Like she would be if she couldn't leave her past behind.

She got paid $300, laid out in rows of twenties, more than halfway to her goal, but it took her whole life to still be short of the goal. And, there it was… her life didn't have the same meaning anymore.

On the way home, she thought someone was following her. Feeling paranoid, scared and alone, she stopped and looked behind herself several times. Just the normal masses of humanity scurrying about their business in the big city…

***

Ellen was in the kitchen, waiting for her supper of instant noodles to cool off, wondering how to solve her predicament.

The phone rang. She answered it, reluctantly.

Doctor Hopewell said, "Ellen? I'm sorry. I've had to reconsider my earlier estimate of my expenses. The price will need to be $1,000 per treatment. Nothing less, and even then, I'm still losing money. Do you want to continue with the treatments?"

Do I want to live and at what cost?

At any cost…

She briefly considered why he was doubling the price now – probably because he knew that she had no other choice, and, she'd do whatever she needed to in order to live. *Bastard.*

"Yes. I'll get the money somehow." The words tumbled out of her mouth automatically.

"Call me when you do." He hung up.

She wished that she could cry. It would probably help. She felt cold. Out of touch with everything. The symptoms of shock, possibly.

She left her supper untouched, shut off the lights, got into bed, lay flat on her back and pulled the blankets up to her chin. She stared at the water-stained ceiling, heartbeat thumping. What was she going to do? She knew she couldn't muster that kind of money. She drifted off into sleep, thinking about her imminent death.

***

A rustling noise awakened Ellen.

Someone was in her bedroom!

Immediately, she thought about her money – luckily, it was stashed in her mattress.

The shadowy intruder moved toward her dresser, eased open the top drawer and fumbled through her underwear, socks, scarves and other personal items. The robber pocketed several goods then opened the next drawer, intent on stealing what little valuables she still had left in her possessions.

Surely, someone like that wouldn't leave any witnesses behind.

She didn't dare move or breathe.

Oh my God! She inhaled sharply when a misty white light suddenly appeared behind the thief. She could see the brute thug as he turned toward the soft light. He was a snarling young punk, apparently thinking he was confronting some helpless old lady. His expression transformed into wild panic immediately.

He tried to flee. Too late.

The light swallowed his right arm all the way up to the elbow, holding it immobile, while he frantically struggled to free himself, much like an insect caught in the relentless path of tree sap oozing down to the ground. The luminescent air became scarlet-tinged as blood flowed freely from his arm. Not a drop fell to the floor.

His nearly breathless scream was suddenly squelched as the light enveloped his head and absorbed it. The massive spray of blood was ensconced by the cloud of light which flared with actinic bursts of released energy as it devoured the burglar piece by piece like a hungry praying mantis picking apart its prey, delicately and without hurry.

While she watched, mesmerized, various objects clattered to the floor: a set of keys, a large knife, a wallet, clothes and her stolen items.

Damn! Was that some tooth fillings?

She was astounded by her change of fate. Minutes ago, she thought she'd be dead at the hands of a prowler.

Now, despite trepidation with fear, she also felt… better, undeniably rejuvenated and supercharged with healing energy. The doctor's drug cocktail may have already altered her perceptions, so that she saw this apparition, but it was definitely real, not some hallucination.

The loose dregs of unleashed energy must have healed her, for now… like it did twice before, just by accidentally being within the area of effect and, despite having been unintentionally attacked before, she knew this supernatural entity would be her salvation.

But, at what cost?

Someone just died. Horribly.

She then noticed, with alarm, that the light was floating towards her. She held up her hands in supplication. "Wait. I can help you," she pleaded. "I know what you want," her voice cracked. "And, and… you probably know what I need."

The cloud stopped moving.

"I can bring people to you." She was thinking of Doctor Hopewell when she said that. He was a horrible person – who knows how many patients he'd destroyed with his evil greed? She also thought of other bad people worthy of sacrifice. She knew she'd be wracked with guilt, but she needed to live. Terrible decision, but then again, she was always good at making the tough choices.

Two more light spheres appeared behind the first.

All of them waiting for her.

"Sooon," she crooned, with a wicked smile, and picked up the phone.

THE BRACELET

The store was musty with obscuring mists of incense that floated in passive laminar layers and stirred like an angry swarm of bees when disturbed. Antique lacquered cherry wood and smoky glass facades displayed a precisely arranged selection of medicinal plants, animal parts and minerals. The exotic smells of distant lands evoked a tingling sense of the mysterious unknown within the old Chinese man's shop.

The old man's hands fluttered in calming supplications before his visitor.

"Business has been slow," the old man murmured. "I've no money today."

Johnny Yee watched the old man's wrinkled face scrunch into an enigmatic smile, which could mean 'so sorry' or 'bite me' or both at the same time.

No money? Johnny thought, incredulously.

"This is a Chinese apothecary." He leaned over the shop counter, peering closely into the old man's eyes. "Many people come and go from here. It should be a gold mine of money!"

The old man's body odor was repulsive – Johnny

stood back up, once again showing his intimidating height advantage over the frail old man.

The old man's dry voice cracked, "Not everything revolves around money."

"Let me speak plainly. If you don't pay, your protection comes to an end."

"Protection?" The old man chuckled softly. "From whom? The Triad? That's not protection–"

"Do you want me to make an example of you?" Johnny asked, taking a chance, considering that the Triad had given him strict orders not to hurt anyone, at least not this time.

"Do whatever you will, but first, may I ask a question of you?"

The excessively polite cultural customs of Johnny's elders sometimes grated raw upon his patience.

"What is it that you desire?" The old man's eyes locked with Johnny's and wouldn't look away.

No time for this crap. I've got a date tonight... "You play a dangerous game," Johnny growled with dark undertones.

"Please tell me," the old man pleaded. "There is nothing to fear here."

What?!? "I take whatever I want, whenever I want! I'm afraid of nothing!"

Johnny opened his jacket to expose his holstered handgun.

The old man flinched, appalled, his body shrinking slightly, yet still holding his ground.

"Of course not. I do not mean to offend, only to assure you of my intentions. Obviously, a brave man such as yourself is fearless. But, surely, you have something you desire? Something you covet?"

"What's it to you?"

"In exchange for the sanctity of my humble life, I offer to help your wish come true."

"How can you do that?"

"I know a great many things. Please…"

Johnny frowned, then sighed and said, "There's a woman. Su Kim. I've loved her since–" He remembered the fateful day when she first came sashaying into his aunt's luxury trade goods store. He couldn't keep his eyes off Su Kim. She was drop–dead gorgeous: an enchanting mix of beautiful Chinese genes and flashy American mannerisms.

The familiar spiced up with the glamorous, he had daydreamed. His aunt had smacked his head, telling him to get back to work stocking the shelves, also warning him to 'stay away from that woman'.

The old man waited patiently for Johnny to resume talking.

Johnny continued. "Well, she's everything to me. But no matter what I do, buy her gifts, clothes, jewelry, take her places, pay attention to her, well…" He had given up his aunt's job and began working for the Triad to earn more money. All to please her… "She still sees other men. Rich men." Johnny shrugged as a hollow empty feeling overtook him. "If I could just get her attention, I could make her love me." When she fell for him, he'd change her unacceptable attitude, she'd show respect or else he'd beat it from her.

"You want me," the old man's expression softened, "to make her love you?"

"Yes. The possibility of never having her would be unbearable."

"What is her love worth to you?" The old man questioned with scrutiny.

"Everything."

"Then that is what it will cost you," he said. "Please wait while I get what you need." The old man shuffled behind the counter alongside the back wall of stored dry goods.

"And what do I need?" Johnny asked, curious despite his skepticism.

"You need the ingredients." The old man plucked an index card from a small box file. "Ingredients for your love potion." While reading from the card, he began removing sealed paper bags from various glass enclosures and placing them on the countertop.

"You're not going to make a potion for me?"

"I can't. This love potion is for you. Love is a very personal thing. You must create the potion yourself. I just provide you with the ingredients."

The old man finished pulling items from the enclosures. He scribbled down a numbered list onto a yellowed scrap of paper.

"You will both need to drink the potion at the same time. This is powerful magic, so not much is needed, maybe a sip or two for each of you," he said, handing Johnny the paper.

"Follow these instructions. Make sure you grind the materials into a fine powder," the old man said as he gestured to the six paper bags. "Then, let it dissolve into a liquor of your choice."

"You want me to get her drunk?"

The old man giggled. "The alcohol helps activate the potion's components."

"Yes, yes, yes," Johnny agreed, snorting gruffly through his nose. He was going to be very busy tonight before his date with Su Kim.

"The most important component of the potion is tears. Since it is love you want from her, they must be her tears of joy…"

Johnny tuned out the old man. *She's never truly happy around me, even when I do nice things for her.* But she was happy when she was with other men – he had seen it whenever he was with her.

"…You must be very careful," the old man droned

on, "this is a love potion and love is like a delicate flower that–"

"Flowers!" Johnny slammed his fist against the glass counter, shattering it instantly. She had laughed at his flowers! Nothing seemed to work – she wanted more and more and more every time he saw her! The back of his hand struck out of its own accord at the old man.

The old man flew backwards, bounced off the dry goods back wall and crumpled to the floor. He cowered, holding his shaking hands up, as if to ward off further attacks. *The Triad won't like that! Got to get out of here…*

Johnny grabbed the list and the ingredient bags from amongst the glass shards. Sucking on several deep cuts to his fingertips, he ran out of the apothecary using the back alley exit.

Inside the shop, the old man groaned when he rose stiffly to his feet. A wide smile broke out across his face. He laughed repeatedly while he cleaned up the mess.

***

Later that evening, Johnny sat alone at one of the nicer reserved tables within the classy Lee Ho's restaurant. He tapped the side of his water glass, keeping tempo with his restless thoughts as he watched the front door entrance that gave him an etched glass view of the city street. *She's late. As usual. Why does she do this to me?* He took comfort in the knowledge that tonight, everything would change, and she would become his love slave. *No more of this arrogant behavior – I will own her and make her all mine!*

Strangely, he felt a momentary pang of reluctant sadness in his pursuit of Su Kim; he had lost something of himself as time went on. As a stock boy, he led a simple wholesome life. Now with the Triad he had to do unpleasant dangerous things, but at least the pay was good, and except for today's performance, he was appreciated for excelling at his duties. Luckily, the old man was still alive and not injured. His group leader had told him that he'd better control his emotions, or else. Being disrespectful to the community's elders could have a backlash – it would be bad for business.

They'll get over it. They need me as a right hand.

He sighed and finished off his glass of water. His forlorn gaze fell upon the front door entrance.

Once again, he wondered where she was.

He'd been waiting for half an hour.

He hated not being in control. Despite his recent rise in income, the woman still toyed with him; he was at the mercy of her free-spirited whims.

Patience, that will all change after tonight, he convinced himself.

Reaching to the table's center, he grabbed the expensive bottle of red wine and angled it to catch the overhead chandelier's light. *Looks good.*

Earlier, using a syringe, it had taken a great deal of perseverance to replace some of the vintage wine with the potion. He had then sealed the pinprick cork hole and brought the bottle with him. *Ten-dollar corkage fee. And some people complain about the Triad's extortion...*

He tensed as he waited for her.

A BMW sedan had pulled up to a stop in front of the restaurant. A well-groomed white man in an expensive suit helped Su Kim out of the front passenger seat. She touched his cheek and slid her fingers through his hair. They held each other tight while they kissed, long, deep and passionate.

She doesn't even bother to be discreet. Why won't she kiss me? Johnny gouged his fingernails into the tablecloth as Su Kim parted company with the man.

She waved energetically at the car as it pulled away. Then, almost as a casual afterthought, she entered the restaurant.

Angry as he was with her, he couldn't help being entranced by her presence. She was a beautiful woman blessed with a natural grace that was confident and engaging, her every move accentuated by an elegant outfit that showed off her body.

The waiters fawned their attention over her. One of them escorted her to Johnny's table.

Johnny helped her into her chair, practically shoving the waiter aside.

She adjusted her hair and flashed a coy smile at him when he sat down opposite to her. She glanced at the menu before her and raised a hand into the air, snapping her fingers. Apparently, she'd been here before and knew what she wanted.

Two waiters instantly arrived on both sides of her. One waiter replaced the empty water jug on the table and filled the empty water glasses, taking his sweet time about it, while lingering at Su Kim's shoulder and blatantly gawking at her. The other waiter took her order with animated enthusiasm. He then took Johnny's order with far less attentive interest. Both waiters finally left Johnny and Su Kim.

"You're looking beautiful as always, Su Kim," he managed to say. He always felt shy and smitten around her.

"Am I? So nice of you to notice, Johnny. Is that what I think it is?" She poked a daggered fingernail at his $150 bottle of wine. "That'll do," she quipped after a cursory view of the label. "I could use a drink."

That'll do? It's damned expensive and it's one of your favorite wines. What's wrong with you?

A waiter appeared before she could raise her hand for assistance.

"If you please," she pointed to the bottle.

"Of course," the waiter said, using a corkscrew to pull out the cork with a solid pop. He filled her glass part way and offered it deferentially to her.

She downed the wine in a single slurp. "More," she demanded imperiously, holding the glass out indelicately for a refill. The waiter refilled her glass, then filled Johnny's and left them. She downed the second glass before he could even raise his glass in a toast.

It's funny how I sometimes miss my culture's rituals of polite behavior. But only when I'm around her, Johnny thought.

When she finished pouring herself another glass, he said, "I want to offer a toast to our good luck and fortune."

She smiled, an uneven, crude, crooked smile, and clinked her glass against his, saying, "How quaint. You sound like my grandfather…" She chuckled ruefully and downed the drink in one swallow.

Damn, she drinks like a fish. To keep pace with her, he gulped his wine down with irritated regret. *This is the good stuff. We should be savoring the flavor by drinking it slowly.*

He refilled their glasses.

The wine helped him to relax as he listened how her day went: the hectic schedule of appointments for dress fittings, shoe and accessories shopping, hair, nail and salon time, the list of sophisticated agonies seemed endless. *Everything is still the same. Did I mix this potion correctly? Maybe it needed to be used right away? No, the old man said nothing about that. I used the ingredients in order. Wait. The old man said to use her tears… but what could that matter? Tears are tears. Mine will work just as good. Damn, she's so…beautiful in this light.* He stared at her with rapt adoration. *I could do this all night long just to be seen with her.*

He used to find her self–centered babbling to be annoying, but tonight, it was actually quite endearing. Her charming anecdotes further encouraged the need within him to protect her, take care of her and make her happy and be with her and only her.

When she finished off another glass of wine, he took an exquisitely wrapped box from his suit pocket and slid it across the table to her.

"What's this? A gift?" She snickered, slamming her glass down on the table, spilling red wine droplets onto the white linen tablecloth. She grasped the box with sharp fingernails, digging past the bowed wrapping of royal blue paper. Within seconds, the box was opened and she pulled out his gift. She held the jeweled bracelet up to the light overhead, evaluating its worth with a practiced eye.

Even with his improved fortune, the bracelet had set his finances back. He would be collecting debts for the Triad for a long time.

"Very nice," she admitted as she slipped it onto her wrist. "It's about time you showed me how much you care about me."

Averting her tearing eyes, she gazed down at her lap, pursing her trembling lips as she suddenly became quiet.

I give her all I have and she treats me like this? Is this damned potion working? He shifted in his chair. A trickle of cold sweat crawled down the back of his fitted dress shirt. *Oh well, it doesn't matter. As long as I'm with her. I know what she wants and I can make her happy. It's not all about having things my own way – it's about what she wants. That's what's important. Why has it taken me so long to realize that? Wait! What's going on? She hasn't changed! I'm hopelessly in love with her? Oh no...*

"You need to take better care of me," she sobbed. "I

feel hurt when you neglect me."

His heart sank as he looked at her.

He realized that he'd do anything for her. When he told her that, her face lit up with the sweetest smile he'd ever seen in his whole life – the same smile she gave so many times to all of her other male friends.

"I'm so happy," she purred. "Johnny, I know I'm often a very demanding woman, but now that I know you love me, and you accept me for who I am, I can finally feel safe and secure because I know that you'll take care of me.

For starters, I need a better apartment…" and on and on she went, giving him a list of her every desire.

Deep inside, his resolve crumbled away like a ritual offering of his body's ashes spread into the winds; willpower replaced by a blissful acceptance of his tragically obsequious relationship with the love of his life. He knew he'd do everything he could for her, even if she still behaved like an obnoxious, spoiled peacock and dated her other male friends, or even if he had to take on a more aggressive role in the Triad and eliminate his rivals to climb up the chain of command, because even if he ended up working himself to death or getting killed, he loved her more than anything else in the world.

***

After dinner, Su Kim visited her grandfather at the apothecary shop.

"Honorable Grandfather, your alchemy has once again succeeded. He took the potion. Now, he'll do whatever I want – his influence in the Triad will help us greatly. Soon will come the day when we take back our community from the corrupt scum of this city…"

The old man smiled beatifically.

"Su Kim, I am very fortunate indeed to have such a clever sorceress for a granddaughter. So, Su Kim, who shall be our next mark?"

A SLICE IN TIME

Robert Watson thought, *How do I feel?*

It was a common enough question. But when asked by a staff psychiatrist at a mental health facility, it contained an uncertain depth of hidden meaning that required a carefully staged reply.

The doctor sat opposite to him, staring at him, never blinking, and patiently waiting as if time had no meaning. The wall clock's hands never clicked, ticked or moved; stuck at 11:55.

Robert's cracked leather chair groaned as he fidgeted. At least ten other old musty comfy chairs filled the therapy room, haphazardly arranged. His eyes darted about, searching for insight, inspiration, answers, anything but the truth.

The windows, all of the windows, were painted over – for the millionth time, he wondered, *Why the hell did they do that?* Considering the lack of decent lighting within the building, it was a profoundly stupid idea. The dim fluorescents hanging above were a dull egg-white color, strangely caught in half-spark, never twitching, buzzing, or flickering, casting a ghastly pallor down onto the doctor's face.

The bald, bespectacled doctor seemed to be immune to the building's sweltering heat as he awaited Robert's reply… not a drop of sweat on him. Robert sweated profusely.

The doctor spoke. "Shall I repeat the question?"

"Uhhh… no. How do I feel?" Robert felt distracted, spacing out the words to gain more time. *Oh, what the hell, just say it.* "I'm afraid. Not of, uh, what I saw. I'm afraid the hallucinations will return."

"You've only had one hallucination. And it hasn't recurred, correct?"

"Yeah, thanks to your help."

"You've rationalized that it wasn't real. But something's still bothering you about it. Let's revisit what happened, shall we?"

Robert sighed. He was tired and exasperated. He didn't like sharing his emotions. Over and over and over. The doctor always probed, an indelicate intrusion into his life, as if memories and emotions were something physical that could be surgically extracted, disassembled, categorized and reconstructed.

And so he was hesitant as always, not wanting to mention certain things that would provoke other intrusive questions. "Uh… um," he stuttered, "we were strolling about downtown North Conway, my brother Alex and I. We had just taken several hits from a doobie, and…"

He watched as the doctor scribbled in his notepad, then resumed talking. "Well, we were totally stoned. We just had a slice of pizza and were walking back to his car when we saw…"

"What did you see?"

Robert frowned, then continued, "People… that is, everyone else… they stopped moving, stopped breathing… like they were frozen in time and everything else was too. The wind wasn't blowing anymore, falling leaves were suspended in midair and the clouds didn't move across the night sky. After that, I don't remember anything."

He hated this. He didn't want to remember what it felt like to be crazy. Maybe that was why he could only remember so much, and not too much.

"Why do you think it wasn't real?" the doctor queried.

"It couldn't be. I must've been trippin'. I'll never do drugs again, that's for sure." Robert snickered on the inside because all the patients received medication at meal times.

"Very good. We'll keep working on this. See you at group."

The doctor softly closed his notepad, stood up and left the room. Robert followed soon thereafter.

He had some 'unstructured free time' to himself until the group session. He remembered the term from long ago, when as a teenager, he had spent some crisis intervention time in a psych ward.

Shuffling down the long corridor, he passed by many patient rooms, wondering why almost all of them were unused. The activity room was also empty – everyone must've been taking a nap. That was understandable. He often felt tired himself. Lost in foggy thought, he ambled back to the therapy room and sat down to wait for the group session to start.

Soon enough, the other seven patients shuffled into the room and sat down. They were all young men with scruffy hair and unkempt beards. Their emotions were moderated by drugs: antianxiety, antidepressant and sedatives to smooth over the mental edges of their lives – nightmares were common.

Robert half-listened as a patient, Thomas, asked where the new guy was. No one knew. The new guy had freaked out in group last night, babbling something about aliens among us. *UFO nut.*

There was a scattered chorus of nervous giggles when his friend Bongo asked if anyone knew the doctor's name... no one did.

The chatter died as the doctor entered the room and sat down facing the semicircle of patients. His eyes swept across the group as he said, "Who would like to begin?"

The doctor's dreadful words washed over the uneasy group.

Robert was reluctant to talk. He suspected why he was an amnesiac; that opening up certain mental doors could be dangerous, especially if you stumbled upon some awful hidden truths. It was a horrible feeling to question one's own reality.

"We can only get better if we share our experiences and learn from them..." the doctor prompted.

Someone gave a low rueful chuckle. It was Jake, seated to Robert's left. Jake usually kept to himself.

The doctor directed his attention onto Jake.

"You don't believe that sharing is healthy?" The doctor asked, his voice monotone and measured, as always.

"What should I share? That I'm freakin' insane? Hmm?" Jake scowled, obviously perturbed.

"Your fellow group members can help validate your feelings," the doctor said.

Most of the group nodded their heads.

Jake struggled, agitated, as he expressed himself, "I have dreams-"

Robert felt a moment of shock creep up on him. He had dreams too. The drugs took the ragged scary edge off them, but he often woke up, panicked, sweaty, shouting.

No, no, no, he thought, but Jake went on.

Jake practically spat his words out as if they were poison. "There are dark shadows, I don't know what they are, and they make noises, a deep grunting, like… like how an ape would talk if it could."

For Robert, the room's hot air became even more stagnant, damp and smelly. New beads of sweat crawled down his skin.

"It's like…I'm the only one awake in the world and I shouldn't be. The shadows notice me and they…" Jake shook his head. "It was so real, ya know. I don't know what to believe anymore." He put his hands over his eyes and started sobbing.

Murmurs of support came from the group.

The doctor spoke, "Thank you for sharing with us. I'm sure we can all relate to your experience."

Uh, hell YES.

"Would anyone else like to share?"

No one responded to the doctor's query.

The doctor continued. "Our brain tries to make sense of everything around us. It organizes patterns into familiar shapes that we can attach meaning to. Sometimes, we are deceived by what we think we see and we have delusions that can impair our judgment. Very good. Dinner awaits in the cafeteria."

Visiting the cafeteria was the only time they were allowed to leave the second floor.

Robert hated the hallway – he was afraid of the dark. Or, more accurately, maybe what could be lurking within it. He had no idea what other rooms were down here, or, even where the staff stayed: that is, the doctor and the chef.

His spirits picked up considerably when he entered the cafeteria. The room held many metal folding tables and plastic chairs and it was far too spacious and accommodating for the needs of only eight patients.

He grabbed a tray, plate and utensils, all of them

flimsy plastic with no sharp edges. Shuffling down the short line, dinner was slopped onto his plate.

The doctor handed him a plastic cup of water and dropped a pill onto his tray. The pill, a strong sedative, was administered to knock the patients out at night. Robert thought it was odd that pills were never dispensed in a small paper cup. He thought that was standard operating procedure in all medical facilities, but not this one.

His friends Bongo and Reefer caught his attention, waving him over to a distant corner table, far away from everyone else.

He joined them and started to eat his meal.

After the doctor left the cafeteria, Bongo said, "Reefer and I, we think we're being watched. Studied."

"Why? We're nothing special." Robert asked.

Reefer replied, "They want to understand how we think."

"The doctor…" Robert said, between mouthfuls of food, "he wants to understand what we're going through so he can help us."

"Dude, we're not being paranoid," Reefer lowered his voice. "Doesn't it bother you that none of us remember how we got here and that we've never seen anyone come or go? It's always just us here, man."

Bongo said, "And remember when the doctor asked what's-his-name, Edgar, why he felt sad about not remembering what had happened to his daughter?"

"Yeah, but Edgar, he's delusional." Robert stated.

"Don't you get it?" Reefer stopped eating. "The doctor, it's like he can't even begin to relate to our emotions and that other freak, the chef, is even worse. And how come there's only eight of us staying here? This building is huge. It was built to hold at least a hundred patients."

Bongo answered. "Maybe it's like Jake said, we

shouldn't be here. We're a mystery. They don't know what to do with us."

"The government wouldn't do that – study us." Robert said.

"I'm not talking about the government. Something else is going on here." Bongo stopped talking as he watched the doctor reenter the cafeteria.

"Well," Robert pointed out, "Brenda was released. She's no longer here."

Reefer said, "Who knows."

Right then, Robert made a momentous decision.

Normally, he would've downed his sedative with a slug of water. Instead, he went through the motions, appearing to swallow the pill, but palming it in his left hand.

After dinner, they returned to their bedrooms to go to sleep.

None of the lights worked in the bedrooms, so, when he closed his bedroom door, he had to stumble through the darkness using the hallway light seeping through the door cracks.

He dropped the pill into the room's toilet and flushed it down.

He wondered if he was doing the right thing. Not only was he opening himself up to nightmares, he was turning his back on what the doctor was trying to do for him. But he needed to find out what was going on.

After everyone was asleep, he'd go for a walk and explore the building.

Slipping into bed, he tried to stay awake, but failed soon enough.

The dream returned.

The entire world was frozen in a stark abomination of reality, a surreal pause that held everything transfixed, with two exceptions: Robert and his brother Alex. But there were other things…

Alex pointed to shadows flitting about on the other side of the street. The shadows were in the vague shape of stunted creatures, menacing in nature; they seemed to phase in and out of space and time. They'd move, vanish and reappear elsewhere as they picked up frozen people and casually tossed them onto a large pile.

His eyes refused to focus correctly on the shadows. The depth and outline that defined their shapes would slip away just as his eyes attempted to pull the separate parts together.

Alex sprinted across the street towards the shadows. Robert yelled at him to stop…

Alex slammed into a shadow that had appeared out of nowhere. It was as if Alex had hit a brick wall. He crumpled to the ground and lay still.

The shadows hovered over his brother, seemingly curious. They began to coalesce into horrific creatures…

Robert screamed and woke up. Breathing heavily, sweating, grasping at his bed sheets, he looked around his dark room to reassure himself that he was awake. The nightmare started to fade.

As helpless as he felt now, he noticed that at least his thoughts were clearer because the cumulative effect of the drug was wearing off.

He got out of bed. The air was brick-oven toasty as usual, but the chilling sweat rolling down his body gave him a brief tickle of respite from the heat.

Easing open his bedroom door, he listened to the snores rumbling from the other bedrooms.

The way out of the facility would be on the first floor, where the staff was staying, most likely. He'd need to be careful. Especially since nighttime was also when patients appeared and disappeared.

He stepped out into the hallway and walked to the elevator along the ancient wear marks in the grimy linoleum.

At the elevator he hesitated, at the moment of finality; what he did from here on could change his life.

He took the elevator down to the lobby. The lobby was illuminated with the constant half-shadows of fluorescents.

Walking closer to the thick metal entrance doors, he noticed that they had small electronic connections on the door frames. They were probably buzzer-locked. *Might set off an alarm... oh, what the hell...*

He pushed on the door. It wouldn't budge.

There had to be other ways out. Most of the facility was unused, so maybe they forgot to lock everything up.

The wear marks on the floor continued as he walked to the cafeteria. They reminded him of the trails that ants would leave between their lair and a food source.

In the cafeteria, the lights were on, as usual, but no one was in there.

In the long hallway, it was pitch black on his right, but... *hmm*, to his left, as his eyes gradually adjusted to the darkness, he saw two doors outlined with a pale light.

That was promising. And scary... he hated the darkness.

With uneasy trepidation, he walked toward the first door, which was adjacent to the cafeteria. He pushed it open.

The room was a large kitchen with many commercial-grade cooking equipment and tools. The far end of the room was hidden underneath a floor-to-ceiling pile of large empty food cans. Feeble light suffused from a dirty skylight.

Letting the door swing shut, he continued onward.

He passed several doors on his left, but those were dark and led into the center of the building, not towards the outside of the building, where there could be an exit door.

He pushed open another glow-lighted door on his right.

Beyond the door, there was a huge open-space gymnasium, lit from far above by two pale skylights. The gymnasium was used as a storage room, for what he couldn't see exactly, but the indistinct shapes occupied most of the floor at the far end of the court, just beyond the reach of the revealing light.

He walked closer to the shapes, squinting into those shadows. What he finally saw made him flinch back in sudden alarm.

No... no ... no!

It was just like his dream.

Those shapes; they were people! Arranged haphazardly, standing with different postures, maybe the last position they experienced before they became frozen, paralyzed, placed in stasis, or whatever it was...

It was real. All real!

He forced himself to creep through the haunting forest of statues towards one of the doors on the outside wall. There were more people, in sitting, reclining or other awkward positions, stacked high, against the far wall, like cords of firewood.

Who did this?

What if Bongo and Reefer were right? What if they were being held captive, subjected to bizarre experiments and studied by some mysterious intelligence, by something not human?

He stopped walking.

A young woman was posed in still-life before him.

It was Brenda. She was a patient, a Goth rebel, who had been violent in a group session – she had been terrified. She had disappeared that night.

He had missed her...

She was now an exhibit in this grim collection of unfortunate souls. A tear forming, Robert caressed her face. Her skin was warm, soft and pliant. There was nothing he could do for her.

Why is she here? His next thought chilled him to the core: *Why am I here?*

He felt an overwhelming need to leave this room, this building, this… nightmare.

With a running leap, he slammed his body against the nearest outside exit door. The door moved slightly. He leaned hard into it and it broke free of whatever had been gumming it up, snapping open with a harsh screech.

Outside, the night sky was overcast with low unmoving clouds.

He had expected a wash of cool air to refresh him when he left the building, but, instead, it was even hotter outside. Worse yet, he began to feel queasy from the eye-stinging bite of foul air pollution.

This place wasn't anything like North Conway. Where was he?

Staggered about the rocky terrain surrounding the building, there were virtually endless piles of vehicles, appliances, and essentially anything metallic, stripped apart and scavenged. Each colossal mountain was at least a hundred feet high, undoubtedly the collective result of lifetimes of work, yet he couldn't see any signs of rusting on the metals, a telltale sign of time's passage.

All around, there were no trees, no grass, no insects, and no topsoil. It seemed there was nothing organic, or even once organic, for even the rubber tires had been stripped off certain older vehicles as well as other once-living parts, such as leather from seats.

In the near-distance, just beyond this hellish scene, he saw a sickly blue-green light sputtering upon the dense cloud cover.

He was afraid, but he had made a pact with himself to learn the truth. He moved towards the lighted area, stepping along a winding path that snaked through the wasteland.

On all sides, he saw that huge foundation stones had also been cast aside within the chaotic tangle of debris. Other more common non-organic items appeared as well, and in more frequent, larger quantities. It was like the basic building blocks of his entire world had been ripped apart, polluted and cast aside, forgotten and useless.

The thick cloying industrial stench grew worse as he walked towards source of the nauseating light, soon to reveal itself, just around one more mountain.

When he saw what caused the light, he was stunned.

Against the gloomy landscape, a densely-packed web of spindly towers waved high into the air, disappearing within the murky atmosphere above, their sinuous interwoven lengths discharging tiny sparks that sprinkled downward like a crackling rain shower.

The writhing towers sprouted like tentacles from glowing structures, not buildings as he knew them, but pulsating blobs, clusters of huge oblong monstrosities from whence the striking brightness radiated strongest. Roiling gases billowed forth from the structures and blackened the skies above, despite the unnatural illumination.

Every vestige of his sanity was assaulted by this otherworldly view.

And he saw movement outlined against the structure's light. Fleeting shadows at first… then…

He saw the creatures that spawned his nightmares. Except, this time, they were clear, distinct and undeniably real.

He had no idea what they really were, but, to him, their appearance came straight out of pages of folklore. They looked like hobgoblins. Huge heads, wiry arms and legs, powerful hands and crude features. Their naked, misshapen bodies were bald and hairy, in no particular consistency of location, and some of them had odd tools in their hands as they…

Oh my God…

They were assembling their structures, slowly, carefully, methodically; crafting their odd creations using plants, trees, animals… and people! People frozen in time, plastered, melded and assimilated as raw material grafted into their constructions that hummed with repugnant life-force energies.

The hobgoblins worked with life the way an artist worked with clay: arranging, kneading and sculpting, cutting away useless parts as needed. It was as if they didn't realize that the organic material they used might have been sentient. Or they didn't care.

Suddenly, it occurred to him that they must've been working for a long time on the sweeping vista of enormous structures. And that everything he once knew was long gone, maybe along with all of mankind.

It was as if the natural world was frozen in time, except for him and a few others, and the hobgoblins as well as their structures. Maybe the hobgoblins weren't even a part of this world, or even this universe; maybe they were from another dimension, subject to different laws of reality, allowing them to manipulate time and space anywhere throughout this universe.

He felt so hopelessly lost.

"Robert," a voice said, close behind him. It was the doctor.

Robert looked at the doctor. He was offering his hand.

"There's nothing for you out here," the doctor said.

What is all this?

He turned to look back at the odd structures.

The hobgoblins had stopped working. They were staring at him, standing completely still, as if they didn't want to startle him, but were intensely curious.

Then, one of them changed its appearance, transforming while it loped to him, becoming taller and wider as it changed into a middle-aged man in a blue mechanics jumpsuit.

It stopped several feet in front of him, its face devoid of expression, but looking so human. Its mouth moved and deep, clicking grunts issued forth. Its eyes then flickered towards the doctor behind him.

"Robert, you've had a relapse," the doctor said. "I can help you. Come back inside the building."

He felt the doctor's hand upon his shoulder. He went numb all over, collapsing in slow motion towards the ground.

"Come into the gymnasium…" The doctor's voice grew distant.

Robert faded away into unconscious oblivion.

DEVOURERS OF ETERNITY

There was nothing like a steaming-hot and mysterious Louisiana cemetery to draw out the haunting creepiness of the night world.

Louise stumbled through the ancient graveyard, breathing heavily in the humid darkness. She weaved around tilted, cracked tombstones to avoid the deep, sunken depressions in the forgotten holy ground.

They're right behind me. The thought gave her a desperate burst of energy.

She knew what the two gang members would do just before they killed her. The gang, the *Cajun Riffs*, had a score to settle with her. She had been a girlfriend for one or two of the *Riffs* at different times, but when they insisted she also be a drug runner…

No one was allowed to quit the gang, so she ran through the night until she was on the verge of collapsing from exhaustion.

She struggled to focus. She needed to see her surroundings so she wouldn't fall. Headstones and angel statues were illuminated by the full moon. Monolithic crypts rose from the inky shadows cast by sprawling, kudzu-draped oak trees. The strong moonlight plunged the landscape into a stark polarization that held no shades of worldly grey.

This was a bad idea. As far as Louise could tell, there was only one way in or out of the enclosed cemetery, unless she wanted to climb over the tall, jagged-spike fence. She didn't have the energy for that.

A yell cracked across the still humid air. "There she is!" The voice sounded very close.

It made Louise run wild, without thinking, panicked and sobbing. The hitch in her left side took her breath away, a debilitation now joining the pain in her legs, which had already spasmed repeatedly with vehement protest.

She knew the gang members almost had her. Could she shake them loose?

Suddenly she saw a large crypt nearby. She decided to backtrack her trail by going around it.

In the arch above the crypt's rusted gate entrance, there was a family name chiseled into the marbled stonework, but its exact wording was lost under the drooping shadows of clinging kudzu vines. The crypt was incredibly old, probably from before the time when the French sold the territory to the Americans. It was once an ornate monument to the eternal, but now it was defiled by the passage of time.

Louise staggered into the relatively cool darkness behind the overgrown crypt. Her despair became momentarily overwhelming; disorientation disabling her as she fumbled about, hands held before her.

She wondered why she was trying so hard to survive. Why not just die, like the meaning of her life had on that fateful day over a year ago when she'd left home, forever. In woeful contrast, her stepfather's sexual abuses and her mother's drunken denial were nothing compared to the evil Louise encountered in New

Orleans. The city streets corrupted the meaning of her life and desensitized her with an anesthetic of indifference, until she was almost ready to be sacrificed, her heart cut out, on the civilized altar of profound misery.

But she kept struggling through the darkness, hands extended forward, searching. She moved away from the back side of the crypt, using the overhanging tree shade to conceal her actions.

"I see you, Louise!" a French-accented voice yelled.

Damn!

Louise bolted from her cover, tripped on a tree root and landed hard on the damp mossy ground. The earth gave way beneath her and suddenly she was tumbling down into a stygian darkness.

Somehow she landed on her feet, but at an awkward angle that caused her to lurch forward with her hands smashing into the thick debris that covered a firm stone floor.

Her mouth opened in agony; a silent scream. The pain in her hands seemed endless; taking her breath away, it was so immediate and pervasive. Her chest finally heaved, and Louise let out a short yelp. She tried to stop hyperventilating. She calmed herself, trying to take her mind away from the pain, especially in her right ankle.

She kneeled carefully back on her legs and was shocked to realize that it was actually cold down here – a very strange and musty discomfort, considering that it was never cold in New Orleans in the summer. Moonlight filtered down from the opening of the hole above, just enough for her to see that she was sitting in a large area about thirty feet underground. There were shadows flitting across the walls about twenty feet away. *Maybe it was a cave?*

The ground felt… odd. She remembered the same

sensation from once before – she had gone to a bar that served endless peanuts for free as long as you kept drinking. The peanut shells had covered the floor of the bar. They crunched, cracked and split.

This felt similar, but also a little gooey. And something on the ground tickled her... with light twitching movements. *What?*

As her heartbeat settled, she heard an odd, high pitched chittering. It was a collective surround-sound of multitudes, a sound that ripped right through her composure and left her trembling and shaking, as fear overtook her rationale.

What?

She had no idea what it was, but it seemed to originate from everywhere.

She couldn't breathe as the sound became louder. And it crept closer... closer.

Then, from the opening above, she could hear her pursuers as they drew closer, snapping her out of her unknown fear into a known dread, far more real and dangerous.

"She went behind this headstone-"

"Yes, but where is she?"

"She has to be nearby. Look, what have we here? A rabbit hole? Did Alice fall down into Wonderland?"

"Ma Cherie, it's time for you to come out, or else we'll have to come get you!"

Frikkin' Creoles, all psychics, half in this world and half in the next. She frowned, exasperated, but knowing it was her heritage too...

"Look at that drop. She's not going anywhere. Let's see if there's another way down there."

"That crypt might have a basement. Here... shine your flashlight down there."

I'm in a crypt! She cringed in the darkness.

Loud smashing sounds echoed from above. They

were breaking into the crypt!

The rustling sound around her became more agitated. She had to figure out where she was – she had to get out of here!

Louise reached into the pocket of her black leather pants and took out her lighter. *Good thing I took up smoking after the world had gone to hell.*

She flicked the lighter. It sputtered wanly, then flared to a full flame, creating a small sphere of illumination in the darkness, which was now suddenly alive with movement in the shadows.

Her eyes adjusted. She wished she had never turned on the light.

Surrounding her were hundreds, thousands, maybe hundreds of thousands of them: unblinking tiny red eyes, watching her, the faceted reflections of numerous insects, a species that scattered underneath the feet of the mighty dinosaurs and yet outlived them all, and would undoubtedly outlive mankind… cockroaches. Millions of them.

The burial chamber's walls, ceiling and floor were pocked with holes, the porous limestone like Swiss cheese. Out of those holes, the unusually large, caramel-colored cockroaches skittered forth. Their frenetic movements made the skeletons in their wall niches writhe, as if they were alive and getting the flesh stripped from their bones, undoubtedly a taste the roaches acquired throughout the graveyard.

Normally, Louise knew that cockroaches would flee from any light, but this horde surged closer to her, a rolling wave of individuals that behaved as a huge whole, a carpet that would soon engulf her.

She turned off the lighter as the roaches surrounded her. Her heartbeat rate escalated with fear. She shuddered as the first of many serrated insect limbs tickled and scratched her sweaty skin with their frantic movements.

The cockroaches crawled all over her, bristling with wispy feelers and sharp barbs. They scaled her back, her chest, and inside her blouse. They began scurrying about wildly on her shoulders, racing up inside her pant legs, and getting caught in her hair. She held her eyes and mouth firmly shut and flailed her arms, frantically trying to brush them off.

Above and behind her, a door was being pried open. Metal scraped loudly against wood and stone. Apparently, her pursuers couldn't open the door the regular way – *maybe it was a secret door?*

The cockroaches seemed even more agitated by this new raucous noise. Some of them bit into her skin…surprisingly painful bites that excised tiny scallops of flesh from her.

Louise knew the end was near, either from the multitude of cockroaches causing her to have a heart attack, or, from her pursuers deciding to kill her in this dungeon. She started to scream.

The door above suddenly shoved opened with a crack of splinters. Bright light from the crypt abruptly flooded the burial chamber. She could sense the intense change in light even with her eyes squeezed shut.

Suddenly the cockroaches moved away from her like algae-green swamp water dripping… oozing intimately down her body.

She heard the two *Riffs* race down the stone stairs to the chamber, where she sat on the floor.

One of them cried, "Lord in Hell! Look at the critters here, 'tis disgusting." Both of them had flashlights and were shining them about.

"And looky, there's Louise, the biggest critter of all!" The light haloed brightly around her. "Louise, you really didn't think you could lose us, now, did you?"

"Ah, not to worry girl, you gave us a long chase, but

it was very exciting! And we *love* to see you scared. Tell you what; we'll be sure to give you a quick death. Maybe after we have some fun with you, no?"

Louise heard the sound of a gun being drawn from a holster. Terrified, she realized that the room seemed much brighter somehow. Cockroaches were on every side and seemed energetic, almost angry as they flexed their wings and legs.

The gang members were behind her, probably three of them, maybe ten feet away. She saw that they were blocking the stairs; blocking any escape. Just ahead of her was a narrow crawlway that was sunken into the floor – it was probably once a small aquifer offshoot from an underground river – could she escape through that?

One of the gang members said, "Little buggers don't like the light."

"Ouch! One of them bit me!"

"They can't – ouch! What the hell? They're biting me too!"

"They're attacking us!"

Desperate cursing followed as more and more of the cockroaches skittered and flew towards the men. The stomping crunch of squashed bugs became frantic and the cursing escalated into bellows of raw fear.

This was her only chance…

Louise dove towards the crawlway.

She slid below the rim of the floor and squirmed into the smooth crawlway. She felt like she was swimming through a pool of bugs.

A gunshot thundered loudly within the chamber. *They shot at me!*

She inched further along into the crawlway, her ankle throbbing. More cockroaches appeared, drawn to the disturbance, possibly beckoned from across the entire cemetery…

In the crawlway, a massive wave of the huge monsters streamed over her for a long time, sounding like poker chips tumbling in a near-empty dryer, drowning out everything until they finally passed into the chamber beyond.

The screaming in the chamber soon transitioned to gruesome choking and gurgling noises. She could hear the sounds of shoes flailing against the floor but soon the sounds became more and more sporadic.

Don't look back, she told herself.

She lifted herself up into a sitting position in another open area. She didn't dare flick on the lighter still held tightly in her hand, but she could see a little more now that her eyes adjusted to the dim light. She was in a small natural cave.

There was nowhere else to go. She was trapped.

She sighed, and awaited her fate, slumped against a footstool that had been left in the middle of the cave. Near the stool were a hurricane lantern and five small chests. Could there be something to help her in any of the chests?

She flipped open the cover of one of the chests. Tarnished gold and silver reflected back at her. There were coins inside all of the chests. Very old coins.

Louise sifted her fingers through the cold thick metal pieces. The chittering of cockroaches eventually faded away in the other chamber as she thought about her life's circumstances. She could change everything if she could get out of there… with some of the coins.

With a prayer spoken to the spirits, she filled her pockets with gold and silver. If she survived the night, she'd come back for more later.

She turned around and went back through the crawlway. She had no other options. She couldn't hear the gang members anymore; perhaps the cockroaches had scared them off. Perhaps they were gone.

It was tighter than she remembered. She wondered how she had made it through so quickly before.

Finally she reached the chamber and saw that most of the cockroaches had retreated out of sight. But it hit her that the gang members had not left with the insects.

A thick layer of splattered carapaces surrounded the ghastly remains of three human beings. The bodies, still clothed in shredded rags, had been stripped clean of their flesh. She could hear faint scratching coming from within the skulls.

She didn't know why she felt so numb. She understood on a primal level that what she saw should terrify her. But she stepped carefully past the blood-wet skeletons, and the nearby pistol and two spent flashlights, then climbed the stone steps upward. There was an iron slat on the stairs, which was been torn from the crypt's now-open outer door.

Once in the crypt at the top, she pushed the secret door closed; if you looked very closely, you might see some out-of-place marks on the stone wall, and that would be all. Her pursuers were very clever to have found the hidden door – lucky for her and unlucky for them.

The precious coins in her pocket felt good. Louise now had the power.

She stepped out into the moonlight and closed the outer door to the crypt. A whole new world awaited her, one where she'd no longer be afraid of what the darkness held.

EDGE OF DARKNESS

She was waking up.

Michael watched her with trepidation.

She was a scavenger, his age— twelve or so— surprisingly well fed.

Her eyelids fluttered open. She looked around, groggy, probably trying to understand why she was sitting on a chair in a dimly lit room.

She focused on him, sitting on another chair, facing her, three feet away.

Her eyes popped open wide with fear. Her mouth gag moved, bobbing in and out, with each wild breath. She struggled against the rope that held her body to the chair, only now realizing she was also bound at her hands and feet by plastic tie-wraps.

She stopped squirming. Her muscles trembled as she slumped back in despair.

"Don't cry out. You don't want *them* to hear. If you don't listen…" Michael said, the final implication left unsaid. While he wasn't a cold-hearted person, he certainly had a good instinct for self-preservation. There were millions of the infected creatures outside, roaming the city ruins, obsessed by a relentless hunger. The creatures would eat anything: people, animals and each other, preferably in that order.

His captive fixed her gaze on him and after several thoughtful seconds, nodded her head.

He leaned forward and removed the gag. She licked her dry, cracked lips.

"Would you like some?" he asked, holding up an unopened bottle of water.

She nodded eagerly.

He twisted off the cap and slowly poured the water into her mouth.

She drank greedily. Not surprising – good water was hard to find. She finished off the bottle.

He began to wonder if she could talk. *Just my luck*, he thought. He hadn't been around anyone for years… and he missed conversation.

"Why am I here?" she squeaked, surprising him.
"You were being attacked by the creatures when you fainted, I guess you were out cold. I saved you, just in time," he explained.

"If you saved me, then why am I tied up?" she asked the obvious.

"Just being safe. I don't know you yet…"

"Let me go," she pleaded. "I didn't do anything to you!"

"You caused a ruckus – the creatures noticed. I can't let that happen again." He shook his head. "I don't want them to discover I'm here."

"It wasn't on purpose. Really… I couldn't help it. The zombies noticed me because… I laughed," she started laughing again, hysterically. "I laughed when one of them farted."

A farting zombie?

He laughed, too. It was a nice feeling. It had been so long…

"Okay, fair enough. By the way, how did you do that? Walk among the zombies?" he asked. He liked her use of the word 'zombies'. It was less frightening than the truth – lost souls living in a mindless hell.

"If I tell you, will you let me go?"

"Maybe."

She rolled her eyes with a sigh. "You have to behave like them… and smell like them."

"What were you doing outside?"

"Looking for water." She paused, and then said, "You seem to have plenty of water."

A cold sweat suddenly chilled the back of his neck. He had a closet full of bottled water.

"I don't have much, but it looked like you needed it. What I don't have is… food." He had finished his supply of stale crackers long ago and was down to slurping ketchup mixed in water.

She smiled pleasantly, even though her pale lips cracked even further from the effort.

"I know where there's food," she drawled.

"Where!?!" the desperation in his voice surprised him.

"I can't explain it to you. You wouldn't be able to find it. At least not by yourself."

"What are you suggesting?" he asked, confused.

"I give you some food and then you let me go. You get what you want. I get my life back. And actually, you did save me from the zombies, so… I owe you."

"That's it? Nothing more?"

"Some water would be nice. If you can spare it."

"I knew it. Nothing's ever free."

"Well… we both have something the other needs. Look… I'm asking you to trust me, even though you shouldn't… just like I have to trust you. You can take whatever food you can carry. There's all kinds of candy bars."

"Candy bars?" his mouth began salivating. He remembered their delicious sweet taste from his early childhood, before the world went to hell.

"Yeah. I discovered a storage closet. Under some rubble. Inside, there were boxes and boxes of goodies. I moved them to my hiding spot."

He thought it through. There was enough ketchup soup to last maybe another month if he was excessively frugal, and when that ran out, he'd have to go searching outside, continually, without rest, with the zombies wandering about, waiting to make a meal of him. And also… his health was failing; his energy was being sapped by starvation. He needed energy now, while he could still do something rational about his fate.

"If you lead me there, I'll give you four liters of water," he offered. "You can even take them with you. I'll give you one of my backpacks."

She thought about it for several heartbeats, then said, "Okay. It'd be a good idea to leave now… it's still daytime, right?"

"Yep." He pulled out a small pocketknife from his back pocket and flicked it open. "Now… before we leave, you need to tell me that you'll do as I say."

"I will. Don't hurt me," she whimpered.

"Stay still. I'm going to cut the tie-wraps…" He freed her legs first, then her arms, then he untied the rope around her body.

She rubbed her skin where the plastic tie-wraps had chafed through the crusted grime coating her body.

"When we're outside," he frowned, "if you need to talk, just whisper and only when I'm close to you."

"Of course."

"Oh, how were, uh… are you able to smell like them?"

"I masked my scent. I used a rag and wiped up some… pus and blood from a dead zombie," she cringed. "I keep it in the open bag around my waist."

The sour tang of old stale sweat emanated from him – disguising that would be a challenge, but she smelled far worse than he did.

"I know where to find a body. Where's your hiding spot?"

"On the opposite side of the park. Near the tourist shops."

"Hmm… okay, let's get ready."

While she stood up and stretched, he went into his adjacent bedroom, grabbed two small backpacks, put one on himself, and then opened up his storage closet, which was stacked high with cases of bottled water. He grabbed four water bottles, added an extra one, and put them in her backpack. He also grabbed a large belt pack and secured it around his waist.

He mouthed a silent heartfelt goodbye to his stuffed animal collection arranged on the bed. He often talked with them. They were complete idiots, but regardless, they were good company.

On the way out, he picked up his baseball bat. Some blood was etched into the wood's grooves – he'd missed that spot during his cleaning. At least it wasn't on the surface, so there was little chance of his getting infected on contact, besides, he'd probably need to use it again today.

She was startled when she saw him return with the bat.

He grinned unevenly, an uneasy feeling considering that he hadn't done it in so long. His facial muscles didn't feel right.

He handed her the backpack that contained her water.

"I gave you five bottles of water."

"Thanks."

"You're welcome."

He didn't know why he was being so nice to her. It wasn't easy for him to trust anyone… he was all alone, and had been for about three years, ever since his parents were killed by marauders… right in front of him. He had escaped. He ran and ran and ran, and ended up being chased by zombies, until he evaded them in his current hideout, a top floor room in a garish hotel that had probably been on the verge of being condemned long before the apocalypse. And now he was going to leave this safe house. It was the only security he had known for years, since... he lost his parents.

He refused to cry.

She was watching him closely.

"What's your name?" he asked softly.

"Lenore."

"Lenore. That's a beautiful name. I'm Michael."

"Hello, Michael."

"Shall we go?" he asked.

She nodded.

He slid the bat underneath his backpack. It was uncomfortable and awkward, but it wouldn't fall out as long as he didn't move around too much.

He opened the door to his safe house.

They stepped out into the cold murky day. He peeked over the edge of the balcony. Three stories below, there were no zombies in the open rectangular courtyard, only some broken heaps of furniture and an empty swimming pool.

"All clear," he said.

They went down the staircase, across the courtyard and into the tiny hotel lobby.

There was no sign of zombies on the street outside, but that meant nothing, they could be hiding, lying down, or out of plain sight.

"Stay away from walls, doorways and cars," he warned. "Always keep some distance clear around you."

"No kidding? You think I was just born yesterday?"

He opened the lobby's front entrance door and peered outside. In the parking lot, there was a scattering of derelict cars. Still no zombies - live ones at least.

Silently, he led her to the bodies of two zombies, lying sprawled on the oil and blood stained parking lot pavement. Like most zombies, these two were freckled with oozing white pustules on their slime-encrusted, swollen and deformed bodies.

This morning, he had been out on an unsuccessful food-scouting foray when he was drawn to the sound of her laughter, the first human sound he had heard in a long time, and then... her scream of terror. These two zombies were about to eat her alive when he came running over and crowned them with the baseball bat. When the battle was over, he noticed she was lying on the ground, having fainted during the zombie attack.

He gazed down upon the zombies. They almost looked at peace when they were dead. No longer fever-driven by the End-Times-Plague.

Almost three years ago the Carni-Virus variant had destroyed civilization within several months, leaving behind the scattered remnants of mankind to fight off overwhelming masses of the walking dead.

They weren't actually dead, but close enough to it, for in addition to the Carni-Virus' fever destroying the mind, the body was slowly ravaged by the fever's side effects, a destructive necrosis of the flesh, until, in the end, the mindless creatures were no longer even vaguely human.

He tore off a strip of cloth from his outer shirt and reached down to rub it thoroughly over one of the bodies. Good thing he wore gloves.

"Ugh," he griped, wincing at the ripe stench as he shoved the gooey strip into his belt pack. "Now I smell as bad as you do."

She chuckled.

"Okay. To the park?" he suggested.

She nodded.

Thereafter, they pretended to shuffle along like the zombies, occasionally reeling and staggering in their footsteps, just in case there were any zombies watching as they walked through the city.

The entire downtown community had been razed through years of vandalism, fire and weather. On the streets, amid a maze of rusting cars, the common artifacts of an ancient life had been strewn onto the cracked pavement, where healthy shoots of grass sprouted up next to the desiccated bones of the long dead.

He always felt a desolate sense of hopelessness whenever he saw what was left of the world. Everything... homes, cars, possessions... once considered to be important, was now decaying away into ruin, much like the kindness of humanity.

Lenore picked up a chewed plastic doll from the street, hugged it to her chest and snuggled it gently into her backpack.

So innocent.

Up ahead, the chilling sound of rending flesh distracted him away from his thoughts of Lenore.

Three dogs were tearing into a zombie that was lying on the ground, still twitching. One of the dogs casually looked up from its gruesome meal. It growled menacingly, then continued with its feast unperturbed.

Michael was considering how to avoid a confrontation when suddenly, all of the dogs became alert, ears shifting about, looking around, sniffing the air, homing their noses toward the street ahead.

A group of zombies – over a dozen of them – were advancing upon the snarling dogs.

The dogs charged the zombies. The dim-witted

zombies tried to grab ahold of the much faster dogs, but to no avail. The dogs were snapping, biting and ripping, slowly but surely inflicting grievous wounds upon the zombies.

He realized that it was time for them to leave, before other zombies arrived, who'd be attracted to the loud, violent sounds of imminent death. He and the girl quickly ran away, circumventing the slaughter. At the crossroads ahead, they resumed their plodding pace as they encountered more zombies swarming toward the fight. Soon, they left the chaos behind them. They could relax again.

He happened to glance at an overturned newspaper dispenser as they walked by it. The curled paper pressed up against the viewing glass was brown and wrinkled, but several fuzzy words survived the years… The Living Dead. There were other words that he could pronounce, but the meanings were unclear: Outbreak, Apocalypse, CDC – Hope For Cure.

War, famine and pestilence had followed in the wake of the Carni-virus pandemic. Civil society had disintegrated as the ranks of the zombies swelled. It only took a single drop of blood, sweat or even a sneeze to become infected – and the infected attacked anything with rage, teeth and nails. It was a miraculous tragedy that anyone had survived. Maybe he and Lenore were immune to the Carni-virus, unlike the poor zombies around them.

They reached the park without incident. A lingering wisp of gray smoke drifted over the ornamental stone wall surrounding the park.

He looked at Lenore and said, "A fire – must've been a lightning strike. From the storm last night."

"We could go around, but it'd be a longer walk." She shrugged, looking apprehensive. "Risky."

"You're right. Let's just keep going," he whispered.

They stepped through a park entrance: a colorful wrought-iron arch depicting children and animals frolicking together. Tall, thick, overgrown hedge walls sectioned off the parkland. There were several playgrounds and picnic areas in here that he had enjoyed long ago, and in the center of the park there was a short maze of hedges and a memorial statue.

The smoky air grew thicker as they walked, a powerful cloying smell that blended with something else, something intriguing, an ancient savory smell – hamburgers frying on a barbeque grill! Up ahead, a long section of hedge wall was ablaze with huge flames roaring skyward. A car had crashed into the hedge wall. Bullet holes dotted its burning body. The gas tank had exploded. Several charred zombies, still on fire, lay on the burnt grass near the wreck, twisted into horrific shapes of agony.

The intoxicating aroma of freshly cooking meat made him drool involuntarily.

He was revolted by his reaction. This wasn't the alluring aroma of a barbeque. This was the God-awful smell of burning people, the flesh of the infected, but he was so impossibly hungry that his survivalist mind registered this possible alternative: the zombies could be eaten.

Lenore stood transfixed, solemnly watching the shimmer of warm flames crackle upon the zombie bodies.

"Could you do it?" he asked in a hushed tone after he glanced around – no living zombies were nearby.

"Do what?" she whispered.

"Eat them. If you had to?"

Her face cringed with disgust. "Ugh – no. You'd catch their infection."

"Yeah… I guess so."

A sharp gunshot cracked across the air. Then

another. And another… it was coming from beyond the hedge wall on their right. *Someone else was here!*

They shuffled to the hedge passageway and observed a sickening sight. On top of a gazebo, a camouflage-outfitted man fired a military rifle at a horde of zombies, advancing on him from all sides across a large rolling field of dead grass.

Must have a death wish…

They had to leave, quickly, before the chaos got out of hand. By the time they made it to the desired park exit, the sporadic gunfire switched to bursts of automatic fire.

Once outside the park, they shuffled down the narrow street full of souvenir shops through a veritable river of zombies being drawn to the gunfire. The pervasive stench wafting off the zombies almost gave him the dry heaves. One of the zombies, once a young boy, stumbled and bumped into Michael, splattering nauseating pustules across his clothes. The zombie spun away, stumbling again, then stood straight, sniffing the air.

He and Lenore tried to walk away as quickly as they could without attracting attention. He heard a gurgling cry erupt behind them – the boy zombie was now shambling towards them, attracting the curious attention of other passing zombies.

"Run!" Lenore mouthed, in a forceful whisper.

They sprinted around many confused zombies, but eventually the zombies ahead of them noticed what was happening and started to close in on them as well.

"Right side… in the alley!" she screeched.

He hoped there was a way out… he'd seen what zombies could do if they cornered a person.

The alley, about fifteen feet wide, was obstructed with overturned garbage cans. They leapt over cluttered mounds of debris.

Sounds of enraged calamity grew behind them; the zombies were having a difficult time pursuing them and began fighting amongst themselves.

She stopped to open up an alley door. It was locked. So was another. All of them were locked at this far end. They couldn't go back – some zombies had made it past the raucous fighting that had broken out.

"Fence," she yelled, pointing to the alley's end only a short dash away.

Despite being terrified, he sighed. He hated climbing.

She had already nimbly scaled a series of old garbage cans and was pulling herself over the tall wooden fence.

Exhausted, he took a deep breath and jumped up onto an aluminum can, then continued upward onto a taller green plastic container.

She was already somewhere on the other side of the fence.

He grabbed onto the fence top and placed his foot against the fenced wall, trying to leverage himself up and over. His foot slipped and came down hard onto the container, causing it to suddenly tip and fall away from the fence. The container slipped out from underneath him, leaving him hanging from the fence top, suspended four feet off the ground. He tried to pull himself over the fence, but his feet couldn't get any traction – the fence was slick with wet mold.

A zombie was lunging toward him, at his ankle height, mouth open wide for a ravenous bite.

Noooo!

Lenore grabbed him by his arms and painfully yanked him up and over the fence top, away from the reach of the nail scrabbling, mouth foaming, teeth chomping zombie. He was now safe atop a huge garbage dumpster, breaths coming in ragged gulps, standing next to her.

He looked back.

On the other side, there were now three zombies howling down below and even more were arriving. They made clumsy, maniacal attempts to climb the fence when they saw him.

His baseball bat lay on the ground near the crazed zombies. All he had now was a tiny pocketknife – hardly sufficient to protect himself.

At least I'm still alive…

He suddenly realized that he would've been dead by now if she hadn't pulled him over the fence. She had saved him.

She motioned for him to move away from the fence.

On this side, there was no alleyway. They were inside the enclosed parking area of an apartment complex; surrounded by the blackened shells of burned-out buildings, derelict cars were parked forever underneath reserved sun-shaded spots. There were no zombies here that he could see.

"Wait. Let's rest," he wheezed. She nodded immediately, even though she seemed to be fine. She must get a lot of exercise – not an easy thing to do on a starvation diet.

"Thank you for rescuing me," he said, smiling awkwardly. "They would've gotten me for sure if it wasn't for you."

"Sure," she said, smiling back, a flicker of a grin.

"No…I mean it," he persisted.

She nodded, dead serious, when she said, "My pleasure."

"Is it much further? Your hiding place?"

"Well, this wasn't the way I intended on going, but… I think it's just outside the gate… to the left. Not too far."

"Okay. Let's go."

They walked toward the parking area's exit. Near the main gate, there was a pedestrian access gate. It had a turn-knob on this side. He opened the access gate and they walked out onto the street.

There were no zombies in sight.

Whew! Good luck...

"There it is," she pointed towards the end of the block, where the road ended in a T-junction with another road.

He laughed when he saw it, then quickly stifled himself.

"Chez Jacque le Gourmand? A French restaurant?" he said. "Everyone and everything looking for food and you hide in a French restaurant?"

"Best place. Food places were picked clean long ago," she answered, looking surreptitiously around the neighborhood. "So no one would think to look there."

"Kind of makes sense," he conceded.

She chuckled when his stomach rumbled. "I know exactly how you feel. It's been a while since I've eaten, too."

They tread cautiously down the street.

The restaurant's walkway was framed by a lengthy canopy of blooming roses, red, white, and blue in color. A faded black plastic-covered chain stretched across the arched entryway, attached to stout pillars on both sides, undoubtedly sufficient to keep out meandering zombies. He followed her as she ducked under the chain. She pulled open the restaurant's thick wooden door for him. The door had black fleur-de-lis patterns nailed into it.

They entered the ostentatious dining area of the restaurant. From the light of narrow stain glass windows, he was amazed to see intimate tables set with elegant cushioned chairs, crisp white table linens, romantic red candles, formal silverware, engraved napkins and silk flowers in fluted vases. It was perfect –

a vision of heaven right out of the past, unaffected by the rest of the broken, dirty world. It had a woman's touch, as his mom used to say. Lenore was definitely handy to have around.

"Lenore," he said, reaching out to touch her shoulder.

She turned to face him.

"I just wanted to say thank you," he murmured. "This food of yours, it'll save my life."

She smiled sweetly.

"Michael, you saved my life, too, so… I'm glad to help you."

He smiled back.

She likes me!

He experienced an unusual euphoric feeling. Maybe this was what love felt like. It certainly made no sense when it came to survival, but he didn't care… He'd have to find a way to ask her to stay with him in his safe house. They'd do so many wonderful things together… cards, board games, all kinds of fun…

"It's in the back," she said.

She led the way through the dining area, then down a short hallway. She held open one of the two swinging doors that had signs saying 'Employees Only'. They entered into another short hallway that had office doors on both sides before it opened up onto a spacious kitchen area. Stoves, ovens, sinks, cabinets, storage racks, and preparation tables dominated the room with a well-organized flair of precise efficiency. Even the pots, pans, plates, cups and mixing utensils were perfectly arranged in overhead shelves and storage racks. The people who once worked here had a passion for fine dining.

At the far end of the room, beyond the illuminated area defined by the skylights, he saw a wall of meat lockers and pantries obscured in the shadows.

"There," she pointed. "On the table ahead."

He finally saw it. About forty feet away. Just at the edge of darkness. How could he have missed that? It was a low stacked pile of cardboard boxes, many of them sliced open; exposing some of the decadent treats he used to love.

Whooping with laughter, he ran to the table and scooped up a double handful of candy bars. Their dusty wrappers crinkled – he forgot about that sound! He slowly lifted them up to his nose and inhaled deeply. A faint whiff of chocolate, caramel, nougat... it had been so long. He shivered in sweet anticipation. He then realized that there was also another faint smell lingering in the air – the smell of rotting flesh. He dropped the candy bars and looked over his shoulder to Lenore.

She was backing away. Toward the door. She looked... wary.

Something's wrong! She sees something!

He scanned the room around him. His eyes locked onto something just beyond the furthest table away. In the shadows, he saw a small river of blood pooling around a clogged floor drain, the source of which was piled low, in the corner, a haphazard jumble of human body parts, flesh gnawed away, pared down to cracked bones and stringy cartilage.

Oh no, the zombies are here!

His eyes darted about for a weapon, anything, anything, anything... Leaping up, he snatched a long handled cooking pot from an overhead rack. Other pots and pans spilled to the floor, crashing with an echoing cacophony of noise.

He crept backwards, away from the shadows, watching for movement. A door thumped closed behind him. He turned-

Lenore stood amongst a group of feral children, about a dozen of them. They blocked the only way out of the kitchen.

It finally came to him that zombies wouldn't have left a neat pile of leftover bones in the corner. Someone was eating the zombies…

"You've been eating *them*? The zombies? But you said you'd never eat *them* because you'd get infected!"

"Silly boy," she smirked. "*We* don't eat the infected. That would be insane."

Understanding dawned upon him. His mouth drooped open in numb, trembling shock.

"I told you not to trust me," she chuckled, as the group of children advanced towards him, knives drawn.

WITCHES HILL

October in New England is when the world begins to die. The dreadful cold arrives like the last shovel of dirt on a grave, sharp and bitter with a stinging chill, curling the fragile leaves of maple, oak and cedar, their dying desiccation cracking with a riot of vivid red, orange and yellow, rustling on quivering grey branches, until finally breaking loose, spiraling to dark soiled land steeped in tradition, folklore and mystery. But, like the ever-present pine trees, which held their needles close, something of the past always remained behind through the endless winters ahead.

The country town of Jonas Mills, Maine had almost 600 souls in it, a post office, a school, a volunteer fire department, and a small general store, catering to the tourist traffic that sped past the sleepy town. History itself had passed by the town. It was once a thriving community of over 8,000 during the industrial heyday of the narrow gauge railroad. Most of the remnants of those years— buildings, houses, and fences, the evidence of civilization— all lay rotting in collapsed shambles, obliterated by time and reclaimed by the ancient forest.

To Larry Wilcox, the recent relocation from the New York suburbs to live here, in the 'sticks', was a lifetime change of epic proportions. It was a stunning dislocation of the senses akin to moving to a foreign country – there were some similar patterns to existence, such as food, shelter and clothing, but everything else was 'different'. 'Different' was his wonderful experience of living in Maine, exploring the wild-flowered fields and quiet shady woods surrounding his family's rustic farmhouse, breathing in the refreshing clean air, and best of all, frequent visits to his Uncle George and Aunt Mary's house, several towns away, where he spent the Summer playing games with his cheerful cousins, swimming and sailing, slurping on juicy watermelon and gobbling down hot apple pie. All wonderful things that he was wholeheartedly grateful for.

The next season, autumn, changed everything: midway through, the onset of harsh weather, fewer outside activities, and the start of seventh grade in a new school. 'Different' also became the oppression he endured from some mean kids at school. Now, aside from being a wispy-thin, longhaired, shy boy, he was also an 'outta-stater', someone not from here, not to be trusted, and as such, the target of farm boys who inherently disliked 'city-slickers'. It was hell. He tried to be nice, say the right things, but it was awkward at best: he didn't dress in practical jeans and lumberjack shirts, he was bored to death in school, he could barely understand the local accent, he was prone to idiotic bragging whenever he could gather the courage to talk, and damn-it-all, everyone knew about sex except him.

Being invited to go Trick-or-Treating tonight was an opportunity he couldn't miss out on. Sure, it was absurdly childish for him, he'd done it about three years ago back in the city and felt ashamed by the immaturity of it all, but now, apparently, it was about being clever and scamming candy from reluctant homeowners. At least, that's what he could expect tonight per Danny Louis and Jimmy Watt, his local newfound friends. He'd been reluctant to go on the outing until he heard that Jimmy's hot sister, Lorraine, would be accompanying them. Larry had a helpless crush on her.

She was all he could think about on the mile long walk to the agreed-upon meeting place, Danny's house. The two boys watched him approach from the house's pebble driveway, staring at him wide-eyed, mouths half open, like he was a disgusting cockroach that dared to venture into their presence. Lorraine was nowhere in sight.

"Lorraine's busy." Danny smiled widely with a contemptuous leer. Jimmy snickered.

Larry knew that his resulting expression and posture undoubtedly exposed his devastation. He wasn't good at hiding his emotions.

Maybe she didn't come because of me... he wondered, miserable.

"You like my sister?" Jimmy teased, his incredulous fake smile showing off brown-stained teeth.

Embarrassed, Larry stuttered, "So, um, what are we going to do? Do we have a ride?"

"You tired?" Danny drawled.

"Uh, no," he lied.

Danny shrugged, "Then let's get going." He and Jimmy started fast walking alongside the uphill road. "What the heck is your costume, anyway?"

It took him a disappointed moment to realize that they were walking, not driving to the trick or treat site. He scrambled to catch up to them.

"Uh, a pirate," Larry panted, feeling ridiculous. "See? Red bandana, eye patch, striped shirt and booty bag." The booty bag was from his childhood – it was yellow linen with an orange pumpkin sewn on it.

They both cackled with laughter at him.

To distract the conversation away from himself, he asked, "What are you guys dressed up as?"

"Jeez, what are you, a numbie?" Danny quipped.

"Yeah, a numbie?" Jimmy echoed like some cheap stereo feedback reverberation.

He learned not long ago that a 'numbie' was a numbskull, a local term that described someone afflicted with profound stupidity.

"We're dressed as farmhands!" Danny bellowed, apparently angry or exasperated or both, a difficult concept to express with a smooth, easy-going Maine accent that pronounced farmhands as 'faaam-hans'.

"Ah, good one!" Larry beamed.

Larry didn't get it. They were dressed in plain, dirty, ragged clothes, same as always, except they each carried a stained pillowcase. He wasn't a snob, but he didn't think highly of certain types of laziness. How much effort would it take to wash their clothes? He became especially aware of their body odor because he was trailing behind them, trying not to breathe in their stench too deeply, especially when the headwind picked up now and again, spraying roadside leaves into their faces. Larry didn't bring a jacket, so he shivered whenever a gust of wind crept up through his clothes, frosted his skin with pinprick shivers, and clawed its way out across his backside.

Thankfully, they drew closer to the first house, that of Danny's closest neighbor. It was a timeworn, cozy doublewide trailer surrounded by a short white plastic picket fence. Garishly colored cardboard skeletons, black cats and haunted houses were taped on the inside panes of several curtained window. Real spider webs draped over the front door porch light. The light was on – the sun had disappeared below the horizon hours ago.

Danny and Jimmy giggled in anticipation, then

knocked on the door, serious and contrite expressions congealing on their faces.

After a grumble, slow shuffling, and a wet cough, an elderly woman popped open the stubborn door. She wore an orange sweater and a faded black witch's hat and had real straw-like white hair. Her knotted shrunken hands firmly held onto a plastic pumpkin stuffed with 'fun-size' candy bars.

The woman looked them up and down, blinking, then squinting in consternation, her face twisting into an ugly grimace, she said, "Danny, you're a little old to be trick or treating."

"Uh, yes ma'am, we're..." Danny improvised, voice sweet at honey, "Uh, we just wanted to go out one more time, to remember what it was like to be kids again."

Jimmy reached for the bowl, grasping fingers spread wide like grubby bird talons.

"No ya don't, ya hooligan," she growled. *What's a hooligan?* Whatever it was, Larry silently approved of the woman's rebuke.

"Sorry! Jimmy's hungry. He hasn't eaten at all today," Danny confided with a chagrined expression.

The woman looked from Danny to Jimmy. She reached into the bowl and gave them one candy bar each. She was startled when she noticed Larry behind them, reacting as though he'd just snuck up on her with the worst of intentions. Shaking her head, she gave him a candy bar as well, albeit in a gentler manner than his companions.

"You children should be ashamed of yourselves," she grumbled as she slammed the door. Inside, a lock bolt slid into place along with a chain lock.

Danny and Jimmy jumped in the air and high-fived each other as if this was the greatest accomplishment in their life. Larry felt sickened by the cheap vulgarity of it all.

"Whatcha think of that?" Danny asked.

"Cool!" Larry replied, almost convincing himself.

"Yeah! That's how we roll, man!" Jimmy said.

The next house up the hill was a cube-shaped, two story farmhouse.

Cows mooed from within a nearby barn as Danny knocked on the door. Inside, a chair slid across the floor, heavy footsteps plodded closer and the door opened. A huge man filled the doorway, huge but beefy with real muscles built from long hard labor, dressed in a blue jean overall and smudged white shirt. Squinting through small round glasses, he bellowed with laughter, "Ethel, come lookie here! There's some limp wrist pansies begging at our door for handouts!"

Backing away, hands held up, Danny babbled, "Suh-sorry mister, sorry to have disturbed you. We'll be moving along now. Sorry sir..."

They beat a retreat back to the road. The man's scorching insults carried in the air, chasing them as they scurried up to the last house on the hill.

Before Danny could knock on the door, a voice screeched from within, "Go away, ya idiots!"

They shuffled back to the road. No new houses in sight. There were probably more on the other side of the hill. They walked slowly up the hill.

What the hell am I doing? It was already dark outside. Despite the soft glow of the sickle shaped moon, the Milky Way's splash covered the sky from end to end. The stars were always so beautiful here...

"That didn't go well," Danny understated.

"Worked last year," Jimmy said, "Oh no, the city slicker must be disappointed."

"Well, we got something better for him..." Danny pointed to where the road crested ahead. The tombstones of an old graveyard dotted an enormous hillside on the left. "You wanna look for some ghosts?"

"Uh, sure..." Larry replied.

"You believe in spooks, right?" Jimmy asked, lips pursed like a duck's bill.

Larry hesitated, thoughtful, "I think it's possible they exist."

"Oh yeah? Me too." Danny said, suddenly serious. "A few months back, some little kids saw a ghost, for sure, in this graveyard." He improvised a medley of ghostly sound effects. "Anyway, they got all worked up and bawlin' when they got home. Must've seen somethin' wicked cool, I think, but the sheriff went by and found nothing." Eyebrows raised with a mischievous smile, he asked, "Still wanna take a look?"

"Oh wait… In the graveyard at night? Isn't that illegal or something? What if the sheriff drives by?" he reasoned, feeling like a prude.

"That's what makes it fun! Wait a minute, you're not afraid of ghosts, are you?" Danny asked, making an obvious dare, just like all the juvenile delinquents Larry had ever known.

"Yeah, afraid of ghosts." Jimmy repeated, wiping slobber from his mouth onto his shirt sleeve.

"N-no, I'm not afraid, but-" Larry felt trapped.

"Then it's settled. We're going." Danny nodded briskly. "You're gonna like this. Betcha don't have graveyards like this in the city."

Leaving the road, they stepped over the fallen remains of the rusted iron perimeter fence that once guarded the graveyard. Larry's steps became snagged in the long dead grass, so he had to constantly lift his feet up to avoid dragging them. Stumbling once into an unseen sinkhole, he watched his path carefully thereafter, for there were a great many other small hollows half-hidden on the hillside. In the illuminating dusk of the starry moonlight, sparkling rime-cracked tombstones, leaning this way and that, marked the hillside with an exposé preview of inevitable death. Everything at this point was fast on its way to becoming reduced to shades of white, grey and black. The surreal experience prompted him to comment, "This place looks really old."

"A-yah," Danny agreed. "Around the days of the Salem Witch Trials, there was a church up on yonder hill."

"No way! Really?" Larry looked at the graveyard's hilltop, but only saw crooked tombstones – no church.

"Check out the headstones. Some go back to the 1600's. The town abandoned it all long ago, around when the railroad shut down." Danny sighed. "Bad luck all around."

Larry glanced at the weatherworn headstones as they passed. Most were crudely made, barely even markers, but some were large stone plates with finely carved names, dates, details and memorials, guardian angels even, engraved for a forgotten life lost on a sad lonely hillside. One was for a twelve-year old girl who died in 1821 from consumption. *What's that?* It was overwhelming... "This place should be a historical landmark," he sighed.

Danny looked thoughtful, "Guess people don't want that. My mammy says this place is cursed. Not exactly something to brag about."

"Witches' Hill!" Jimmy blurted out.

Danny followed up. "Yeah, witches, well, the church was Christian, but something bad happened… real bad. I don't know what. At nighttime... black magic, summoning demons, and so on. Proper townsfolk finally had enough of that and burned it down. Hung those pagans, too."

"Wow! Creepy!" Larry said, suddenly wishing it wasn't nighttime.

"I'll say. The spot's right…" Danny looked around.

They'd reached the hilltop – it was quite large. "Oh, here it is!" He pointed to a rectangular depression in the ground. Rimmed with lichen-freckled foundation stones, it was about ten by twenty feet in size, but its depth was unknown, being obscured by a wild profusion of raspberry vines that grew here and nowhere else. They walked to the foundation's edge and looked down onto the raspberry patch.

"This is where those kids saw the ghosts?" Jimmy asked, somber voiced.

"A-yah, them ghosts could be watchin' us right now... Hiding down below," Danny said with theatrical melodrama, "Go find out Larry!"

Larry felt a hard shove from behind and was launched into the foundation hole. He fell with an embarrassing yelp, entire body crashing through the raspberry vines, scratched, torn and bleeding in a tangled confusion beneath the thick canopy of leafy vines, outstretched hands and knees sinking deep into a muddy mulch.

It didn't take long for him to realize the ultimate betrayal of his friendship. Anger began to build, boiling up through the pain and humiliation.

"You sons of bitches! When I get outta here, I'm going to get you, get you back, and I'll never give up, no matter how long it takes, I'm going to hurt you bad."

"Oops," Jimmy said, then cackled wildly.

Danny laughed too, though not as wholeheartedly. "Gee, I'm sorry city-boy, sounds like you hurt yourself. You need to be more careful..."

Larry was fuming with hatred but soon became preoccupied with something else besides their heckling. He was sinking deeper into the mulch and couldn't pull his hands or knees out; it felt weird, as if he were being sucked down into a vine-barbed quicksand. He was quite relieved when he discovered a solid unmoving structure beneath the surface.

C R A C K!!!

The ground opened up.

Mouth stretched open in a scream, raspberry vines snagged on his body, gouging, ripping and spinning him further as he tumbled through a newly formed hole into a dark open space below, landing on his backside with a hollow thump against a cold hard surface, knocking the wind out of him in a wheezing groan. A massive avalanche of painful objects thundered down onto his legs. As the downpour of falling objects finally lessened to a hissing trickle, he could hear his 'friends' laughing, far away, above and distant from his ringing ears.

The hole he'd fallen through was sealed off – the darkness was complete.

The brutal agony of it all made it impossible to breathe for an eternity in the smothering darkness. Stunned, he realized that he'd hit the back of his head. Hard. Fresh pain sprouted from there like fiery tree roots growing into the soil of his brain. Fighting the sudden urge to vomit, he shifted his head to one side and spit out bloody phlegm from his mouth, several times, the last time succeeding in removing a thorny vine fragment.

Carefully extending his sliced-up hands, he discovered that his lower body was covered under a large mound of debris. Apparently, when he had fallen through the ground, some of the foundation wall had also collapsed, plunging him down with him into a subterranean chamber of some kind.

He shifted his body, trying to sit up, and failed... instantly regretting it. His scream echoed in the small space. Something heavy, probably a large foundation stone, had pinned his right leg. The pain flared like an electric arc drawing acidic razors across his nerves. After several minutes, he stopped screaming. The intense pain had subsided gradually into a prolonged ache with intermittent sharp stabs of agony. His leg was broken.

The ringing in his ears diminished to the point where he could hear Danny clear enough, from a muted distance, asking, "You okay, Larry?"

"HELP ME!" He screeched, throat raw, the effort of talking amplifying ragged pulses of pain to rage about inside his skull. He definitely had a concussion.

"You okay?" Danny again.

Even now, Larry was amazed by their stupidity. *Idiots!*

"No!" He tried to calm himself. It helped slightly. "Send help!"

"Okay! Don't getcha panties in a bunch!" Danny's voice faded. "…going for help. Watch out for the ghosts!" Laughter, then nothing. They must've left.

I'll just stay here then. Like I have a choice. I don't even know where I am.

Anger helped him to not lose it – he was so scared that he wanted to cry. Despite the anguish, he happened to remember that his cell phone was in his front left pants pocket. No chance of calling coverage, but it did have a flashlight app. He'd have to clear away some of the debris from his waist to get to it. His fingers, already raw with scratches and gouged cuts, stung when he heaved aside damp clumps of dirt that landed with a soggy plop on the floor. He also shoved aside some big stones, the size of honeydew melons, which rolled away into the humid darkness. Finally, he was able to reach into his pants pocket, careful not to shift his pants too much, for his broken leg was aching fiercely. Painful as it was, he knew from his boy scout's first aid class that his leg should be hurting much more. *I must be in shock.*

He pulled the phone out delicately, grateful that the protective case didn't get snagged in his pocket. The dim glow of the screen setting was like an explosion of revelation upon his mysterious surroundings. Even that was too bright, scoring a red globe into his retinal images. Squinting as he switched on his flashlight app, its stark illumination seemed to make the enveloping darkness leap forward to attack it in violent resistance. Eyes squeezed shut instantly, it probably took him a good minute to adjust his eyes enough to see.

Much like he expected, the debris pile that covered his lower body was comprised of mud, gravel, and rocks, some of them heavy foundation stones, and roots still grasping onto clumps of rich soil. The jagged end of a thick hewed, half-rotted timber plank stuck out of the pile, unfortunately reminding him of what his broken leg might look like underneath the rubble. The mountain of debris rose in a steep slope to the ceiling, closing off the rest of what must've been a larger chamber, such as a basement or root cellar that was maybe connected to a cave, for the floor and walls had a smooth, mildly-undulating surface of a water worn aquifer. The walls, however, had been further modified by crude notches, the kind often found in a mine, to accommodate the placement of square wooden beams that supported the sagging disarray of ceiling planks, some of which still remained despite the cave-in, bulging only four feet above him.

Short people back then.

Even though his pain would probably escalate to excruciating, he felt the nagging compulsion to look behind him. It was clearly a bad idea… but he had to know. He just couldn't stop thinking about it.

His leg went on fire when he twisted his body to look. He bit his trembling lip to contain the scream. Through tear-blurred vision and panted breaths, he saw the oddest thing ever.

Within reach, the edge of a colossal heap of cracked

and splintered bones extended back to a rounded, pictograph-covered wall about twenty feet away. Amidst the pictographs, there was a bas-relief carving of a stunted man-like creature, whose hunched posture suggested an easy transition to either standing to crawling on all fours, somewhat reminiscent of a rat or mole, for it had a stubby tail, huge hands and feet, all completely out of place with a narrow head and oversized bulbous features that inferred a crazed feral ferocity. More details developed in the light – his eyes widened further with a sharp intake of breath. There was blood spattered on the bones, some of it new with cracked blobs, rivulets, and bubbles, and also attached like a gossamer of spider webs, stringy pieces of gristly cartilage. He could tell that they were mostly animal bones, but… *OH MY GOD…* some were human. Looking up from a shattered human jawbone, heart pounding, his eyes fixed again on the wall's monstrous carving. Suddenly dizzy, the bizarre spectacle spiraled away into red and black dots that led into unconsciousness.

* * *

Shivering in the gloomy dark, he awoke to the sound of persistent digging from above: shovels scraping, objects shifted and thrown aside, occasional grunts of exertion, and snippets of conversation, such as, "might shift", "watch your hands" and "over here".

It made sense. He remembered the accident. One of his 'friends' had pushed him into the pit of an old church foundation and he fell into a hidden chamber far below.

His legs didn't hurt as much as they should. Actually, apart from occasional spikes and twinges of pain, his whole body felt numb after lying on the cold, wet, and hard rock surface for who knew how long.

I'm so tired. Wait! I'm in shock. Definitely in shock. No sleeping!

Fingers groping, he searched for his cell phone and found it, lying face down and damp with beaded water, inches away from his left hand. It wouldn't turn on, even though he tried many times, desperately, before realizing that the battery was dead.

He was alone, freezing, in the cold dark.

Throat parched and voice no more than a scratchy whisper, he tried calling out and failed. He had no saliva, so, cringing, he dipped his fingertips into the tiny puddles he felt around him and licked off the moisture. It tasted like sucking on a dirty penny, but, eventually, his throat felt less raspy and sore.

"Help!" he managed. The digging noises didn't stop. A muted siren's wail drew closer. When the siren switched off, he called out again, "Help! I'm trapped! HELP!" The strain caused his head to momentarily throb in teeth-grinding pain.

The shuffle of above ground activities halted.

He heard much better now. "Larry! This is Fire Captain Enright. Are you okay?"

"My leg's broken," he gasped, forcing the words out into the dank, earthy air. "Can't move!"

"Okay. Stay still. Don't talk. Conserve your air. We'll have you out soon."

The activity above resumed.

He thought there was an echo, but there wasn't... it was actually more scrabbling noises from the other side of the pile that covered him.

The rescue crew were also creating a side entrance! It reminded him of how some Chilean miners were saved from certain doom when their rescuers bore a hole into the ground at an angle to reach the trapped miners.

Brilliant! Won't be long now!

To distract himself from the spurious pain, he thought about what the Captain had said... 'Conserve your air.' The air was dreadfully oppressive, stuffy and sticky, but at least he could breathe. The chamber must have an air supply from the surface somewhere.

He then remembered what else was in the dark with him.

Bones! Those bones! And that carving! He began to hyperventilate. *Damn it! I need to calm down. Calm down. It's gonna be okay. They can't hurt me. Stay awake. You have a concussion and you're in shock. You can do it Larry*!

It worked. Concentrating on the sound of digging, he felt less anxious. The digging from both fronts was getting much closer. The work above was proceeding at a more deliberate, cautious pace, probably because they were right over him and could easily dislodge debris onto him. He started to worry again... A heavy stone falling from above could be lethal. He wouldn't be able to see it, let alone dodge it. Then again, he was glad that he couldn't see what was behind him. *What was that stuff anyway? Get me the hell out of here!*

Small rocks and dirt crackled, tinkled, and hissed as they spilled down the debris pile enclosing his legs. He sensed the earth shifting around his feet.

They're close!

From above, a pinpoint of intense light also ventured into the Stygian darkness. It hurt to look at the hopeful intrusion of light.

"Larry!" The fire captain's voice boomed.

"I'm here!" His voice hitched from a spasm of pain.

"Okay, don't move. We're moving some planks. Shouldn't be long." The hole above suddenly increased in size – large enough to show the fireman silhouetted against bright klieg lights. The light inundated the dust-mote chamber, making Larry squint and look away into the darkness, headache blooming into ice-cold claws that ripped into his eyes.

"I see you!" Larry said, gasping. "You can tell the others to stop digging."

"What? Hey Larry... just hang on, buddy, we'll be right down there."

Ouch!

Underneath the pile covering him, rough hands were scraping debris away, incidentally gouging his feet. Someone was tugging on him from the other side. A large rock shifted off his injured leg. He screamed, veins popping out upon his forehead and neck, eyes unfocusing, mind and body beginning to seize up with a heart stopping miasma of cold shock.

From a pain-fogged distance, he heard the rescuer above saying, "Hurry up! The debris is shifting!"

Dirt and rocks rippling around his legs, several pairs of wrinkled, dead-white hands reached from the debris and grabbed his waist. They were muscular, knotted hands the size of dinner plates, with stubby fingers ending in thick chisel-like fingernail nubs that pierced his jeans, tearing furrowed gouges into his flesh as they yanked on him viciously, pulling him deeper into the debris pile. He thrashed about in sheer instinctive terror, pain excruciating in its intensity, but all to no avail. He was pulled into the loosened soil, dirt filling his screaming mouth, his last sight before succumbing to the darkness being a frantic rescuer leaping into the chamber and reaching for Larry's outstretched, spasming hands and failing to grab them.

Deep into the earth he went, taken by the underdwellers.

DON'T WORRY DADDY

Robert cringed on the inside.

Here it comes…

The charade of introductory pleasantries had been exchanged around the conference room table: at one end, River Rock Elementary School's principal, Maggie Holms, smiling like a game show host; Tad Wheeler, school psychologist, in a relaxed pose, yet watching closely; Edward Graves, Daniel's prissy fourth grade teacher; and himself, alone at the far end, Robert Locke, Daniel's single-parent father.

The principal nodded to Graves, who, before speaking, a-hemmed and dabbed his flighty tongue tip across white-pink cracked lips, then said, "Mister Locke, as you know, we've called this meeting to discuss your son's behavior…"

Robert's instinctive fears tingled, threatening to well up and ignite into panic, but he was determined not to lose it in front of these people.

"…And," Graves plodded on, "it has been perceived that your son's aggressive tendencies have of late become increased." Graves looked up from his papers to his colleagues, who, except for the psychologist, reflected supportive glances back to him like he was a faithful dog starved for attention. Graves then pointed his gaze to Robert and raised his eyebrows, expecting… no… demanding a response.

Robert was still stuck on processing what he had just heard.

What kind of pompous ass uses the word 'perceived'?

Also, the term 'aggressive behavior' was mystifying to Robert. His son Daniel was a sweet kid, kind and friendly, though, many people never bothered to look past his appearance. They saw a frugally dressed, sickly thin, tender youth who needed squeaky metal leg braces and crutches to hobble about. Often enough, some people just hated him for being different, or worse yet, for no discernable reason whatsoever.

Robert knew that some kids older than Daniel had picked on him yesterday afternoon in the school playground. Daniel said he was shoved around, knocked down, kicked and laughed at. Robert was furious. He wanted to report them to the school authorities, but Daniel had pleaded with him, "Please don't worry, Daddy. I'm okay. Those kids are just idiots, afraid of everything, so they behave like jerks. Promise me you won't say anything…"

Robert suddenly realized that he'd been thinking far too long when he saw the impatient expressions of the school staff. Even the principal's plastic smile drooped at the edges, as if melting from within, from some wicked fire of annoyed petulance.

"Is this about yesterday? Daniel didn't want to raise a fuss," he closed his mouth and smiled kindly, even though his jaw clenched in a spasm that ground his teeth together. "So… I decided not to bring it up. Apparently, something else happened that I'm not aware of?"

The psychologist spoke, eager to respond with a Socratic question, "What do you think happened?"

"Daniel said that three kids… were mean to him… treated him poorly."

The principal's pleasant smile transformed into an indulgent smirk, "Be that as it may, we've heard a different story from the three other children."

"And?" Robert was confused, and, then, not hearing a response, said, "What did they— the other children— what did they say happened?"

"They all said the same thing." The principal frowned, making the raccoon mascara around her eyes sink inward like empty fire pits at a campsite. "The children were joking with Daniel, attempting to cheer him up, when he pushed one of them down."

Angry despair filled Robert's soul. He wouldn't be able to keep his promise to Daniel… he had to say something. "Wu-what? Daniel can barely stand, let alone push anyone. And, point of fact, after they knocked HIM to the ground and called him a 'crippled freak', one of your precious angels kicked Daniel in the gut and stumbled – that little monster lost his balance and fell down. He wasn't pushed down! It had nothing to do with Daniel!"

The teacher, Graves, pursed his lips together before saying, "If that's the case, then why didn't you report it?"

Robert hesitated. Daniel was waiting in a nearby room. He'd be able to hear everything. "My son asked me not to say anything. He was embarrassed. He has had enough problems without being 'perceived' to be a snitch."

The teacher started to respond in outrage but was interrupted by the chilly tones of the principal, "Mr. Locke, all we have to work with are the facts. So… you're telling us that you didn't think Daniel's point of view…"

Point of view?

"…was sufficiently credible or else you would've contacted us like any responsible parent would."

Responsible!

"You've put this school in an awkward position and even though you don't appear to be taking this seriously, I assure you that the parents of those three traumatized students are."

Eyes suddenly dry, Robert blinked, feeling the surreal moment of insanity squeeze in against his rapidly beating heart. "I-I am taking this seriously," he said, voice shaky, "And, I think you've got this story all wrong. Now… I've been tolerating this school's lack of oversight for the longest time, but I will no longer stand by and allow my son to be victimized any longer, do you understand? And, you know what, I'm going to make sure that he'll get some training, martial arts training, so that he'll be able to protect himself and- "

"No, Mr. Locke, he won't be allowed to use martial arts," the principal's caustic response dissolved the rictus on her face. "We don't condone violence here at River Rock. Your son is hereby on suspension for two weeks. Make sure that when he returns, the violence doesn't return with him or else you'll have to find other accommodations for your child. Oh, on a personal level, it may behoove you to consult with an attorney. The parents who contacted me may not be as forgiving as we are concerning Daniel's behavior. Good day, Mr. Locke."

***

What a way to start the weekend.

Robert's numbed hands gripped the steering wheel as they drove away from the school. He felt cold and tired. He sometimes wished that he could slip away into a permanent oblivion, but he couldn't – his son needed him.

Daniel slouched on the front passenger seat, unusually somber; he knew that he'd been suspended.

Need a distraction. Friday, Pete, oh yeah!

Peter Nichols was Robert's friend from the shipyard where they both worked. Pete had offered to set up a special Karate program for Daniel a few weeks back.

"Hey… would you like to go see Pete tonight? Watch a class?"

Daniel looked thoughtfully into Robert's eyes, then said, "Okay, Daddy."

Such a trooper. Robert's heartbeat fluttered from emotion.

It was a pleasant ride to Pete's Karate class held at the Community Center. Daniel was curious and asked many questions. Most of them Robert could answer. Some he couldn't, like "Do ninjas use Karate?"

When they got there, Daniel couldn't wait, he hopped out of the car and slipped on his crutches in record time. His crutches and leg braces creaked loudly as they entered the building.

The class had already started. Young students, all of them with white and orange belts, stood at attention, lined up in rows, listening to Sensei Pete.

Pete acknowledged them with a nod. He turned over the class to his assistant instructor, who was also a black belt. Pete smiled warmly as he shook Robert's hand then bent down before Daniel. "Why… hello there Daniel," he said, putting his hand lightly upon Daniel's shoulder.

"Hello Mr. Nichols. My Dad and I have been talking for a long time about coming here. Can you teach me to do that?" Daniel motioned with his head towards the students who had started one-on-one fighting matches.

"Ah, sparring. Yes, I can teach you something like

that. All it takes is hard work and dedication. From what you're Dad tells me, you've got what it takes. I think you're capable of doing great things. Do you, Daniel?"

Daniel glanced away, then said, "I hope so, but I get afraid. And… I can get… angry. I don't… wouldn't want to hurt anyone. That's not good."

"We all feel that way from time to time."

"Dad wants me to protect myself against the bullies at school. I don't want him worrying about me…"

"It's good to care about your father. Those kids, they shouldn't be picking on you. You know that, right?"

"Yeah," Daniel replied, sounding uncomfortable. "Dad says that everyone has the right to be treated decently."

"Yes! Quite true! You have the right to protect yourself. By allowing others to hurt you, you're actually teaching them that it's okay to hurt others as well. Do you understand what I mean?"

"They'll treat others the same way they treat me, so I need to stop them?"

"Yes!" Pete laughed. "You said it even better than I could. So, do you think it's important to stop people who would do that to you?

There was a long pause while Daniel thought it through. "Yes, I do now…"

"Right. Or else they'll never learn. Daniel, I went ahead and wrote up a special training plan for you after speaking with your father. He thought you might need – and enjoy – this class. It'll use your strengths, that is, you're low to the ground, have a solid base to protect yourself, and... you do have two formidable crutches at your disposal. Ready to start?"

Daniel looked at Robert.

"It's okay," Robert nodded, smiling.

"Yes, sir," Daniel replied to Pete.

***

They were at home.

The Karate practice had gone well. Daniel learned a few basic defensive moves. He seemed to glow with a new purpose in life and chattered away about it until bedtime.

Robert sat on Daniel's bed near the pillow. Daniel held a picture book in front of him. They began their nighttime ritual of reading a short story picture book together. When they finished, and the book was laid on the nearby dresser, Robert fidgeted with the bed covers; making sure that Daniel's body— especially his feet— were tucked in. He adjusted the top blanket to give extra coverage to Daniel's shoulders. Even California had its cold nights when you lived near the Sierra Nevada Mountains. "Sorry about today, kiddo. With those mean kids and all."

"I don't like it when they hurt me. But Pete, Mr. Nicholls, said it was okay for me to defend myself, so I don't... uh, won't feel so bad. I'm sorry, Daddy. I just... I don't want you to worry."

"Oh well, yeah, I do get sad, sometimes, that's, uh, just who I am, but... I am so proud of you, you know that?"

"Yeah. I love you, Daddy."

"I love you too, kiddo. Now, get some sleep." Robert kissed Daniel on the forehead, turned off the lamp and left the room, leaving the door cracked open. He walked down the night-lighted short hallway that connected the two bedrooms, the bathroom and the living room, which also led to the kitchen. He entered his bedroom and closed the door softly. Turning on the light, the room appeared as an organized clutter of furniture, books, folded clothes, a computer and the desk it sat on, that held utility bills neatly laid out in a row.

There never seems to be enough money. Good thing Pete isn't charging for the classes.

Thinking about the classes perked up Robert's spirits until he looked at the phone's answering machine on the table nightstand near his bed. The insistent red LED blinked, indicating that one or more of the bill collectors had left a nasty message.

Gritting his teeth, he turned the volume down and pressed play.

One message.

The ID flashed. It was his ex. He groaned. He would've preferred to listen to one of the bill collectors.

"Uh, yes, Louise here," she rasped, "I heard that Daniel was in a fight today. What exactly are you doing about that? Fine parent you are. No wonder Daniel has problems. Why are–"

He switched off the playback. His ex's drunken ramblings weren't what he wanted to hear now. Or anytime actually. She did almost nothing to help with Daniel's upbringing, but always had plenty to say about Robert's shortcomings. Sighing, he realized that regardless of her abusive nature, she did have a right to be concerned about their son.

Daniel didn't do anything: he didn't deserve a stressed-out father, an alcoholic absentee mother, a crippling disease, and being the target of mean kids everywhere. Robert felt like he failed... *it shouldn't be this way for Daniel.*

It wasn't all bad, Robert knew that, but *damn it!* Robert began to weep silent, bitter tears for his boy.

***

Robert's parents had given him a little money with the strict instructions: use it only for fun and entertainment. The timing was good for an outing.

Early that morning, during a quick breakfast, Daniel was so excited when Robert told him where they were going. He talked with Robert for the entire hour-long trip to the amusement park. When they got there, the park was practically empty, almost as if they had the entire place to themselves.

Daniel wanted to see the first dolphin show at 9AM.

They had about a half hour until then, so they decided to walk around and see the sights on the way to the dolphin amphitheater. On the way, Daniel squealed with excitement when he saw that a bungee jump ride was open. The ride allowed you to bounce up and down on a trampoline, and each jump launched you high up into the air with the aid of bungee cords attached to your waistline.

The ride operator sat inside a fenced area looking as bored as you could get. The cashier at the entrance gate set up her tray of cash in the podium's register.

If Daniel could, he would've literally been jumping up and down with unrestrained excitement. *He could do that on this ride.* He looked at Robert with eyes pleading; smile wide, and energy revved up.

The price was outrageous – $10 – but Robert wanted the day to be a special memory for Daniel. He did some quick mental calculations in his head. He could cut back his lunch meals at work for a while… "Okay tiger, go for it."

Daniel took off at top speed, which was maybe a quarter as fast as any other kid, and more of a ballet of precise maneuvers than anything as haphazard as running. Robert burst out laughing. He was too tired from a restless night's sleep to keep up with Daniel who raced to the ride about a 100 feet away, up a slight inclined hill.

The cashier started making a call on a radio, probably to get the go-ahead to start the ride. Daniel had already made the dash to the gate and waited near the cashier at the metal chain-link fence. The cashier glanced at him and grinned, then turned away. Apparently, she was waiting for someone to answer her on the radio.

Another boy approached the ride just as the cashier started talking into the radio. The other child was about Daniel's age, pudgy, but strong, the type who always seemed to have an offended look on his face. He stepped in line ahead of Daniel and slammed him aside with what was certainly a hockey hip check. Daniel skidded backwards, as his left metal crutch scraped along the fence until he landed flat on the ground.

The cashier turned towards the noise as she switched off the radio and slid it into her belt holster.

As Robert ran to Daniel, the burly boy thrust a ten-dollar bill in the cashier's face. She looked at the ride operator inquisitively. He shrugged and nodded. She reached forward to open the entryway gate, but the boy had already opened it before her and ran inside to get fitted for the ride's body harness.

She helped Daniel to stand up just as Robert got there and with a distant expression of sadness, stepped away to let Robert attend to Daniel.

Daniel seemed a little dazed but flashed a smirk with a chuckle.

Robert wanted to scream in rage. Not at the ride attendants – they had no idea what had happened. He wanted to scream at that horrible child. His hands clenched in tight fists. He was trembling when he noticed that Daniel was watching him. Robert quickly buried his anger and asked, "You okay?"

"Sure, Dad, I feel great. Nothing to worry about. Trust me."

They watched the boy. He told the ride operator, "Shut up, bitch, and let me start." Surprised, the operator clipped short his safety speech and did a final check on the boy's body harness. His eyes roamed the four bungee cords attached to the harness— two on each hip— following them up to the elevated poles that held pulleys and back down to the ground where they connected to four enormous concrete blocks.

"Go for it, dude," the operator drawled and backed away, hands up.

Watching the brat child, bouncing higher and higher, up to 20 feet above the trampoline, laughing and hooting, reminded Robert of every single injustice that had been laid upon Daniel. The bitter memories went back over the years, abuse after abuse, inflicted by evil monsters such as that pudgy boy.

You hurt my son. How dare you be happy! Robert let his imagination wander free. Horrid malignant thoughts emerged about what he'd like to do to the boy. *Let him... feel something. Something for what he did to Daniel. Let him... fall. Just like Daniel did when he got knocked to the ground.*

Robert concentrated on one of the pulleys. At the spot where it hooked into the pole's eyebolt, he imagined the pulley material stretching, melting, splitting, and pulling apart, atom by atom. He'd been in a trance of hatred for a while before he noticed Daniel staring up at him with an odd look on his face – almost joyful in a sad, reluctant way.

Oh my God! What have I done! This is wrong. Violence, thoughts of violence, don't solve anything. God please forgive me.

Daniel looked away. He watched the kid on the ride. Bouncing up and down, braying with laughter like a donkey, he was definitely enjoying himself.

Suddenly, the pulley that Robert had thought about snapped clean with a loud pop, sending the kid plummeting from the sky to the edge of the trampoline.

The kid smacked hard against the springs where the connected with the surrounding support frame. Something wet crunched inside the kid's body as he was hurled back into the air again, upside down and off-balance. The operator leapt forward and held the kid down on his awkward return to the trampoline.

What. Have. I. Done?

The operator yelled to the cashier, "Call the paramedics!" It was difficult to hear him – the kid was wailing loudly, clutching at his right ankle, which was bent at an unnatural angle.

Robert struggled with his horrified feelings as he turned to look at Daniel.

Daniel was beaming with amusement, serene and confident and happy.

Robert heard Daniel's sweet voice inside his head.

["Don't worry, Daddy. Everything is going to be A-Okay. I'll never let anyone hurt us ever again."]

GIVE 'EM HELL, MR. CARTER

Beyond the wing curtains were the jaded attendees of the 23rd Southern Paranormal Symposium listening to the young emcee announce, "Mister Robert Carter is our next speaker. We've all heard of his remarkable new discoveries regarding proof of the afterlife. Ladies and gentlemen… Mister Carter!" Either lack of interest or the sweaty afternoon heat brought a scattering of halfhearted applause as Robert took a deep breath and stepped up to the podium. As they firmly shook hands, the young emcee grinned and whispered an encouraging, "Give 'em hell, Mister Carter!"

Robert quickly pulled his presentation file up on the podium's hidden computer, clicked the icon for his presentation and turned to the large screen behind him where the opening page loomed overhead. He placed his speech's bullet point notes to one side of the computer and grabbed the remote clicker for his slideshow. Robert looked down at the wooden crate sitting at the base of the podium and nodded, then he raised his face to the audience. Several people glared at him, but many of them appeared to be mildly bored: stretching, yawning expansively, gazing vacantly up at the room's vaulted ceiling or flipping through the program booklet. He tested the microphone with a cheerful "Good afternoon!" A few people acknowledged him as he smiled widely and stepped away from the podium to the center of the stage. "Thank you for that wonderful introduction. I hope you are all enjoying this year's Southern Paranormal Symposium, and hello, I am Robert Carter."

The big screen behind him showed his name, credentials and contact information:

Robert A. Carter, Paranormal Investigator
PhD Psychology, MS Physics, MS Electrical Engineer
ParaBob@sureglobal.net

What struck the audience most on the large screen was the background picture of a six-story concrete and redbrick building. Random parts were quite oddly out of focus and it seemed to have been abandoned for some time, evident from cracked and missing windows, the boarded up first floor and a rather verdant overgrowth of weeds surrounding it.

"Today, I'm going to talk about the Waverly Hills Sanitarium in Louisville, Kentucky. As you can see, since its closure in 1982, the facility has fallen into a state of disrepair."

A few tired chuckles wafted from the audience.

"The site has been renowned for supernatural events. On several occasions, these events were witnessed by professional paranormal investigators, but none of these instances have ever been captured on film or instrumentation, subsequently, they are accepted, but not validated as authentic, beyond any shadow of a doubt. I'm here today to present evidence of the supernatural occurrences that my team experienced at that site." He clicked onto the next slide showing four men posing steadfast in front of the Sanitarium. "This is the research team. From left to right, George Elliot, James Tyler, myself, and Steven Prendergast. All of us have dedicated our lives towards research into the paranormal." He gazed across the audience, a few had succumbed to the sticky heat and were nodding off, but some were paying close attention, or at least, looking directly at him.

"After receiving permission to enter the property, we planned on a weeklong stay, with both day and night surveillance, and brought along sufficient equipment and supplies to allow us to maintain such a rigorous schedule."

A hand rose in the audience, Robert nodded to a college-aged man who asked, "What instrumentation did you bring?" After his query, he smiled to a young woman sitting beside him as she adoringly gazed back.

"The usual standard instrumentation: ion detectors, EMF meters, particle detectors, remote IR readers and static electricity detectors." Robert flipped ahead several slides and stopped at one displaying an arrangement of typical instruments. He then slowly clicked ahead, slide by slide, showing actual setups of the remote sensing instrumentation. "As you can see, we had a variety of options open to us and took full advantage of them. Our main data acquisition computer was the hub of our operations. And…" Robert hesitated, "I also used equipment of my own design."

Groans erupted from the audience, someone even grumbled "experimental" in a crude slur.

"Please, let me explain." He advanced several slides ahead and displayed a varnished wood box the size of a small suitcase with several dials and gauges on its front. What struck the viewers most was a thin web-like skeleton extending from its top, like a miniature satellite dish. Robert used the laser pointer to circle around the gauze-like metallic array. "This is the transceiver, and below, are various controls, the red dial being the electromagnetic, or EM output signal gain. Um, actually I brought it with me…" He removed the device from the wooden crate and placed it on top.

Someone began to laugh hysterically.

"This is my device. It is used to communicate with the spirits. I created it by modifying an original design. I found the design in a notebook. The notebook was passed down to me by my father and his father before him and so on. The notebook belonged to Jacob Carter, my great-grandfather. He used to assist the original designer, *the* Thomas Edison. *My* design is a derivative of the original Edison design. One that has much more power. Much more…"

The audience became quiet as one person stood up; it was Harwood Jenkins, award winning author and speaker, renowned in the field of parapsychology. "Sir…" He drawled out, as if that were a question, "Edison never made such a machine. No prototypes, no specifications, schematics or physical drawings were ever found, and even the press at the time thought that he was mocking the paranormal community. For you to follow the path of such preposterous malarkey, means that you are also delusional, unscientific and disrespectful of this esteemed community. And if, as you so wildly suggest, he did design one, why would he choose to never reveal it? Perhaps because it was too dangerous, hmm? Though, I doubt that. More likely, it simply never existed. What have you to say for yourself, Carter?"

"Through a lengthy period of experimentation, I happened upon several improvements. I incorporated them into my final resonator design, which is still patent pending, so, hopefully you'll understand if I keep most of the details a mystery."

"Theoretically, my apparatus was quite the effectively built device, but I had to fully test it under controlled scientific conditions. Otherwise, my results could be construed as coincidence or interference from other sources, known or unknown."

Robert silently stared at Jenkins for several seconds as though he were frozen in place. "Why…" Robert blinked several times, "That's a very good observation, Mr. Jenkins. Thank you for pointing that out. You have recounted exactly what I was going to say regarding the paranormal community's known understanding of the Edison invention. And, of course, I would never think of maligning the good nature of this community, let alone presenting anything but the truth, if you would be so kind as to let me proceed?" Jenkins shrugged and sat down with a dark frown set on his face. Snickers and leering glances showed the audiences amusement with the terse exchange of words. Robert wiped the sweat from his brow with his handkerchief and carefully placed it back in his pocket before continuing. "As I said before, this book was passed down to me. I never claimed it was by Edison, only that it came from his lab. I know the handwriting well, it's written by my great-grandfather."

He clicked onto another screen, showing an overlay of several detailed sketches. A few members edged forward and read intently as others smirked or whispered to each other. "Here are… some… of the manufacturing details: dimensions, tolerances and so on. These are a few of the drawings included as foldouts in the book." Robert ignored the many who dismissed his work and spoke to the few that showed interest.

Harwood Jenkins raised his cane above his head and waved it about, "You've actually done this? Used this…

device?"

"Yes, I could not come before you if I hadn't. Thus, after extensive functional testing in my lab, I arranged for my team to assemble at the Waverly Hills Sanitarium, a known site of psychic disturbances that some say have gone back as far as a hundred years." He clicked the screen through several photos of his team setting up instrumentation, halting at one of a man in an electrician's blue jumpsuit. "Here's Steven Prendergast calibrating a motion sensor in one of the building's long corridors. We had a video feed of every main area routed to our central computer along with stationary and mobile video setups for each location. The stationary video feeds were continuous while mobile feeds were activated and controlled by the motion sensors. If there was any movement or temperature variation, the video equipment would track and zoom in on that location. Oh, at nighttime, we also engaged infrared equipment, thus, covering ambient and infrared spectrums."

A curious looking bespectacled man called from the back row, "Where did you get your funding?"

"We were independently funded by Mr. Elliot, our team's computer network expert, who has a great passion for investigating the unknown."

"Lucky you…" the man quipped.

"Yes, I agree!" Robert chuckled modestly, "We had access to the best equipment. It was the first time I've ever had the right tools for the job." Several people giggled in sympathy while some scowled at him with envy. "We setup our control center in Room 502, as the 5th floor is well-known for its paranormal activity. Many ghost-hunters speculate to be sure, that most activity in the entire building is within that room. Some would also say that the 4th floor is just as active, but that floor's entrance had been padlocked closed for safety reasons." Robert realized that many blank looks were directed at him. "Oh, pardon me; I've assumed that everyone knows about the history of the Waverly Hills Sanitarium. Well, in short, it was built as a tuberculosis hospital in 1910 when this horrific disease ravaged its way across America. It was woefully believed that the best treatment was fresh air, sunshine, good food and plenty of rest, but people still seemed to die no matter what was done for them." He waved a hand toward the screen, "A great deal of research was conducted here, and while well-intentioned, the gruesome investigative methods practiced by desperate doctors and nurses upon the patients resulted in… a great many people leaving in coffins from the questionable treatments. Over 8,000 people died there. So commonplace was the presence of death that, when they rebuilt the hospital in 1926, they constructed a hidden tunnel that had a motorized trolley to transport bodies from the morgue to waiting railroad cars. With so much misery having occurred at that site, it is no wonder that this once-elegant building became a nexus for paranormal activity." His sigh added to his sorrow, and a few more within the audience seemed less speculative. "The hospital was finally closed in 1982, but it was considered haunted long before then. Doors slamming shut for no reason, objects falling or even being thrown when no one was there, people hit by unseen hands, flickering lights, unaccounted footsteps, unearthly sounds and voices heard… and odd aromas, like baking bread or formaldehyde, have been smelled, and… of course, ghosts have been seen." The very mention of these ghoulish atrocities seemed to peek the attention of more of the audience and several hands were raised, almost politely. Robert finally noticed this change and pointed to a teenage girl in the front row,

"Yes?"

"What was it like inside?" she asked, with a hushed voice. "I mean, was it, like, creepy? Did you feel like something was watching you?"

"Hmm. We certainly thought it was spooky. Aside from entering a known paranormal site, the site also had other occasional residents: homeless drifters from what I've heard. We saw some evidence of old cooking fires and there were also trash piles, mostly on the lower floors. But... it looked like no one ever made it a permanent home, except for the ghosts, maybe."

Laughter rippled through the audience.

"In general, it was much like what was televised on one of those ghost hunting TV shows. The place was run-down: the concrete walls were moldy and wet, covered by graffiti and peeling paint, and the waterlogged rot of decaying wood and plaster saturated the summertime air with a powerful stench... yes, that's it, it was much like the smell of lingering death, one could imagine. And, the huge building was so silent and still that even the slightest sound could be heard from far away. So, whenever we heard something, we were often quite startled."

Robert pointed to an elderly professorial man who was taking notes. He boldly asked, "What's so special about Room 502?" Then softly added, "Why did you choose it?"

"Excellent question." Robert glanced upward with a thoughtful expression, then continued. "The 5th floor was where the emotionally and mentally ill – and outright insane – patients were kept. Its isolation was hoped to prevent their unsettling behavior from disturbing the other patients." His eyes narrowed, "Stories claim that some of these patients, and even a staff member, jumped from the easily accessible fire escape window in Room 502, falling to their death onto the hard concrete below. It is also believed that, in 1928, the head nurse hung herself from a chandelier just outside of Room 502. The area has been considered a hot spot for paranormal activity. Much like a lightning rod attracts lightning."

"And in this case, the building, and especially the room, attracts the spirits from beyond?" The man queried.

"Quite so! You must be a reporter?" The man nodded to Robert's question. "Well, this was the best site we could think of, and our success was greatly enhanced by the usage of my machine. Hmm... I seemed to have gotten a little bit ahead of myself." Robert clicked the presentation back to a screen shot that showed three bulleted descriptions of the R&D process with a picture next to each one. "The first step in the R&D process happened quite by accident. I had just installed the red dial," he aimed the laser pointer at the machine's dial, "this is for EM output. Oh, I forgot to say, when the dial is turned to zero, the device is switched off. And, uh, while I was adjusting it-" Robert sighed. "Something happened. As luck would have it, I had been recording my activities at the time, and afterward, I could've continued onward, but, I admit... I was afraid." He felt a slight chill at the nape of his neck. "The second time was after I convinced Mr. Elliot, my working partner, that something unusual had happened when I used the machine. We tried the experiment at his house, across town, about three miles away and sheltered within a deep valley near Stone Mountain Park, in a notoriously bad spot for radio and TV reception. Oh, and to keep the signal pure of outside electrical influence and instability, I modified the device to use an independent DC power supply, a battery that is. We achieved... several good recordings at his house. Our third test was with our team, assembled together at the Waverly Hills Sanitarium, quite the field trip away from Atlanta, our team's hometown. I brought some video with interesting sound bites from each test."

Almost as an afterthought, Robert asked, "Would you like to see and hear them?" There was an overwhelming reply of YES from the audience, Robert smiled graciously and quickly searched the computer for the files. "Is the sound hooked up?" Robert glanced about for the young emcee, who gave him a smiling thumbs up. Robert clicked on the first video. "This was shot during my accidental discovery at my home lab. The voice you hear… well, it was enough to convince me. And frighten me." The image on the large wall screen showed Robert carefully fitting the red dial onto a plastic control spindle extending from the box. He then turned the dial a short notch clockwise as he listened to static hissing from the machine's speaker, though the noise seemed to emanate from all around, as if it had no single source, as if it came from everywhere. The video showed Robert literally jumping out of his chair when what could be described as an unusual voice said, "It's cold." It was a childlike voice, and easily heard, yet it seemed only a murmur. The video stopped, leaving Robert's image frozen in time near the machine. Some people began to chuckle, though most appeared to be shocked, yet skeptical.

The audience calmed down as Robert continued, "There's more, but it's less distinct. I didn't try it again at my house. But, even though I was afraid, I knew I couldn't let this go, so I contacted my friend, George Elliot, also a paranormal researcher. He said that the voices could be a conventionally transmitted noise, like radio or TV. One thing to note, amongst the voices and background static in the other recordings, there were other less distinct sounds, rasping and crackling sounds, like something huge was being torn asunder. We didn't know what it was at the time." Robert pulled his shoulders back, "The second experiment was conducted at Mr. Elliot's house. We still used a digital video camcorder to record the experiment, but you'll see that Mr. Elliot has a much better camera, the recording quality is much better."

Several nervous laughs bubbled from the audience as the large screen showed the machine with the output EM dial at one-quarter turn from zero, much more than the slight tweak given before. The laughter stopped as the air around the device seemed to shimmer like a mirage of rippling water on a desert horizon. With each pulsation of a low frequency rumble, the video feed began to skip several frames at a time. Bands of white-noise interference traveled down the recorded video. Then, there came a voice as fragile as crisp autumn leaves saying an oddly cryptic, "Why do you torment me?" The video stopped suddenly leaving the stunned audience staring at a snowstorm of hazy static.

"We have many recordings from that night, but… to stay within my allotted time, I need to press onward, to the crux of the story. Our major discovery. You see, contact with the spirits improved exponentially at higher intensity of the electromagnetic signal. We knew we were onto one of the greatest discoveries of all time. But, I had an uneasy feeling, like maybe we shouldn't be meddling in things we didn't quite understand."

"It's about time you admitted that, Carter!" Harwood Jenkins heckled from the audience.

The audience roared with laughter as Robert deeply frowned, but he quickly redirected his shock towards capturing the audience's attention. "What do *you* think is out there waiting for us?" Robert took, and now held their attention. "Well, I'm here to tell you, because it's the right thing to do, to advance the knowledge of science, and to honor a friend. It would be what he'd want. For the truth is, my machine does work… but in ways we didn't anticipate." Robert clicked onto a picture of a long corridor. "We setup our third experiment on the 5th floor of the Sanitarium. We cleared away broken furniture and removed debris from the test area. It was night when we finished setting up our base of operations. It was a nice sized room, which was once a nurse's station. Stagnant air filled the room. Fresh air would have been quite welcome. While we collected an abundance of evidence, I'll show you the videos with the most dramatic results." Robert clicked on the third video. "This is a split-screen view of Room 502 and the control room where our team carefully monitored the data." The large screen showed a disheveled empty room dimly lit by the pale moon while the other half of the screen showed Robert's team watching him adjust the machine's red dial to the halfway mark. Robert closed his eyes and listened to the video's sound. The color began to drain from his cheeks, dissolving his friendly demeanor and leaving an anguished, pale, forlorn and stilted face.

Startling the audience, a whispery yet oddly resonant and silky voice demanded, "Why are you here?"

Robert answered firmly, "To prove the existence of the afterlife!"

"You need but look around," was announced with grave wisdom as the audience began to feel unnerved.

"You are all already dead." Harsh words, bluntly spoken, from a voice no longer wispy with ethereal tones. "You just don't realize it yet."

The video of Robert and his team showed them as confused and scared as most of the audience. The video shut off. Robert opened his eyes; people seated near the stage could see a thin trail of tears from his right eye. The audience quietly watched Robert; most too scared to do anything else, some were nearly catatonic.

"That was but a small sample of the dialogue. The rest of it ventured into other more disturbing interactions, during which… well… the voice seemed to know what we'd want at the most primal level and tempted us with those vulgar subconscious things that we'd never even dare think about."

"The voice also somehow created a hypnotic sensation where the current tangible reality blended seamlessly with our deepest nightmares. It was truly terrifying, for the source of it, it didn't seem to be right. It seemed… evil."

"And while this was happening, the room— and soon the whole building— it all began to shift, as if the dimensions of our world were being stretched to accommodate another overlapping plane of existence, one *very* different than our own. A deep subsonic hum was shaking the video cameras, warping the images out of focus until finally, they shorted out, but not before we obtained some extraordinary footage. The following videos show some of the last recorded details."

Robert clicked his remote to advance the slideshow. The wall screen had four partitioned videos showing eerie apparitions coalescing from the moonlit shadows and moving about within various murky rooms and corridors.

"The noise became all encompassing. The video doesn't quite capture it, but the noise had intermittent undertones that were unsettling, worse than fingernails being drawn across a blackboard; it was like… a dull razor slicing across overly-tight violin strings, which were ready to snap apart, violently. I started to see things as my vision doubled. Within our area, fleeting shadows appeared in the room, taking form, mostly of a frightening aspect."

"I saw…" Robert's voice cracked, "I saw people I once knew. Some of them seemed to be warning me."

"When I heard my dear friend and teammate James Tyler screaming, I shook off my entranced lethargy and turned the red dial back, turning off the device, but the lasting momentum of its effects took a while to dissipate, seemingly taking its time like the slow inevitability of a great stone door closing shut."

"The entire incident took place in a matter of several minutes, but, as you might guess, it seemed to last much longer. And the consequences lasted a lifetime… Tyler was dead."

Carter sighed deeply. The sound reached the back of the auditorium, it was so quiet.

"Like me, the others were shaken up by the turn of events and the terror of what we had just experienced."

"To be honest, looking back in retrospect, we were unprepared for what could happen. After all, this had never occurred before in the history of mankind. And then suddenly, contact! Beyond all doubt. But not the kind we would've expected."

"And what we saw, well, the human mind may not be capable or prepared to handle such things. We think that's what happened to Tyler; he had a heart attack, though we may never be absolutely sure why."

Robert looked towards the audience, seemingly unaware that they were there.

Harwood Jenkins rose slowly. As he spoke, his angry voice held an indignant righteousness that flashed like lightning in his eyes. "Oh, I think we all know what you did, Carter, using unconventional, untried experimental equipment and techniques. It's clear as day that your reckless need for attention and power has driven you to the point of harming your fellow compatriots in order to get ahead. You said that Tyler died of a heart attack – well, it was caused by you, you heartless monster!"

"No no no!" Robert sputtered over the mike. "It wasn't me. Something happened to us. I told you about –"

Jenkins's loud sarcasm crushed Robert's reply.

"Here at the Southern Paranormal Expo, you have repeatedly demonstrated that you are a careless idiot, mocking us all as you pretend to be a scientist, with utterly no care or concern about the dignity of others, who you trample upon with your profane insensitivity, thereby bringing down the credibility of all your fellow investigators, and now, you reckless moron, you've killed someone! And… you whipped up this paranormal farce to cover it up!"

Robert took a deep breath and stared out across an audience of confused, agitated and hostile faces. "I admit that I had some previous difficulties with the quality of my research, but… but you don't understand."

"We actually made contact!" Robert words came out quickly. "And… something horrible happened. And my friend died. He would want me to let others know that we were successful. So… as far as future testing goes, I think that with careful controls in place, this research can be continued – "

"You evil bastard!" Jenkins barked. "You would do anything to get noticed! Was your friend's life worth it? Or was he just another casualty in your crusade against real science?"

"No… he was my friend. The machine, it wasn't just a communication device… it was like… a gateway… to who knows where," Robert said, but it looked like no one heard him above the verbal assault that Jenkins continued to unleash upon him.

At this point, Jenkins had the audience quite worked up. "Murderer! I think the authorities should be encouraged to take another look at your activities. I, for one, will make this happen! Anyone else here want to stop this scoundrel from killing other people?"

"Enough!" Robert spoke to the chaotic audience. "The police cleared me and my group of any wrong doing. This experiment was all done in the name of science and there was… the accident… it was…"

"Accident? Is that what you call it? You are a dangerous fool! You killed your own friend in a cold heartless desire to advance your own pathetic career. And now, you revel in the glory of your detestable behavior behind a flashy slideshow of lies and deceit!"

Robert's face twisted into an insensate mask of rage. "You mindless, pompous… know-it-all! You want proof? Damn-it-all!!! You want proof!?! Here it is! Here it is!"

Robert strode across the stage to the device and melodramatically turned the red dial all the way to its endpoint. The EM output of the machine was at its full power.

Thunder cracked outside the meeting hall. The sunlight coming from the windows suddenly darkened into a blood-red shade as the sky filled with angry storm clouds. The wind picked up to hurricane level, buffeting the windows with loose debris.

A menacing hum rumbled throughout the building's structure. The room's old wooden support beams swayed, creaked and cracked as the earth moved.

Unattended chairs and tables vibrated and skittered across the floor in all directions.

"Now do you believe me!?!" Robert howled.

From the whirling turbulence growing above the machine, frosty air billowed forth in rolling waves of white mist, turning opaque as it took shape into eerie forms both unreal and unknown. Ghostly phantoms dashed and darted above and through the startled audience, passing through chairs and people, sometimes lingering to engulf a person who fell into trembling nightmarish screams before the phantom dashed on. Those few who held onto their sanity still screamed and ran about, causing more havoc and mayhem, even the few escaping the auditorium went screaming into the night. The apparition's torturous attacks continued, claiming nearly everyone with paralyzing fear.

"Welcome," a disembodied voice said, dripping with honeyed venom, coming from everywhere at once. "Behold the one thing you have waited your entire lives to discover – your own mortality!" The voice's laughter became lost in the painful rumble of the space-time continuum being split open like a ripe orange.

Robert had been laughing maniacally up until he heard the voice.

His sanity apparently rattled, he bent down and quickly tried to turn the red dial on the machine.

Robert looked quizzically at the red dial held in his hand, dazed, finally realizing that he had snapped it off. Most of the plastic spindle was still connected to the dial he held – it was a clean, flat break. He pushed it back into the machine and turned the loose dial back and forth, frantically. It didn't work – it would no longer turn the inside-dial's controls.

Robert yelled for someone to bring a sledgehammer or something, but no one heard him at this point. The gates of the afterlife had opened onto this world.

"What have I done?" he wailed. It was the last rational words he ever spoke.

Then, all hell broke loose.

THERE'S NO PLACE LIKE HELL

Ice storms wreaked havoc across the planet; no place was safe from their unrelenting fury.

Jonas Haskell was caught outside in one of these storms.

Just ahead of him, the narrow country road was delineated by the surrounding snow-covered forest. The bent branches of pine trees leaned overhead, further dimming the feeble midmorning light, yet still allowed hard ice pellets to hammer down from the low grey clouds. The relentless patter reminded him of delicate bones cracking in a meat grinder.

His Anorak parka, ski pants, thick gloves and hiking boots did little to protect him from the cold. Trudging forward gave him some warmth deep inside, but that was drained away by the fierce wind that seemed to pass right through him.

He tried not to dwell upon his chilling circumstances. Secluded, alone, in the near-dark, his memory of some overheard news flashes kept coming to mind: people across the world had been seeing shadow creatures... frightful things that struck at the core of primal fear.

A loud crack echoed in the woods to his left. Snow tumbled from a low tree branch, the wood snapped clean, its raw insides exposed.

He blinked several times to clear his vision – he thought he had seen a dark shape retreating furtively into the wood's inky blackness.

It's all in your head. Jonas thought.

He realized that he wasn't thinking clearly.

The farmhouse. He needed to get to it. He needed to see his family.

I'm so tired. Maybe I could lie down just for a minute.

Despite the curious allure of taking a snow nap, he readjusted the chafing straps of his backpack and slogged onward down the road. Each step pushing through the rolling snowdrifts took an active effort of willpower.

They never had weather like this before in Maine; this was something altogether unusual, something terrible, out of control, like something polar explorers would experience.

Squinting through frosted eyelashes, he could just barely see the dull glow of the farmhouse windows.

The welcome glimmer of golden light came from the kitchen woodstove, the living room fireplace, and maybe some scattered candles.

As he got within a few steps of the farmhouse kitchen entrance, he heard the sound of his family talking inside. The snow had accumulated halfway up the front door. He stumbled and crashed into one of the front door's curtained windowpanes.

The chatter inside stopped, chairs screeched on the floor, footsteps approached, and the door stuttered inward in stubborn reluctant movements.

They seemed surprised to see him: his mother,

father, two sisters and two brothers.

Jonas started to say something but wasn't too sure if anything sensible came out as he slumped towards them. Half asleep, he knew that he was guided upstairs to his old bedroom, his outer clothes removed, and helped into his soft warm bed.

***

When he awoke, he was lying underneath many layers of comfortable blankets. The ambient light thrown from the bedroom window reduced everything to shades of bleak charcoal grey.

Kneeling nearby, his mother reached out and gently stroked the hair on top of his head.

"We were concerned about you," she murmured. "That was a very stupid thing you did, you know."

"Yeah. I thought it would be easy," he croaked, voice scratchy. "I used to walk that road all the time."

"Yes, you did," she replied wryly, "but not during the worst Nor'easter ever. Didn't you notice how dark it was getting?"

"Um, yes, but-" he stammered. "Hey, I was stranded at the bus station. No one picked up the phone when I called."

"Of course, we didn't. The phones have been out for almost a week. Power's been off as well, like everywhere else by now."

"Oh, I should've let you know beforehand that I was coming to visit."

She nodded.

"Well, Jonas, we're just glad you're here. The supermarkets had closed awhile back, so, we won't be having our traditional Thanksgiving meal, but we'll make the best of it. Come downstairs – dinner is almost ready." She kissed him on the forehead and left the room.

Jonas felt remarkably refreshed.

When he eased out of bed, his body immediately began to shiver. The sting of bitter cold air helped to incentivize him to dress quickly. The temperature warmed considerably as he went down the stairs and entered the living room.

His younger brothers, Jeremy and Elias, not yet teenagers, were stretched out like cats, lounging on the carpet near the bright roaring fireplace.

They looked up from their ongoing war of toy soldiers when he greeted them, and both of them said, "Hey," in stereo. They went back to playing as he passed through the unheated and unlit dining room that connected the living room and kitchen.

His older sister, Patricia, stop talking just as he entered the candle-lit kitchen. She had been saying something about "without warning…"

"That's enough of that, now," his mother said as she smiled at Jonas. "Look, sleepy-head is up and about." She was poking a wooden spoon into one of the three tall pots that steamed on the wood stove's cast-iron surface. The aroma was of boiled hot dogs, sweet baked beans and potatoes, probably fried in bacon grease. No turkey this year, but the food would be tasty nonetheless.

His two sisters were sitting around the kitchen table. Patricia's face looked guilty for an instant before she put on a forced smile. His other sister, Mary, nodded curtly to him while cracking open a walnut.

His Dad was finishing shoving some split logs into the woodstove's firebox. He forced the door closed, stood up straight with a grunt and walked over to give Jonas a bear hug, saying "Glad you could make it, son. Here, grab a seat by the table."

"I'm soooo glad to be here." Jonas sat down on one

of the 1960's style kitchen chairs. It creaked, as always – he laughed. "It's been a long time."

"Ain't that the truth?" Patricia snorted.

His father glanced at her with mild disapproval, then said, "How was the trip up from Boston?"

"Yeah, we were surprised that you made it," Mary quipped, a bit snippy. "I mean, what with the weird weather and all…" she amended.

Patricia dovetailed onto her sister's conversation, "Lots of things happening, we saw it on the web, at least until we lost power. Did you… experience anything unusual while you were traveling?"

Jonas almost laughed aloud – what were they expecting him to say? The world was freezing to its death with no end in sight. "Uh, nothing unusual," he shrugged. "Except that I was damned lucky the buses were still running. I think mine may have been the last run." He suddenly felt very sad. "There was hardly anyone out driving, but I was able to hitch a ride to the Route 3 turnoff and walk the rest of the way."

"So, you saw no one else?" his father asked.

"Nope. Just the people on the bus and the guy who gave me a ride. A few cars going by, going back to Augusta."

His father's eyebrows crept up a tiny increment. "Well, that's to be expected, no one in their right mind would be–"

Outside, a shrieking bark pierced through the ice storm's raucous tempest, startling everyone. The percussion of wind, snow and hail peppered the house while they held their breaths, waiting to hear the barking sound again.

"Coyote?" Patricia asked quietly.

"Don't think so," his father went to the front window and peered outside. "Would ya look at that. Sleet's coming down hard."

"A-yah." His mother tapped her wooden spoon on the inside of a pot, "Alrighty, food's ready!"

Per tradition, everyone helped bring food, drink, plates, cups and utensils onto the dining room table. Using matches, his sisters lit and placed small tea candles around the tabletop.

Jonas chose three plump hot dogs on mustard-slathered white bread and a heap of beans, all to be washed down with raspberry ginger ale; not much different than what they used to serve at his college cafeteria. While it wasn't the usual banquet at home, the time spent together was special to him, despite the unspoken dread on everyone's mind – mankind's time on Earth was ending soon.

Unfortunately, the food cooled off quickly, so they had to wolf it down while it was still warm. The frigid dining room air seemed to slowly drain everyone's spirits. *Should've eaten in the kitchen.*

"So… Jonas. What do you think of the weather?" Patricia asked.

He shrugged as he glanced at a windowpane – exposed by a gap in the curtains; the glass was frosted solid with beautiful fractal patterns of swirling feathery ice crystals. "I wasn't following the news," he finally answered. "On the bus, people were talking about stuff like… artic weather covering the globe completely… and how the climate change predictions were completely wrong."

"I don't think the storms are going to let up, and everything, everything will get worse. Much worse." Patricia continued. "Before the power quit, the news talked about people acting strangely and doing horrible things. It was as if they were out of their minds, behaving without any moral restraint or remorse, whatsoever. And people… they were disappearing without a trace."

Jonas noticed that the boys were fidgeting anxiously.

A familiar whistling sound arose from the teapot in the kitchen.

"Who's up for cocoa?" his mother asked. The show of hands was unanimous. She went into the kitchen and Patricia joined her.

When they returned, they placed mugs of hot cocoa on the table before everyone.

Jonas sipped on the hot frothy beverage, reveling in its rich chocolate taste.

The cocoa's temporary warmth seemed to perk up everyone's spirits.

Amusing recollections were shared around the table of days gone past – stories that had been told and retold over the years, all of them eliciting chuckles or groans or both. The one where Jonas sleepwalked in his underwear was especially embarrassing to him.

Eventually, the conversation sputtered into quieter and shorter exchanges of words. Everyone's attention seemed to be drawn to the ice storm's constant drumming against the house. Just hearing the moaning wind, wildly shifting and gusting, made Jonas feel uneasy.

His mother noticed him shiver and shuddered herself in exaggerated mock sympathy.

"Seems like the living room fireplace needs some more wood. *Someone* needs to get more ..." She looked pointedly at her husband, one eyebrow arched in suggestion.

His father nodded to Jonas and Mary. Jonas downed the last of his cocoa and followed them into the kitchen. They slipped on their outside clothes and each grabbed a flashlight.

The drop in temperature was shocking when they opened the kitchen's side door. In the hallway before them, there was no insulation at all. The original wood struts and clapboard, erected in 1897, lay exposed with rusty shingle nails sticking out. Spaced along the left side of the hallway, three windows cast a wan grey light upon the small storage rooms that were stripped of internal walls long ago. The faint ambient light left them as they opened the door at the end of the hallway and entered the barn.

There weren't many windows in the barn, so it was almost pitch black. One of the windows rattled nearby, letting in the frosty edge of cutting wind – the weather seemed much colder than it had earlier today.

His father switched on his flashlight. Jonas and Mary followed suit, their beams providing a weak illusion of vision that cut into the murky depths of cold air. The darkness seemed to envelop him, a limitless depth that pressed close to his body.

The barn was huge; rafter beams rose up and disappeared in the lofty darkness above, some four stories to the rooftop peak. Snow had crept in through the gaps of the four small barn doors that led outside. Rooms that were once cow stalls were arranged on all sides except for the huge double-doored entrance on their immediate left and the enormous open-space hay storage area further up on their right, which held at least 20 cords of split, dry firewood, neatly stacked.

"Don't get any small pieces. We want to keep the fire going all night," his father said.

By the time Jonas had reached the pile, Mary had already managed to get a neat stack of logs in her arms. She shook her head, laughed ruefully at him and left to go back to the house.

His father was finished, soon thereafter.

"You got it?" his father chuckled, not unkindly.

"Yeah, it's just been awhile," Jonas replied, balancing some unruly logs in the crook of his arm. "I'll be right there."

His father left him alone with his thoughts.

The whistling wind, looming darkness and bracing cold fueled his latent fears, resurrecting the worst of his childhood memories. When he was a child, this trip to the barn and back terrified him. He believed that monsters were stalking him. As he got older, he realized that there were no monsters – the wind made the loose barn walls creak, the floorboards shift, and the doors rattle. And, he knew that it was easy to let your imagination run wild when you were afraid.

Fingers growing numb, Jonas grabbed the last few select pieces to complete his load of logs, then retraced his path left to return to the house, using his flashlight to guide him.

The kitchen's warmth embraced him, touching upon his exposed skin but leaving the rest of his body chilled.

His mother leaned up against the sink, facing the uncurtained back window, staring out into the dark raging storm with a vacant unfocused gaze. As if mesmerized, she asked, "Where's your father and Mary?"

What?

"Uh, in the living room… I guess."

Patricia's mouth popped open at his response.

"Oh? I didn't hear them come in," his mother said. "Tell your father that I want to talk with him when he has a moment."

He saw that his father and Mary weren't in the living room.

Jonas stacked his wood near the fireplace. The woodpile was very low – he was the only one who had contributed to it.

"Where's Dad? Mom wants to talk with him," he asked the boys.

"Dunno" and "Not here" were the replies.

"Did he go upstairs or to the bathroom?"

"No" and "Didn't see him."

"What about Mary?" The boys ignored him this time, continuing to play with their toy soldiers.

Shaking his head, he wondered what was going on. How could they not have seen anyone? *Oh, I get it, good joke, ha ha.*

Patricia frowned at him when he returned to the kitchen. Apparently, he looked as annoyed as he felt.

"Okay, very funny, the boys didn't see Dad or Mary. Where are they?" he asked.

His mother tensed. "Are… they… outside?"

"I… guess," he answered, confused, "but they left before I did."

"Patricia, help your brother look for them in the barn. I'll check the house."

Patricia slipped her outdoor gear on. He dreaded going outside again into the freezing cold.

Once outside, she asked, "Where did you last see them?"

"At the woodpile," he answered, feeling confused. "Mary left for the house first, then Dad. I finished up several minutes later."

Patricia narrowed her eyes at him.

"What? They're much better at it than I am."

As they walked to the woodpile, there were no telltale signs that any of the barn's outside doors had been opened to the raging blizzard. They checked the rooms as well. Despite their flashlights, the dark still hid its many secrets. There was no answer to their calls.

"They've got to be inside the house," Patricia deduced.

"What the hell is going on?" he griped, regretting it immediately when he saw Patricia's fragile troubled expression.

His mother waited for them in the kitchen.

"No?" her voice trembled.

Dad. Patricia. Like in the news reports – they're missing? Oh my God! No!

They embraced their mother. Comforting murmurs were about all that could be said or done.

After a long minute or two, she asked them to go check on the boys.

Jonas could hear their playtime sounds long before reaching the living room. The boys were oblivious to the tragedy unfolding around them.

He was grateful that they were ignorant of what was going on, but he startled himself when he realized that he was almost as clueless. Where was his Dad? And Mary? *Where did they go?*

He and Patricia left the preoccupied boys to their war games and slipped back into the dining room. With the house rumbling and the windowpanes shaking, it would be impossible for anyone in the living room or the kitchen to overhear them if they kept their voices down.

Patricia sighed heavily, then whispered, "I don't…" Her voice cracked. "I don't think they're coming back."

He took that in – afraid to believe what he had just heard.

"What's been happening?" He asked. "You said something about the weather?"

His mother screamed!

When they ran into the kitchen, his mother pointed at the back window, retreating away from it as she said, "I saw something, outside, right near the window. It was hideous. Like something, something terrible out of a nightmare."

Cautiously, Jonas approached the frost-splotched window. He could only see a short distance out into the continual deluge of the storm, but as far as he could tell, the dark field behind the house only held snow-buried bushes and small trees adjacent to the forest.

"Maybe we're all getting a little stressed out here," he said, forcing himself to speak calmly as he looked away from the window. "Hey, how about I make us some tea and we'll sit down in front of the fireplace and figure this out?"

Patricia shot him a grateful look as she guided their distraught mother towards the now-silent living room.

"I guess I just let my imagination get the best of me," his mother said as she left the kitchen. "I hope I didn't scare the boys."

Soon thereafter, there was another scream.

Teapot forgotten, he ran to the living room.

The boys weren't there.

"Where are they?" his mother wailed.

No, no, no. Not again.

Patricia called out their names. No response.

"I'll check upstairs," he said.

"I'll look in the bathroom," Patricia cried out as he darted up the stairs.

Jonas called out their names as he walked through each of the bedrooms. No one replied, but the house shook with each gust of wind giving him the creepy illusion of a reply. The loose window glass rattled like fragile fingernails scraping across the inside of a closed coffin, giving forth almost no light into the sepulchral gloom. *Damn, it's cold up here!* They weren't on the second floor!

Patricia's expression was grim as she watched him plod down the stairs.

His mother burst into tears when they returned without the boys.

He and Patricia hugged their mother for a long time before they sat down on the couch before the warm fireplace. His mother slumped between her children, her arms draped protectively over them, all huddled together in mutual consolation under a huge blanket.

The boy's army figurines were spread out across the floor. *Where are they?* Jonas had no idea what he needed to do. He felt helpless and afraid. Time passed in an apathetic daze. He drifted into sleep without being aware of it.

He had a dream – traveling through time, across the planet, the continual darkness of swollen storm clouds unleashed perpetual freezing torrents upon wind-torn landscapes of tortured ice. It had happened before, billions of years ago. Almost no life had survived then. This time, mankind wouldn't survive, but something else would, much as it had before. The ancient creatures, emerging from the dark recesses of the underground, could now regain their world.

***

Jonas awoke with a sudden start.

The violence of the ice storm had gotten worse. It slammed repeatedly against the house. The structure rocked on its foundation stones.

The room temperature was sharp with a biting chill. The air hurt his lungs with each tortured breath. He could barely see his breath fogging the area around him.

The room's tall windows were covered outside with layered granules of gritty ice. The candles had long since guttered out. The fire had died down to a stubborn orange cluster of smoldering lambent coals glaring at him like the eyes of a pack of wolves.

His mother's back was to him. He nudged her. Her body was incredibly cold. She didn't wake up.

When he sat up, the blanket slid off his shoulders, giving him an outbreak of pinprick goose bumps.

Patricia wasn't lying on the couch. She wasn't anywhere in the living room. He feared the worst. *Not her too...*

He tried to rouse his mother again. No response. *Damn it, Mom, get up!*

"Patricia!" he yelled.

"She's gone," his mother growled. Her voice was far deeper than it had ever been.

"Ma-mom?" His hand tentatively reached out…

She rolled over to face him. His eyes locked onto her once-caring, once-kind, once-beautiful face as she transformed into something dreadful. Her body shriveled away into the mottled resemblance of a withered corpse. Her hair fell out, leaving behind sparse thick black strands, sprouting from a bumpy, vaguely humanoid head, the grey skin translucent and blue vein-streaked, with lips that creaked open like a gasping lamprey's mouth and no eyes… just smooth blank flesh above a knobby button nose.

The mother-creature lunged towards him, lanky arms reaching out with long, taloned fingers clasping, tearing deep into the meat of his shoulder.

Rivulets of blood streamed underneath his shredded shirt as he pulled himself away. He leapt to his feet and bolted away towards the kitchen.

The monster's laughter roared not far behind him.

Desperately, Jonas yanked open the front door. A landslide of snow-dusted ice pebbles immediately tumbled down onto him. The wave of intense cold attacked his body as he clawed and crawled his way up the steep slope of ice and snow that had accumulated against the door.

He ran away from the house into the shrieking gale-force storm. Wind-driven hail stung deep across his already-numbing body. He stumbled, fell, sunk and pushed his way through the impossibly deep snow, unable to escape the tragic visions overtaking his sanity.

Away from the house, the darkness outside was almost complete. Still, he could see the even darker shapes of more creatures approaching him… they looked like they were once his family.

INVADERS

The sewer maintenance crew was calling it a day. They had worked hard. The weekend was upon them, so now it was time to unwind.

Bryan, the newbie on the team, was especially happy, for after a long shift, the sparkling San Francisco nightlife beckoned to him.

His crew leader, Siggy, led the way out of the vast underground sewer system, cheerfully whistling off-tune like a drunken fool. A huge bear of a man, his dented hard hat repeatedly clipped against the circular tunnel's overhead lights.

Behind him was Bronco, a ruggedly handsome worker who always looked good no matter what he did. Even though Bronco's outfit was splotched with sticky sewer-sludge like everyone else, he looked fantastic, outfitted with the standard protective gear consisting of black rubber hip waders, a dark blue jumpsuit, flashlight-equipped hardhat, and a handheld flashlight.

Doc was also part of the crew. Long ago, he had retired from the Navy and joined on with the City; he liked working, it kept him busy. Once a sailor, always a sailor – he liked telling dirty jokes. Currently, he was making an observation about walking behind Bronco's pretty-boy butt – it ended with "if you ain't the lead dog, the scenery never changes."

Bryan was at the back of the group, also known as the Professor by his comrades. He had recently discovered a new meaning to his life in this subterranean world – he never regretted leaving his college studies behind, much to the amazement of his coworkers.

Bryan carefully watched the placement of his feet as he sloshed through the shallow gray water; he'd fallen several times over the last month. "He didn't have his sea-legs yet," as Doc would say. Underneath the mottled water surface, the concrete was slippery in spots and difficult to see.

Occasionally, Bryan glanced up and saw the swaying backs of his fellow coworkers, all the way down to the approaching tunnel exit, now about the size of a half-dollar coin.

He thought about his date tonight… *Bonnie*. She was really nice.

8:00 p.m. at Fisherman's Wharf…

The ground shifted abruptly.

He fell down; his head slammed against the hard concrete. A thunderous boom resounded throughout the tunnel, louder than an explosion.

When the echoes faded, there was a new sound: the ominous spilling of tons of earth settling around them. Motes of dust sifted downward; thin cracks had spider-webbed across the thick tunnel walls.

Bryan lay on the tunnel floor, staring up at the ceiling illuminated by his hardhat light, wondering what had happened. In an ethereal, detached manner, he noted that the overhead lights were out.

"You okay?" asked Siggy, as he helped Bryan to his feet.

Bryan nodded then readjusted his hardhat, which had taken the brunt of his fall.

"That was a big one," Bronco said, in awe.

"Sure was quick... is that normal for an earthquake?" Bryan asked, never having experienced one firsthand.

Siggy shook his head as he shone his handheld flashlight down the outlet tunnel. About a hundred feet ahead, the exit was blocked by a flat surface of sheared rock.

"Don't think so." Siggy shone his flashlight in the other direction of the tunnel. It was clear. "Looks like we'll be taking a manhole out. Okay. Let's move it. We'll need to call dispatch – there could be an emergency up top."

Bryan understood what an emergency could entail – often, people's lives were in jeopardy...

The somber crew hurried back to the storm drain collection room, where they had been working earlier. It was unnaturally quiet... as if the whole world was holding its breath.

When the crew entered the enormous circular room, the rats scattered, darted about and finally scurried away. The rats had never been spooked by the crew's presence before.

Like the rats, Bryan was starting to feel unnerved and uncomfortable. He looked around, his heartbeat rate crept up, his body grew flush with heat as a cold sweat emerged on his skin. He'd never been in the underground when the overhead lights were out. Before, there was always some meager glimmer of ambient lighting to comfort him. The crew's hardhat lights and flashlights poked into the swimming darkness like spears held by primitive men. The ineffective lights stole away Bryan's night vision, further plunging the huge open space into a spiraling abyss for him.

Dominating the room was a flooded pool designed to accumulate water-drawn debris. Submerged at their feet, the wide concrete ledge that surrounded the pool's rim also extended as a ramp down into the pool.

Nearby, a metal ladder rose to a catwalk suspended far above. The metal-grated elevated walkway provided access into four neighboring tunnels that continuously discharged storm water into the pool. On the catwalk level, there was another ladder that rose up to a street manhole. There was also a phone to the central dispatcher.

"Hey, Professor, we'll be using the manhole above…" Doc announced to Bryan.

Siggy and Bronco began climbing the ladder.

"Thanks," Bryan said, distracted. He noticed that the water flowing from the tunnels into the pool was far less than normal; it was barely a trickle by now. *That's it!* There was almost no noise resulting from the falling water, whereas earlier, the thunderous noise had made even simple conversation difficult to hear.

He followed Doc up the ladder.

When Bryan reached the upper catwalk, Siggy was already on the phone, trying to reach someone. Siggy gave up and placed the handset back in its cradle.

"Phone's out. Bronco, open the manhole," Siggy pointed up the ladder, "and be mindful of the traffic."

Bronco nodded and climbed up to the manhole cover. He pushed against it, struggling mightily, but made no immediate headway.

Doc watched thoughtfully. "Our phones have independent power. And the outside grid is down. Gonna be an interesting day when both of them fail," he quipped.

"Ain't that the truth," Siggy agreed, "Bronco… how's it going?"

Bronco looked down at Siggy.

"Can't budge it. Sorry, boss," Bronco said, sounding embarrassed.

"Okay, come on down," Siggy waved to Bronco. "I'll give it a try."

Siggy pushed with great effort. Bryan saw the ladder's metal rung flex beneath Siggy's efforts, however, the cover refused to move.

"Must be something on top of it?" Bryan ventured.

"Yeah… it's not going anywhere," Siggy said as he climbed down. "Doc… the nearest manhole… it's in the north tunnel?"

"The north will be the closest, yep." Doc motioned with his head toward the other side of the shadow-strewn room.

"Lead the way, Bronco," Siggy directed.

As they walked past the western tunnel, Bryan thought he heard a faint grinding noise coming from the darkness within.

Damn – what is that?

They entered the north tunnel in single file.

The methodical pace of the walk lulled Bryan's thoughts away from the smothering darkness, much like how he had become accustomed, not too long ago, to the sewer's powerful stench and ever-present metronomic dripping of water. He began to wonder what he'd need to do during an emergency. He was determined to make a difference.

I can do this…

He bumped into Doc's backside – Doc had stopped walking. In front of him, Bronco had also stopped walking and was pointing at the ceiling ahead of him.

"Hey, Doc. What is that?" Bronco asked.

When Bryan looked, he saw something completely unexpected: it was flat and black in color, about a foot long, and it had a segmented body with six legs, antennae and bulging multifaceted eyes, all together looking much like an ant, but with frightfully long mandibles.

When the flashlights shone on it, there was a piercing screech and a blur of movement – the ant leapt at Bronco!

Doc lurched back with instinctive fear, knocking Bryan into Siggy.

The ant was latched onto Bronco's leg. He struggled to tear it off, but to no avail; it hung on tenaciously, even when he finally grabbed a hold of its antennae. Then a jet of fluid sprayed from its mouth shot onto his leg. He screamed as the sizzling fluid quickly burned through layers of protective gear onto the flesh of his exposed thigh.

With a savage scream, Doc reached forward and leveraging his body weight, yanked the wriggling ant off of Bronco. Doc smacked the giant insect repeatedly against the tunnel wall. Its loathsome squeal cut into Bryan's head like violent shrill reverberations of sheet metal being torn apart.

Bronco writhed in pain, clutching his thigh, as Bryan dragged him away from where Doc had just finished smashing the ant.

Doc looked back at the crew, holding up the ant and smiling. Yellow ooze dripped from its crushed exoskeleton. He stopped smiling when he saw the raw angry-red blisters of Bronco's exposed thigh.

In the ceiling just beyond Doc, Bryan noticed that one of the wall cracks was considerably wider than others nearby. It was hidden within shadows, but it looked like there was a hole in the wall…big enough for an ant of the same size to pass through.

"Doc," Bryan said, as calmly as he could manage, "there's a hole near you… move away…"

Doc glanced around curiously. When he saw the hole, he walked closer to it.

"No!" Siggy yelled as Doc shined his flashlight in the hole. "Doc, get out of there!"

There was a susurrus of disturbing screeches – suddenly, an eruption of ants boiled forth from the hole.

Doc dropped the squashed ant and turned to run. That was as far as he got.

The horde of ants leapt onto Doc. In an instant, he was covered with angry, screeching insects, several layers thick and growing, crawling over each other to get at him. He screamed in excruciating agony – they were biting into him, slicing off ribbons and chunks of his flesh as he sank to his knees, feebly attempting to pull them off. The smells of burning acid filled the air.

"Doc!" Bryan yelled. He dropped Bronco and rushed forward to help.

Siggy's huge hand pulled him back. "Get Bronco out of here – east tunnel!"

Siggy waded into the growing army of ants swarming over Doc. Siggy grabbed them off Doc and mashed them underfoot, but they only became more determined – Bryan could no longer see Doc underneath them. Bryan lost all hope for Doc when he saw a line of ants returning to their nest hole carrying dripping gobbets of flesh. One of them gripped a hand in its mandibles – Bryan's stomach heaved, and he almost threw up...

Doc!

Bryan lifted Bronco to his feet and helped him hobble away into the east tunnel. In their desperate retreat, the frenzied movement of their hardhat lights caused shadows to streak across the tunnel wall, startling Bryan several times.

Finally, they reached a manhole ladder – the only way out to safety was a long climb up.

Siggy's frantic yells echoed far behind them.

Looking back, Bryan was startled to see Siggy at the

tunnel entrance, flailing his arms wildly against relentless waves of assailants.

Bronco stared, eyes wide and mouth open, at this shocking sight…

Bryan shook him.

"Bronco! Follow me – you can do it!" Bryan yelled.

Bryan scampered up to the top of the ladder. He pushed against the manhole cover with adrenaline-charged strength. It lifted easily. Squinting against the sudden sunlight, he pushed the cover aside and looked away, back down the hole, shielding his eyes from the brightness.

Bronco was just below him, and beyond… at the base of the ladder, Siggy was overwhelmed by a veritable mountain of ants. He struggled for his life helplessly, then fell back, swallowed by the scrabbling mass of clinging monsters, leaving behind an excised forearm with the hand still clutching the ladder.

"Oh my God…" Bryan stammered.

Absolutely terrified, Bryan turned away from the grisly scene and quickly lifted himself and Bronco up onto the street pavement. He quickly shoved the cover back onto the manhole.

Breathing heavily in the rank humid air, he looked around, discovering why there was no traffic…

What the-

They were on a hillside street.

Most of the surrounding houses were in various stages of progressive ruin – cracked, tilted, collapsed and afire. People ran about wildly, screaming in a blind panic. They were being chased by a bizarre variety of huge insects: vaguely similar to wasps, millipedes, praying mantises, spiders… and some things never even imagined… all of them attacking and devouring their new human prey.

There was nowhere to run, nowhere to hide, for

beyond a distance of several city blocks, there were no more houses, sidewalks, roads, telephone poles... no Alcatraz Island, Golden Gate Bridge or San Francisco Bay. There were no reassuring signs of civilization, modern or otherwise. There was only a lush emerald-green forest of strange confiner-like trees abuzz with dangerous-looking alien insects.

The rest of the world had been transformed into an otherworldly version of hell. Or... maybe... this section of his world had somehow come here... wherever or whatever 'here' was...

"Where'd they come from?" Bronco whispered in a small shaky voice.

"Bronco, I think we're in their territory..."

It wasn't long before the two new intruders were noticed...

AMONG US

Utopia Imagination Park
Santa Clara, California, USA
March 9, 2047

Dreams can come true. Unfortunately, there are those people who dream of horrible atrocities, even in Utopia, the world's largest fully interactive, virtual-reality theme park.

Isidro de Vega, a lead park enforcer, was called into action by a security alert regarding a dangerous suspect. Initially, a flurry of conflicting intel lit up the comms channels. The reports became frantic when a massive spree of homicides were confirmed in the park's various adult sectors. Shortly thereafter, a similar pattern began within the adjacent business office of Furry World, his duty sector. The office was placed on lockdown. Remotes had shown office staff being slaughtered by a blur of motion, for the fixed position cameras and recon drones were also systematically destroyed, one by one, by an unknown assailant. Pursuing a homicidal maniac was certainly not the way Isidro had envisioned spending his Saturday evening shift at Utopia.

Isidro was deployed with other rapid response enforcers, a total of six men and women wearing segmented composite armor, including fully enclosed headgear, the bulbous eyeports of which enhanced an overall insect-like appearance, killer insects packing lethal plasma weapons.

Upon entering the office, the elite enforcers split into two teams to perform a sweep and secure recon of the upper and lower floors. Both floors were enclosed, single-level structures, no windows, and a variety of exits, but only one exit was open now, the lockdown access control point that they'd passed through, guarded by a horde of regular park security officers. His team took the stairs to the upper level, two enforcers facing forward, one behind, in a defensive triangular pattern, moving cautiously with weapons drawn, scanning the immediate area on their helmet's HUD modules, keeping comms to a minimum on their helmet mikes. Awaiting them, a huge maze of workstations separated by grey walls, probably several thousand cubicles to a floor.

Their autonomous orders: take the perp down, all other considerations secondary, including prolonged assistance to civilians such as medical intervention. Considering the tragic spread of bodies, those services wouldn't be needed. In fact, worse yet, it appeared that some bodies had been disfigured, parts removed.

Sick bastard! he thought.

Isidro ground his teeth together, thankful that the office's poor lighting blurred out the fine details of the bodies as his team went deeper into the maze.

The overhead lights had been shorted out somehow. The only ambient lighting streamed from the dim holo projections of cubicle computers, the occasional muted wall screens depicting colorful park posters, and emergency lighting strips on the carpeted floor, pointing the way to the closest exit; all flickering islands of luminescence in an ocean of grey gloom.

Each enforcer was equipped with a light baton, typically kept secure in a belt clip. Its intensity could be adjusted from a spherical lantern down to a pinpoint laser strong enough to cut through most tensile steel. Enforcers were often reluctant to use the baton. It was a dead giveaway of your location. He always used his helmet's infrared view, dialed down low to avoided being blinded by a casual look at a wall screen or even worse, exposure to a flash-bang grenade.

Unfortunately, all incidental lighting was to no avail – behind him, there was a grisly sound, an exhaled moan, and a body slumping to the floor. From the shaded darkness, a letter opener had been thrown, piercing the helmet's protective goggles, deep into the brain of the enforcer guarding the rear, dropping her immediately, stone-cold dead. Isidro's remaining companion, also a woman, roared in berserk fury and unexpectedly charged off in the direction of the attack.

"Wu-wait!" Isidro stuttered over his comm, "Don't split up!"

Isidro, still rattled by the sudden attack, followed the chase, stumbling around bodies blocking the way, venturing further into the darker section of the floor, not knowing exactly where his team partner had run but using the distant squishy echoes of sprinting boots as a guide for the general direction to be taken.

A sharp shriek ahead... the sound of running... no more.

He stopped and listened. Just the whisper of AC vents, his heartbeat and shuddering breaths, and the occasional white noise feedback from his comms system.

The dead around him were silent, but seemingly

wanting to tell him something, their mouths open from surprise, fear, or shock, their bodies strewn in awkward positions along the main corridors between cubicles, and in the cubicles themselves; mute testimony untold as to why skin, eyes, fingers, or even limbs were taken and discarded, sometimes nearby, sometimes not, all mysterious, crazy and impossible, perhaps for ritual purpose or some other disgusting trophy gratification. No one left alive. He avoided looking at them when he could – his recent dinner threatened to surge upward at any time.

His imagination was getting to him. The perp was incredibly smart, strong, and dexterous. The ability to throw a letter opener from a great distance through an enforcer's polycarbonate goggle lens was… godlike, and most horrible, all this killing was done with a machine-like efficiency, for in less than a quarter hour over a hundred people had been slain like cattle. All undoubtedly captured, monitored, and evaluated on vidfeed to Command Central.

What the hell is going on?

This message popped up on his side visor: [Backup incoming. ETA 10. Capture suspect now!]

From a PR perspective, it would certainly look better if Utopia could handle its own problems. This disaster was going to become a legendary PR nightmare; his involvement would be put under the probing scrutiny of the amoral, headlines-grabbing, whatever-sells-a-story press.

Isidro saw no movement around him. Nothing also appeared on his helmet's HUD for IR or radar tracking. He was alone up here. No other enforcers on this floor. The killer was waiting for the right moment to strike…

Drops of sweat rolled into his eyes. He blinked until his vision cleared, wishing that he could tear off his helmet and rub his raw eyes, but he needed to keep up the chase, it was vital that the peeps location be known. Moving forward, he slung his rifle over his shoulder and drew out his pistol, in his opinion, a better weapon for close quarters. He also had a stun gun secured to his belt, probably useless in this situation.

To focus himself, he thought about the typical profile characteristics of their perp:

- Usually solo
- Social outcast
- Mentally unstable
- 100% committed
- Fearless, knowing that they're going to die
- Reconned the area layout
- Knowledge of security protocols
- Targets security personnel first
- No hostages

The dry facts helped him break down the insane situation, helped to steady the aim of the pistol in his trembling hands, but all distractions were forgotten when he saw his fellow enforcer lying on the floor ahead. He knew it was her, judging by her familiar pink scarf peeking out from the band of her bodysuit collar. Her head, helmet included, was gone.

Madre de Dios, he prayed reflexively. *What kind of monster would do this?*

He looked away from the body and its spray of arterial blood fanned out onto the floor. *What was her first name?* He wasn't sure... *Carlson?* Something like that. A momentary tug of guilt made him feel sad about not knowing her. He didn't even know the name of her girlfriend, the other enforcer who died first.

He nearly yelped like a whipped dog when he heard the soft singing of Trixie Belle, one of the park's best anime attractions, a sexy, furry fox-human from Furry World. The bubbly crooning didn't originate from the adjoining theme park because the offices were perfectly soundproofed. It was from two cubicles up ahead, about twenty feet away. The singing stopped by the time he peeked inside the cubicle.

No one was there,

Skin tingling, he realized that a desktop holo souvenir was the source of the Trixie Belle tune, probably activated by sound or motion.

The killer was near! His body suddenly chilled. Breathing became difficult as his chest muscles tensed.

A red dot popped up on his helmet's HUD radar. It showed the killer to be in a connecting aisle, perpendicular to his direction, about ten feet away at best. Sweat dripping, pistol leading the way, he quickly rounded the aisle corner…

"Damn!" a man yelled, his voice ringing loud in Isidro's helmet ear buds. It was another enforcer, crouched low against a cubicle wall, plasma rifle pointed at Isidro. "I almost shot you," the man whispered. "Just about sharted my jumpsuit, too."

With sighs of relief, they both lowered their weapons. Sometime during all this drama, Trixie Belle had started singing again, but now, thankfully stopped.

Isidro kneeled next to the other enforcer. "Scanner didn't pick you up until I was right on top of you."

"Huh… walls must be providing some interference, strange though, I saw you. Where's your team?"

"My team…" Isidro processed, still stunned by the abrupt turn of events, "they're dead. That bastard got them." Quiet ensued – it was a difficult conversation to have.

Isidro finally realized that the enforcer before him was from the first floor team, someone who worked in the elite section of the park where designers, engineers, and scientists could interact with their ongoing technical creations. Generally, those enforcers didn't have to deal with the often reckless, perverted general public and their twisted fantasies. On a personal level, Isidro liked working in the endless freak show, except for today's nightmare...

"Dead?" the other enforcer nodded slowly. "Same for me. Came outta nowhere, both of my mates, lying on the floor, bled out by the time I found them. The perp must have a stealth suit. Happened so fast. Never even got a shot off. But I was able to track the perp up here. Lost him in this maze."

"He, or she, attacked us about five minutes ago."

"Hmm. Could be anywhere by now."

"You have a plan?"

"We're on our own. They won't leave the access lockdown point, but help is on its way, so maybe we should wait here and-"

There was a startled cry. No new blip on the HUD. The cry came from beyond the scanner's thirty-meter range, or maybe, it just wasn't registering. Another sound, a whimpering sob, occurred again from the same direction, far away, from the outer edge of the enormous floor.

Definitely a young girl.

The other enforcer motioned with his head towards the sound's direction.

Isidro said, "They told us to take care of this... let's move it."

Off they went, Isidro in the lead, crouching low near cubicle walls. A pair of blips appeared in the periphery of his HUD range. *The perp is near a girl?*

Isidro heard a mumble of conversation ahead, making it easier to traverse a path through the maze of cubicle passageways towards the source. Several times they had to step over bodies blocking their path.

As they moved closer, the lighting vastly improved, due to the row of large management offices lining the floor's outside wall, each office sporting one or more wall screens: colorfully transitioning marketing pictures of the luxurious options available to park guests; amenities such as surrounding hotels, restaurants, events; most of all, the virtually limitless potential of the park depicted within a variety of genres including sci-fi, fantasy, adventure, comedy, drama, children's, and also briefly alluding to the customized packages, often the basest amoral and unethical possibilities, shown in an abstract 'free-spirit' presentation.

IR screen layer flaring with growing halos, Isidro switched off the option and went to regular non-IR vision mode with HUD and radar, his eyes blinking as they adjusted.

A comms screen appeared: [Engage with extreme caution.]

No... really?

They were close. One more turn, and they'd see down an aisle, past two pairs of opposing cubicles, into the manager's office cubicle that held the perp and girl.

The perp, definitely a man, was speaking softly, saying, "What did you see?"

Isidro held up his hand and signaled towards their destination. They crept out into the aisle, Isidro with his pistol held out in front of him. Likewise, the other enforcer followed, rifle at the ready.

The perp's back was to them while he talked to a young girl, probably six or so years old. He was about seven feet tall, a juggernaut of sleek strength, wearing a jet-black full bodysuit, every inch of his skin covered. In his hip holster was an odd weapon unlike any pistol Isidro had ever seen, and, slung in a scabbard across the perp's back, a micron blade easily over three feet long. The molecule-thick edge of the blade could slice through anything, given enough applied force. Certainly sufficient for leaving a gruesome trail of dead bodies.

Isidro's heartbeat raced when the perp asked the girl,

"You saw policemen?"

The girl nodded her head emphatically, her cherubic face illuminated from above by the pastel-green glow of a circular disc device that the perp held up in one hand. "See?" she giggled, similar to a shell-shock victim, clearly overwhelmed out of her senses by the specter of death all around her. She pointed towards Isidro and his partner. "They found us."

Isidro flinched at her revelation.

"Don't!" he boomed, using his helmet's external speaker to project his command. "We have you covered. Gently place the… device… in your hand onto the floor. Do it slowly…"

"Officers-" the perp began to speak.

"Shutup!" Isidro's partner said. "Place the object on the floor."

"Of course." Slowly, the perp bent his knees, laid the device on the floor, and stood up. The device's glow cast underlit shadows on the girl's face, a transformation that made her look ghoulish.

"Officers, there's been a misunderstanding. We're both searching for the… the same killer." The perp's voice was oddly calm and smooth considering he'd just been caught slaughtering an unspeakable amount of innocent people.

What the hell? Effin' loonie.

"Place your hands on the back of your head," Isidro said, watching the traumatized girl in his peripheral view. She looked unhurt, physically at least, and strangely, unafraid.

The perp responded to Isidro's order, "Certainly," and complied, slowly, the fabric of his enviro-stealth suit gliding noiselessly over the hard muscles underneath.

Isidro noticed blood on the suit, mostly on the fingers. Fresh. It trickled down the perp's neck and forearms as he clasped his hands behind his head. Isidro's teeth ground together, no doubt audible on the comms feedback to Command Central.

The perp went on talking, "I work for a secret government program. I track down dangerous aliens that have infiltrated our world. The one… the one we're both chasing is a metamorph. It can alter its body structure, blend in with its background, even become invisible, but… it can be detected by the scanner that's on the floor."

"Alien protection unit?" Isidro's partner snarled with laughter. "Really? Come up with something original. That idea has been around since the turn of the century. In fact, you probably got it from one of those lame-ass alien invasion sims we have. Would've sounded creepier if you said the park's evil spirit made you do it, or that the park's AI created you… spooky! Guess we'll never really know, huh?"

"Officers, please think about what you've seen. This alien is a ruthless killer, feeding off of people's fear, sampling DNA to reconfigure itself as needed, and taking the victim's clothing as a disguise, blending in perfectly. It can't be allowed to escape your trap. If it does, it'll be unstoppable. Please, we're wasting valuable time."

Enough of this…

Irritated, Isidro motioned to his partner. They moved forward, weapons ready, closing the distance.

Isidro's comm system screeched in his ear buds at full volume before shorting out, destroying all transmitting capabilities, defaulting his helmet's goggles to clear, and opening his rebreather ports. Stunned and senses reeling, he noticed that the area was lit up clear as country daylight by the device on the floor.

He squinted against the device's intense brilliance. Too late, he saw the perp turn towards him, impossibly quick, body flexing in the skin-tight suit, no face to see behind the impassive suit mask, no expression from the multifaceted goggled eyes, pistol being drawn…

Isidro's hands had just begun to move his pistol to aim when he heard the unnerving crackle of a plasma rifle behind him.

Surprised, the perp was hit by a rapid succession of dark-purple energy blobs, knocking him down to the floor, ablaze within a sputtering firestorm, body and limbs contorting from the intense heat of ionized plasma, about fifty thousand degrees obliterating everything it touched.

The perp was obviously dead – Isidro could see where the plasma had already burned its way down to the bones in parts and to the floor beneath, and was still cooking the remaining body further, fat crackling, shooting motes of carbonized flesh into the air. Isidro glanced back at his partner, who shrugged and said, "He pulled a weapon on us."

The device's impossibly bright light shone in his face as he looked back towards the girl. He eased his defunct helmet off and approached her, blocking the device's light, trying not to wince from the powerful stench of burning flesh. "Hey, everything's gonna be okay. I'm the shift supervisor with park security – I'm in charge. I'll get you out of here. We're here to help." He showed the girl his best impression of a comforting fatherly smile.

The girl attempted to smile back, as if mimicking a mirror reflection, then… her expression froze, and her eyes grew wide. She saw something behind Isidro.

A shifting, crunching, and creaking noise… clothes being torn and something else, ultimately more sinister… the shining device on the floor being crushed like a bug, its light snuffed out.

He turned in time to see that his partner was no

longer anything vaguely human – he… 'it'… was an amorphous, squirming mass of collective body parts, human and otherwise, rearranging into the ferocious lethality of an uncontested apex predator, reaching out impossibly quick and slicing off Isidro's head before he could even scream.

***

A veritable army of State tactical units arrived on scene. At the last transmission's location, they found a lone enforcer, standing shakily amidst some victims of the attack: an enforcer, head missing; the suspect, a paramilitary psycho killed by plasma pulse fire; and a young girl, reason for death unknown, possible heart attack.

The lone enforcer's helmet code identified him… he was the sole survivor of Utopia's fast reaction force. A hero by all accounts, who had saved the day.

"My partner got him," his voice cracking with emotion, "he gave up his life to protect the girl, but… she too…"

The State's incident commander responded, "We've got it from here. You –" he jabbed a finger at one of his support staff. "Escort this man through the access point for a debrief. And get some medical attention for him while you're at it!"

"I'll be okay, sir," the enforcer said.

"Good work, Enforcer-?"

"De Vega, sir, Isidro de Vega," the enforcer said as he was escorted away.

END

About The Author

Jeff Parsons is a professional engineer enjoying life in sunny California, USA. He has a long history of technical writing, which oddly enough, often reads like pure fiction.

He was inspired to write by two wonderful teachers: William Forstchen and Gary Braver.

In addition to his book Algorithm of Nightmares, he is published in SNM Horror Magazine, Bonded by Blood IV/ V, The Horror Zine, Dark Gothic Resurrected Magazine, Chilling Ghost Short Stories, Dystopia Utopia Short Stories, Wax & Wane: A Coven of Witch Tales, The Moving Finger Writes, Golden Prose & Poetry, Our Dance With Words and The Voices Within.

For more details…

www.hellboundbookspublishing.com/authorpage_par sons.html

https://www.facebook.com/OfficialJeffParsons/?ref= aymt_homepage_panel.

Bibliography

Lost Souls, Chilling Horror Short Stories, 9/24/15,
The New Law, Dystopia Utopia Short Stories, 9/29/16,
The Rain, The Horror Zine Magazine, Spring 2017,
Over and Out, The Horror Zine Magazine, Summer 2016, and, June Selected Writer,
Nothing Personal, SNM Horror Magazine, October 2013,
Eye of the Storm, The Horror Zine Magazine, Spring 2015,
Bruja, Wax & Wane: A Gathering of Witch Tales, March 2, 2016,
The Daisy, SNM Horror Magazine, August 2013,
The Variant, SNM Horror Magazine, December 2013,
At Any Cost, SNM Horror Magazine, August 2012, and Bonded By Blood V: Doomsday Descends, November 30, 2012,
The Bracelet, SNM Horror Magazine, June 2014,
A Slice in Time, The Horror Zine Magazine, Spring 2014, and May Featured Story
Devourers of Eternity, The Horror Zine Magazine, Fall 2013,
Edge of Darkness, SNM Horror Magazine, April 2013.
Give 'Em Hell, Mr. Carter, Dark Gothic Resurrected Magazine, Fall 2017

Other HellBound Books Titles
Available at: www.hellboundbookspublishing.com

Shopping List 2: Another Horror Anthology

Once again, HellBound Books brings you an outstanding collection of horror, dark, slippery things, and supernatural terror - all from the very best up and coming minds in the genre.

We have given each and every one of our authors the opportunity to have their shopping lists read by you, the most wonderful reading public, and have the darkest corners of their creative psyche laid bare for all to see...

In all, 21 stories to chill the soul, tingle the spine and keep you awake in the cold, murky hours of the night from: Erin Lee, The Truth Artist, John Barackman, Serena Daniels, M.R. Wallace, Isobel Blackthorn, Alex Laybourne, Jason J. Nugent, Josh Darling, Jovan Jones, Nick Swain, Douglas Ford, Craig Bullock, Craig Bullock, Jeff C. Stevenson, PC3, David F Gray, Sergio Palumbo, Donna Maria McCarthy, David Clark & Megan E. Morales

Down by the Sea and Other Tales of Dark Destiny

This exceptional collection follows the inevitable path travelled towards truth or justice, whether their own, or from the universe at large:

A tough teen meets his match in an elderly woman who has been ridding the neighborhood of its thugs, one by one.
A repeat drunk driver is cursed to spend the rest of his days trapped behind the wheel.
A pregnant teen murders her parents and devises a gruesome nativity scene.
A woman uncovers a preacher's deadly solution to ridding the world of evildoers.
A serial killer looks to reunite with his estranged mother
The little things you think you see can lead to crippling paranoia, but a little self-surgery can take care of your troublesome eyes.
A young woman discovers her family's fate is to sacrifice themselves to horrific mermaids.
An anxious gardener murders his nosy neighbor to keep the secret about his chemically-enhanced prize rose garden.
A woman is afraid of the dark because it will release the beast that lives inside her.
A woman tries hypnotherapy for childhood trauma and learns her abuser is now her doctor.
A woman tries to forget the murders of her baby and husband by ignoring the proof in the back seat of her car.
Satan seeks revenge on the woman who spurned him by forcing her to give birth to him.
A dying woman returns to her childhood home and encounters the ghosts of her enslaved ancestors.

Blood and Kisses

The definitive short story collecting from James H Longmore - an eclectic mix of dark horror, bizarro and Twilight-Zone style tales of the downright disturbing.

Welcome to the long awaited collection from the writer of horror novels *'Pede* and *Tenebrion*; a foreword by Richard Chizmar (co-author of *Gwendy's Button Box* and author of *A Long December*), 18 short stories, 5 flash fiction and even a poem - all skin-crawling, soul-shredding tales of terror, of the darkest things that skulk amongst the night's inky shadows, and of the everyday gone horribly awry.

Discover the alternative implication of technology becoming self-aware, enjoy the acquaintance of a charismatic new pastor who promises his flock a brand new place in which to worship his God, and spend a little time in the company of a nice young man who is inexorably caught up in his home town's terrible secret. Then there is Cupid's revelation that personally he has never experienced love, yet we discover that very emotion alive and not so well amongst the ruins of a post zombie apocalypse world, and we bear witness to a childhood innocence forever destroyed in a war-torn city. There is more, Dear Reader, much, much more; for within these pages we have devils, demons and ghosts, lycanthropes and demi-gods, all rubbing nefarious shoulders with vilest of Hell's offspring who have slithered from the netherworld to doff their caps and wish us all the sweetest of dreams…

The Big Book of Bootleg Horror 3:
By Invitation Only

A very, very special edition of our flagship anthology series - proceeds going to the awesome Alzheimer's charity *Hilarity for Charity*.

Only invited authors are featured - some of the biggest names in today's horror scene!

Authors contributing:

Jack Ketchum, Michael Bray, Jeff Strand, Chad Lutzke, Eddie Generous, Lance Tuck, Wade H. Garrett, Richard Chizmar and Billy Chizmar, James H Longmore, Jaap Boekestein, Iain Rob Wright, Michael McBride, Edward Lee, David Owain Hughes, Ray Garton & Benjamin Blake

Demons, Devils and Denizens of Hell: Vol, 2

The second volume in HellBound Books' outstanding horror anthology fair teems with tales of Hades' finest citizens – both resident and vacationing in our earthly realm… -

Compiled by the inimitable P. Mattern and featuring: Savannah Morgan, Andrew MacKay, Jaap Boekestein, James H Longmore, Stephanie Kelley, Ryan Woods, James Nichols, P. Mattern, Marcus Mattern, Gerri R Gray, and legion more…

**A HellBound Books LLC
Publication**

www.hellboundbookspublishing.com

Printed in the United States of America